Happy Smith Goes to Brooklyn

An Historical Imagining

Paul Kalb

The characters and events portrayed in this book are fictional. Any similarity to real people, living or dead, is coincidental and not intended by the author. No part of this book may be reproduced, or stored in a retrieval system, or transmitted in any form or by any means, electronic, mechanical, photocopying, recording, or otherwise, without the express written permission of the publisher

Dedicated to my wife, Terry Kalb, a retired English/Social Studies teacher, avid reader, and like me, a dedicated Brooklyn-born baseball fan

"Now, as if to please wayward fans, the Metropolitan Museum of Art has reached into its bottomless duffel bag of curiosities to present an exhibition of early and extremely rare baseball cards. Rows and rows of long-dead ballplayers stare out from the past like the mugshot denizens of the New York Police Department's once-famous Rogues Gallery.

Here is that human snarl, Ty Cobb, so knotted with rage that he alienated opponents and teammates both; he may be the greatest, loneliest player of all time. Here, too, is Cobb's polar opposite, Henry Joseph Smith, an average outfielder for the Brooklyn Superbas who played only one year in the major leagues — but who went by the nickname Happy."

"Metropolitan Museum Opens Huge Show of Baseball Cards," NY Times, 10/13/2013
http://www.nytimes/2013/07/12/arts/design/metropolitan-museum-opens-huge-show

Cover Image: Happy Smith Baseball Card Portrait, T206 BRK American Tobacco Co. Baseball Trading Card, 1910, U.S. Library of Congress Control No. 2008675164, Lot 13163-18, no. 38 from Benjamin K. Edwards Collection

1910 Brooklyn Superbas

(Top left to right): George Bell, Tim Jordan, Ed "Eggie" Lennox, Red Downey, Elmer Knetzer, Frank Schneiberg, Paul Sentelle, "Silent" John Hummel, Doc Scanlon, Harry Lumley, and Bill Bergen

(Middle left to right): Rube Dessau, Jonny King, Nap Rucker, George 8Hunter, Kaiser Wilhelm, Harry "the Horse" McIntyre, Fred Ulrich

(Bottom left to right): Otto Miller, Tex Irwin, Zach "Buck" Wheat, Pryor McElveen, Al Burch, Manager Bill Dahlen, Tommy McMillan, George Schrim, Jake Daubert, and Hi Myers

Note: This photo was taken before the start of the 1910 season and does not reflect trades, acquisitions, and cuts made before the start of play. Specifically, Frank Schneiberg, Harry McIntyre, Red Downey, Paul Sentelle, Jonny King, Fred Ulrich, George Schrimm, and Hi Myers were either traded or released. Players not in the photo including Happy Smith, Tony Smith, Bill Davidson, Jack Dalton, Cy Barger, Dolly Stark, Bob Coulson, Fred Miller, and George Crabble were added to the roster after the photo was taken.

Table of Contents

Lightning Strikes

The excitement throughout the stadium was palpable as "Happy" Smith paced the dugout floor. Despite Brooklyn's poor standing in the National League and the reality that this game on September 21, 1910 was meaningless for either team, the cranks were delirious and were cheering and groaning at every pitch. This was the last of a five-game series in which they were trailing three games to one and their final appearance against the Cubs this season. The Superbas were currently in sixth place, only slightly better than the St. Louis Cardinals and the last place Boston Doves. Chicago was bound for the World Series for the second time in three years (they won the Series in 1908) but the Superba players would soon be heading back to their day jobs for the off-season.

The score was tied at one run apiece in an exceptionally close pitching duel. The Cubs famous right hander, Mordecai "Three-Finger" Brown, was hurling yet another spectacular game. He was the most dominant pitcher in the league, so this was no surprise to anyone in the ballpark. Brown already had 23 wins, the fifth consecutive season he had 20 or more. It was noteworthy however, that "Doc" Scanlon, the fourth best pitcher on Brooklyn's club (with only 8 victories to his credit this season) was thus far keeping pace through the first seven innings, by mowing down the powerful Cub lineup.

Brooklyn's second baseman, "Silent John" Hummel, batting in the three-hole, led off the bottom of the seventh and awkwardly swung through a high and hard, inside, first-pitch fastball without making any contact. His swing was as much in defense to protect his noggin as it was an offensive statement. "Stee-rike One" roared home plate umpire Bill Brennan as if Hummel or anyone in the stands had any doubt. Hummel just scowled but quickly returned to the batter's box where he resumed his crouched stance, tapped his bat to the dirt two times and then waved it slowly and deliberately to let Brown know he was not easily intimidated.

His next pitch was a repeat of the first only three inches closer to his head and this time Hummel wisely, but not particularly gracefully, bailed out and wound up sitting on his rump. Silent John was muttering to himself as he slowly picked himself up and dusted off his clay-stained uniform. His return to the batter's box was a bit slower and more deliberate.

Meanwhile, Three-Finger Brown wasn't paying him any mind as he had turned away from the plate in a half-hearted attempt to conceal his reaction from the umpire, but his smirk was in full view of the Brooklyn dugout and their fans who immediately responded with a chorus of jeers and some choice comments about Mrs. Brown. The reaction was loud enough to drown out Brennan's call of "Ball One."

After taking what seemed like an excessive amount of time before getting ready for his next pitch to allow Hummel some additional time to fume, Brown finally resumed his place on the mound and began his jerky wind up. This time he delivered an off-speed pitch that so fooled Hummel his swing was practically complete before the ball was halfway to the plate. His awkward swing nearly screwed him into the ground and his muttering grew louder and more animated. Once again, Brennan's booming call of "Steee-rike Two" seemed superfluous at best, but to Silent John's ears it was a humiliating gratuitous taunt. In response he gritted his teeth and pounded the bat in the dirt even harder before resuming his spot in the box.

This time, instead of employing his usual stalling tactics, Brown hardly even waited for a sign from the catcher as he quickly delivered the next pitch. The ball seemed to arrive before Hummel knew what was happening. His bat sat in repose as the ball made a resounding thunk into the catcher's broad leather mitt straight over the middle of the plate. "Stee-rike three...Yer Out!" bellowed Brennan in yet another obvious provocation.

Happy thought he detected the hint of a sneer on the umpire's face, further evidence he was testing Silent John to see if he could ignite a spark. Sure enough, Hummel felt obliged to register his discontent in a less than silent manner. He punctuated his comments by kicking up the infield dirt, flailing his arms wildly, and finally spitting in Brennan's direction as he turned to head back to the dugout. His reputation as an outspoken critic of the umpires' abilities, eyesight and sexual habits preceded him and earned him his satirical nickname. Thus, it was not surprising that Brennan tossed Hummel from the game in a matter of seconds.

Next up was Brooklyn's cleanup batter Tony Smith. He wasn't a particularly powerful hitter (one home run, 14 extra base hits so far this season) but he had a pretty decent eye for the ball. Since he could draw plenty of walks and was fast on the base paths, he was generally the lead-off hitter. But since Brooklyn was in the doldrums and didn't really have a bona fide power hitter, manager Dahlen shook up the lineup for today's matchup with the first place Cubs.

While unrelated, Tony and Happy shared the relatively common surname and even though they were both beardless, they were affectionately referred to by teammates as 'The Famous Smith Brothers" after the upstate New York purveyors of cough drops. They both joined the team this year via the pre-season trade with the Cubs and as a result, developed a friendship. Neither had played a single game for the Cubs but had signed contracts with Chicago, making them property that could be bought and sold at will, Happy looked up to Tony who had some major league playing time under his belt (in reality just one complete season with the Washington Senators in '07) but in Happy's eyes he was a consummate veteran and often sought his counsel on both professional and personal matters. Tony took Happy under his wing from the start – in fact, he gave Henry his nickname after noticing how elated he was on learning he made the final cut for the team roster in the Spring.

Tony fouled off a couple of pitches and patiently resisted swinging at the junk that Three-Finger was tossing out of the strike zone. Finally with the count full, Tony got a pitch in his wheelhouse and lined a solid drive to left just over the reach of a leaping Joe Tinker at shortstop. Happy joined the sold out-crowd at Washington Park as they roared their approval.

So, with one out and one on, third baseman Ed "Eggie" Lennox stepped up. Lennox was one of Brooklyn's best hitters – second only to Zack Wheat who had the team's leading batting average and slugging percentage. The crowd eager for instant gratification, tried to stir a large rally and began to shout "Egg-ie! Egg-ie!" Brooklyn's manager Bill Dahlen gently tugged on his left ear, tapped the brim of cap twice with his right pointer, and rubbed the front of his jersey left to right, to signal to his third base coach that the bunt play was on. Lennox stared intently at the coach who relayed the signs to make sure he understood what he was expected to do, fighting the urge to do a double take and give away Dahlen's strategy. Calling on one of your best hitters to bunt rather than swing away in this situation was, of course, an unconventional (some might say controversial) approach. But in a close pitching duel and with the game tied, Dahlen selected the strategy most likely to succeed.

Back in the batter's box, Lennox quickly pivoted to face Three-Finger, crouching low with his bat stretched across the plate. As if he anticipated the bunt was on (was he stealing signs?), Brown let fly a tough, biting fastball that was dropping precipitously as it neared the plate. Lennox was already committed and knew he had to make contact but by the time the ball was upon him it was literally just inches off the ground. Somehow, he managed to lay the bat on the ball before it bounced in the dirt and then jerked his stick backward to absorb as much of its momentum as possible and thus deaden its trajectory.

The ball floated through the air in slow motion straight down the third base line landing about six feet away from home plate. It rolled slowly to a trickle and by the time catcher Johnny "Noisy" Kling reached the ball he had no play at second. He fired to first baseman Frank Chance missing Eggie's back by inches as he sprinted down the line. His throw beat Eggie by a half step on his way to a successful sacrifice bunt.

So, with a runner in scoring position, two men down, and left fielder Bill Davidson at the plate, Chicago's first baseman/manager Frank Chance joined Kling and Brown on the mound for a strategy conference. When play resumed, Brown was keeping a close eye on Smith who was taking a large walking lead off second. Before delivering the first pitch to the plate, Brown stepped off the pitching rubber, whirled around suddenly and fired a bullseye throw to Johnny Evers at second. Smith was leaning toward third and had to lunge in retreat causing his cap to go flying. His dive managed to get him back in just under the tag.

Asking the umpire for time out, he retrieved his cap and dusted off his jersey. After the ump shouted, "Play ball!" Brown began his wind up but again pulled his foot off the pitching rubber and whirled back toward second, only this time he just faked a throw and held onto the ball. Smith returned to second standing up.

Perhaps it was the distraction of having a runner in scoring position late in a tie ballgame, but Brown seemed to lose his concentration and began to have difficulties finding the strike zone.   Davidson walked on five pitches. Two on, two out and the seventh-place hitter Zack "Buck" Wheat came to the plate. Sensing something might be up, Kling called for a pitchout and Three-Finger grudgingly obliged, but the maneuver was for naught as the Superba baserunners held their ground.

Dahlen figured this was an ideal opportunity as it was unlikely they'd waste two pitches in a row on pitchouts. He decided to turn up the heat and on Brown's second pitch, which was low and inside, Smith and Davidson took off attempting a double steal. Kling fired a throw to second which arrived slightly before the sliding Davidson but sailed wildly over second baseman Joe Evers' head out into center field. Smith continued home to score the go-ahead run, but center fielder Solly "Circus" Hoffman held Davidson at second. The sold-out crowd was on their feet. It was a scrappy, unearned run but the scoreboard operator replaced the "0" on the board with the same number "1" he'd have used if it had been an earned run resulting from an extra base hit.

Three-Finger was not pleased and circled the mound mumbling to himself. With a runner still in scoring position he wasn't out of the woods and the Cubs corner infielders played close to the lines to reduce the chance of an extra base hit which could blow the game wide open. Brooklyn's Buck Wheat fouled off a couple of pitches and worked the count to 2 balls and 2 strikes. Wheat then connected with an overhand curve and sent a weak grounder through the right side which threaded the needle in the recently created hole and trickled into right field. Davidson had to make sure the ball would make it through the infield, so he got a late break and held up at third base. Brooklyn now had first and third, two outs and the eighth-place hitter, right fielder Jack Dalton coming to the plate. Still only down by one run and with the pitcher due up next, Chicago decided to grant Dalton safe passage to first base via an intentional base on balls to load the bases.

Dahlen countered this strategic move by calling Doc Scanlon back to the dugout in favor of a left-handed pinch hitter to face Brown. Happy was not surprised at this decision but was shocked when his buddy and back-up catcher, Tex Irwin sitting next to him on the bench kicked his cleats and shouted, "Hey, Hap! Get yer damn butt off the bench, grab some wood and g'won out there fer Christ's sake! "Bad" Bill's callin' yer name, man." Happy's head had been in the game until that point but the idea that he'd be called upon to pinch hit in a crucial game situation was so foreign it hadn't registered that it was his name Bill Dahlen had shouted out.

Like any kid who ever picked up a bat and ball, this was the kind of scenario Happy had daydreamed about from his first neighborhood sandlot game all through his time in amateur ball...to be injected in a critical situation where his performance could influence the outcome of the game... except of course in Happy's fantasy it was a potential walk-off appearance in the bottom of the ninth of a tie game in which a victory would clinch the pennant and not the 7th inning of a meaningless game where he was called upon for an insurance run. But Happy was a rookie with all of 34 games and 79 plate appearances under his belt, so this was a big deal.

It was an especially interesting choice seeing as there were three other veteran Superbas (including another left-handed batter) who had considerably more playing time, acumen and overall baseball experience available on the bench and whom Dahlen usually called on in these situations. So, in fact, his selection of Happy Smith as the pinch hitter had quite a few Brooklyn players in the dugout and thousands of fans wondering what the hell Dahlen was thinking.

Somehow, with Tex Irwin's assistance, Happy grabbed his favorite bat with the initials CS carved into the knob and found himself walking toward the on-deck circle, each step seeming to take an eternity. As a pinch-hitter, Happy was afforded some latitude to take whatever time he needed to loosen up and prepare himself before stepping up to the plate.

Just as people on their death beds are said to be able to see their whole lives appear before their eyes, Happy envisioned these past six months of his professional baseball career as he rubbed his bat with pine tar to get a better grip and swung two bats at once to loosen up.

While taking his practice swings in the on-deck circle, he panned the stands quickly to see if he could see his landlady and new friend, Fanny Goldfarb. He knew she was there but the odds of seeing one in 18,000 plus were pretty slim – especially since she most certainly hadn't paid $1.50 for a field-level seat where he might have been able to pick her out.

He recalled his brief stay in Seattle and the confidence the minor league coach instilled in him before heading for Brooklyn. In his mind's eye he pictured his first glimpse of

Washington Stadium as he stood at the crest of the Brooklyn Bridge and took the final steps that enabled this moment in the sun. He thought of his amateur league coach who helped get him this opportunity in the Bigs.

And of course, he remembered his family back in Oregon, who despite their concerns for his future, encouraged him to pursue his dream. Henry, as he often did, recalled his older brother and couldn't help thinking there was some mistake. He's the one who should be standing here in baggy pants and cleats playing Major League Baseball.

Finally, out of the corner of his eye he picked up an icy stare from the home plate umpire indicating that his patience was wearing thin and Happy's trance was momentarily broken. At that point, for the first time since Tex kicked him in the dugout, he heard the chatter from the crowd. They were as nervous as he was, but the wheels were in motion, and he continued his walk out into the limelight.

Eastward Ho

O n a cloudy and chilly first day of March earlier that year, Henry Joseph Smith left his home in the river city of Coquille, Oregon aboard the 66.5 ft., propeller-driven steamship Echo, owned and piloted by his dad. As they departed, he stood at the stern and waved to his mom and watched for several minutes as she slowly receded on the dock, fading into the past. He then walked to the bow and focused his gaze straight ahead into his future as the oncoming wind whipped the hair that jutted from beneath his baseball cap pulled tightly across his head.

Henry hadn't noticed before departing...but the winds had picked up considerably, creating a sawtooth surf in the usually calm Coquille River. Before long, they were up to speed and needed to brace themselves against the steady chop, chop, chop of the disgruntled waters striking the bow head on. If you could ignore the cool wet spray that accompanied it, the rhythmic pounding that punctuated the steady drone of the diesel motor had a hypnotic effect that Henry found soothing. The moisture, gusts of wind, and cool air had a cumulative impact however, and after a short time the discomfort drove Henry to seek shelter, one flight up in the wheelhouse.

Inside, where Henry's dad Albert kept a steady hand on the ship's wheel and steady eye on the downstream waters ahead, it was drier and sheltered from the wind, a bit quieter. But the low-pitched engine vibration was ever-present making conversation difficult. The tensions under which Henry departed and the fact that his dad was a man of few words, didn't help matters... so they mostly passed the time in solitude, taking in the dramatic mountainous landscape through which the river meandered.

Four hours later, they landed in the port city of Bandon, Oregon where his dad gently pulled alongside the long floating dock and Henry tossed the old automotive tires they used as bumpers over the starboard side and tied off fore and aft before climbing off. His dad cut the engine and walked over to haul Henry's gear onto the dock. He then planted his hands on the starboard rail and swung his legs up and over, leaping to a standing pose in one graceful motion. At 49 years old, Albert Smith was still in fine physical shape. Henry took one last look at The Echo and emulated his dad's dramatic disembarkation.

With a sideways glance Albert spoke quietly, "OK, son...I guess this is it. You be all right getting your gear over to the steamship landing?"

"Sure, Dad. I'll be fine. I've gotta handle my stuff on my own the rest of the way, so might as well start now."

Albert was not comfortable displaying his emotions and his ambivalence about Henry's leaving didn't make it any easier. He reached out for what Henry expected would be a quick hug and said, "Take care of yourself, son," as they embraced.

"I will."

Practically whispering in Henry's ear, "And don't forget to write to let us know how you're doing."

"Of course, Dad. I'll look forward to hearing from you too."

Henry detected the slightest crack in his father's voice, "Your mom especially will be looking for those letters."

Henry began to wonder just how long this hug would go on. After a moment, "Wish you the best of luck kid."

"Thanks Dad. I appreciate that."

Albert nonchalantly raised his hand and wiped something from his face. "Goodbye son."

A few moments later he finally released his grasp, gave Henry a tight-lipped nod, turned and hopped back down to his boat. "I've got this son, go on ahead. Don't want to miss the ship to Seattle."

Henry had helped his dad on the boat for years and the standard protocol was that he'd release all the tie-downs and toss the ropes on deck before hopping back on board. It felt odd to just walk away and watch his father depart solo. After half a dozen steps, he stopped and turned back and stared as his father finished preparations to head back to Coquille. "Bye, Dad!" to which he got a nod and quick wave while Albert simultaneously negotiated the throttle and ship's wheel to reverse course and head back to Coquille.

Henry stood and watched until the wake subsided, and then walked a short way along the harbor and found the ticket office. Inside, he purchased a one-way passage aboard the Independent Steamship Company's J.R. Stetson in steerage class that would get him to Seattle by early evening. This large ocean-going commercial vessel was making its way from San Francisco to Juno with numerous stops in between, picking up and delivering lumber, fish, and other goods. After he arrived, he treated himself by checking into the newly opened Hotel Sorrento situated on top of First Hill and offering unobstructed views west to the Puget Sound, south to Mt. Rainier and east to Lake Washington.

The following morning, he made his way to Seattle's Great Northern Railroad station to purchase a one-way ticket bound for Chicago and begin his journey east. It was only after arriving at the rail station to purchase his ticket did Henry learn of the catastrophe that occurred just the previous day, taking the lives of 96 passengers and crew aboard two other Great Northern trains.

The Spokane Local passenger train No. 25 and the Fast Mail train No. 27 traveling west from Spokane to Seattle, had just exited the Cascade Mountains tunnel at Stevens Pass near Wellington, WA heading west (the very same route he was about to traverse in the opposite direction) but were stopped dead in their tracks for six days waiting for several feet of snow to be cleared from the recent blizzard.

Adding insult to injury, two separate snow removal locomotives had mechanical problems and another two were stranded by rocks and debris on the tracks that had to be cleared by manual labor. The situation became even more precarious when the railroad management fired the work crew needed to clear the debris over a wage dispute.

Then on March 1, a thunderstorm erupted and unleashed torrential rains which, combined with the effects of deforestation from the clear cutting of forest lands and a recent fire, created a perfect synergy of conditions to initiate the most devastating avalanche in U.S. history to sweep down the mountain. The pile of cascading snow and debris, which was ten feet high and a quarter of a mile wide, gathered energy as it descended upon the trains, effortlessly lifting them off their tracks and sending them plunging down a 150-foot ravine. A total of six steam and electric locomotives and fifteen freight, passenger, and sleeper cars were swept away in a matter of seconds.

Miraculously, despite the numerous casualties, 23 survivors were rescued from the twisted wreckage buried deep beneath the snow. Henry read an eyewitness account from a railroad employee, Charles Andrews in the Seattle Times:

> *"White Death moving down the mountainside above the train. Relentlessly it advanced, exploding, roaring, rumbling, grinding, snapping – a crescendo of sound that might have been the crashing of ten thousand freight trains. It descended to the ledge where the side tracks lay, picked up cars and equipment as though they were so many snow-draped toys, and swallowing them up, disappeared like a white, broad monster into the ravine below"*

Henry was moved by this descriptive account of the tragedy and wondered whether Mr. Andrews missed his true calling as a reporter or perhaps a novelist or poet. The excitement and anticipation Henry felt having started his journey was quickly overshadowed by the magnitude of the disaster and its potential to derail his dreams. He wasn't religious but couldn't help thinking, there but for fortune...

The railroad didn't know how long it would take to clear the snow, repair the tracks and restore service so Henry now found himself with an unexpected and disappointing delay. His apprehension over the close call now turned to dread that he'd arrive late and miss his opportunity to make the team. He thought about turning back to Coquille but the idea of going back home even for a couple of weeks was depressing. He couldn't afford an extended stay at the Sorento, so Henry continued thumbing through the same paper in which he read the shocking headline until he found listings for inexpensive housing in the classified ads. He was able to locate a suitable room with an affordable daily rate not far from downtown Seattle.

After checking in and dropping off his suitcase and gear, he located the nearest Western Union office and sent a telegram to the ball club to let them know what had happened and that he'd be delayed. Then he headed for dinner at a saloon nearby. It wasn't clear if he was just making conversation because it was good for business or if he was genuinely friendly, but the bartender soon had Henry recounting his exciting but frustrating saga in great detail.

"We sure love it around here but under the circumstances, I reckon you're not so keen on being waylaid in Seattle for God knows how long. Damn shame 'bout that train wreck... Guessing you're pretty lucky though, seein' as how it coulda been you, but for a couple a days."

Henry had tried to put that thought out of his mind and didn't want to be reminded of it so he was pleased when the barkeep changed the subject to baseball.

"You hearda our local ball club?" Henry knew that Seattle was one of the few West Coast towns that was able to support a minor league baseball team but confessed he didn't know anything about them except that they were known as the Turks and they played in the Northwestern League.

"Well, that's partially right – used to be called the Turks last year and was the Siwashes year before that, but this here year they's callin' themselves the Giants. Don't ask me what for since they got nothin' to do with the Major League Giants from New York City – reckon it's that they got sold again and the new owners are lookin' to start fresh. Take more'n a new name to change up their luck though. Haven't had a winning record in years. Say, seein' as you've got some time on your hands you might wanna go check them out – they're jest startin' their training and they practice right down the road in Yesler Way Park, 'bout a half mile south of here."

Next morning Henry walked over to the ballpark to watch the players working out and tossing some baseballs to begin loosening up. As he approached the field the sounds of balls popping into leather mitts and cracking off wooden bats in the crisp morning air instantly rejuvenated his spirits.

Not wanting to call attention to himself he was content to sit and watch the Giants work out from his seat mid-level on the first base grandstand such as it was. The seating was constructed of only ten rows of rough-cut pine planks supported by two-by-fours, clearly indicating the team's modest aspirations when it came to drawing fans. During their training sessions they weren't officially open for business so Henry was the lone spectator and felt a bit more conspicuous than he would have liked... but he sat the whole day without drawing much notice.

The next day however, manager Mike Lynch noticed Henry in the exact same spot eating a sandwich lunch the rooming house bartender made for him and his curiosity was piqued. "Pretty young to be a scout...what team you working for?" he shouted. Although they were not a high-level minor league club, they did occasionally get a talent scout or two searching for the next Ty Cobb or Walter Johnson.

Not that he took any effort to hide, but Henry was a bit embarrassed to have been noticed so all he managed in response after quickly swallowing a bite of sandwich was, "Not a scout, sir." Lynch knew immediately Henry was telling the truth – no scout would have addressed him as "sir."

"So whatta ya doin' sittin' up there anyway? You know son, our practices aren't really open to the public." And without waiting for an answer, "Ain't ya got a job?"

Henry realized he would have some explaining to do so he put down his lunch and scrambled down to the field level. "Actually, I hope to have one soon...that is, I hope to be playing in the Bigs..."

Lynch burst out laughing, almost choking on his chaw and then turned toward right field and let fly a big juicy wad of brown chaw spit without skipping a beat, "Yeah, I know kid. Everyone thinks they can be a pro ball player – there's nothing to it – just a simple game, right? Figure you'd wander over and join up, take off as an overnight minor league sensation and then get called up to Majors."

"No sir, it's just..."

"Hey, cut the 'sir' crap – name's Mike Lynch, formerly of the Chicago National League Baseball Club. So, I know what I'm talkin' about. Played with The Orphans for one season before they changed their name to the Cubs. Did pretty well too 'till I got my leg busted slidin' into home one game in '02. That was it. End of the career just like that."

"Wow, sorry to hear you..."

"And you can cut that crap too – wasn't tellin' you so you could get all teary-eyed about it. Just a fact, plain and simple. But I do know what I'm talkin' about as far as playin' ball."

"Sorry sir, uh I mean Mr. Lynch, uh I mean Mike."

"Didn't say you could get that familiar!"

Henry turned red realizing this was not going anywhere like he'd planned...Laughing again, Lynch said, "Just messin' with you kid. We're all pretty friendly 'round these parts. So, you any good?"

"Well, I hope so, uh I mean I think so. Coach Howard from Coquille Oregon where I'm from, got me a minor league contract with the Cubs... but they sold the rights to the Brooklyn Ball Club who invited me to their big league tryout... I still can't believe I'm headin' there just as soon as the railroad ..."

"Holy Shit kid! Why the hell didn't ya say so? Invitation from a Major League team? Now that's somethin'! Why're ya hangin' round here then, watchin' this bunch of misfits, half-wits and wannabes?"

Henry was feeling a little less intimidated and gradually told Lynch his saga about getting delayed. "Well, in that case, you don't wanna just be sittin' on your rump getting' soft. Show up tomorrow mornin' at nine a.m. sharp with your gear and you can work out with us. Let's see what you got. Help keep you sharp while you're waitin' for the Great Northern to start rollin' again."

Henry just grinned and let out another "Yes sir!" before he could help himself and as Mike walked away shaking his head as if to say "What a piece a work," it was Henry's turn to burst out grinning. He was thrilled with his stroke of good fortune and relieved his delay wouldn't be a total waste of time.

Over the course of his ten days with the Seattle Giants, Lynch took Henry under his wing. Not many of his players were ever going to make the Bigs and Henry's raw talent was clear. So, helping to mold Henry into a pro ball player was a challenge and source of pride for Lynch. One day after batting practice he called Henry over for a private session.

"Henry, you're gonna find there are lots of talented ball players all tryin' to make it, just like you. Gotta give it all you got and I know you'll be doin' that and then some. But sometimes it takes a few extra little skills to separate out the ones who make it from the ones goin' back home to driving steamboats like your dad - no offense. So, I'm gonna teach you one of those special skills that ain't easy to do... but if you master it, it can make the difference in a crucial situation."

Henry was a wide eyed and eager student. "Gonna teach you how to steal signs."

Henry was visibly taken aback, "Geez, I don't want to cheat - if I can't make it fair and square, I'll happily go back to being a river boat captain. Nothing wrong with that."

"Now see here kid, just 'cause it's called stealin' don't make it wrong. Ain't any different than stealin' bases far as I'm concerned. You got any problems takin' second base from time to time?" Lynch asked.

"Of course not, it's just part of the game," agreed Henry. "Eggs-actly son, so grabbin' a little sneak peek at what the catcher wants his pitcher to throw next ain't no different. You still gotta hit the damn ball! Hell, I know some catchers even tell ya what's comin' 'cause they know you ain't got more'n a one in a million chance of hittin' it anyway. You wanna learn it or what?"

"Well, when you put it that way, it seems ok. Heck yeah, I'm game!" said Henry.

"So the trick's in the timin'. You gotta be smooth and can't let the other team have any clue 'bout what you're up to. Soon as they think you're peekin' they'll be aimin' for your head, sure as shit. So don't ever be turnin' your head 'round while in the box or you're askin' for a beanin'.'"

What ya wanna do is wait for when the catcher's givin' the signs. 'Course you get that information by watchin' the pitcher's eyes and body language. It takes a bit a practice to get the timin' down jes' right. You can practice from the dugout or on-deck circle and even while you're battin' for the first few innings..."

"Kinda like this..." Lynch assumed the pose of a batter standing at home plate in the batter's box waving an invisible bat in the air and staring into the imaginary pitcher's eyes.

"So, when ya think the catcher is just startin' the signs, ya put yer arm up to ask the ump for time out and step outta the batter's box like so. While yer doin' that, ya glance back, real casual and quick-like to make sure he's givin' the time-out signal. Lynch's movements were so nonchalant," Henry wasn't sure he even saw him sneak a peek. "With me so far?"

Henry nodded in response.

"That's when ya gonna get the sign... course you can't be lookin' at the catcher or nothin' and it ain't easy seein' the sign outta the corner of your eye for a jest a half a second. That takes loads of practice too. Plus, the icin' on the cake is to finish up with some kinda real natural-like actin' job... maybe ya got somethin' in your eye or maybe ya gotta muscle cramp that needs attention. Course there's no guarantee the catcher's gonna keep the same sign when they set up again, but if he really ain't suspectin' ya, chances are he won't bother changin' it."

Henry tried to practice these skills and learned the mechanics of Mike's secret art of stealing signs but never really got good enough during his short stay in Seattle to pull it off effectively – either his timing was off and he missed the signs or his actions were so obvious even the bat boy knew what he was up to. Nevertheless, he was happy to learn some of the tricks of the trade and hoped it might come in handy someday if he was lucky enough to compete at the major league level.

Henry was very appreciative of Lynch's efforts to assist him and was a bit sad when he was finally able to resume his long journey east. Lynch wished him luck and expressed confidence in his prospects by promising to look for his name in the newspaper box scores during the season.

Henry boarded the Chicago-bound Oregonian on March 15. It was painstakingly slow in sections especially when the train had to climb the steep grades and switchbacks through the mountains. When they arrived in Wellington the engineer stopped the train for 96 minutes in memory of the recent victims of the avalanche, many of whom were his fellow workers and a couple he considered good friends.

The first leg of the cross-country trip was over 2200 miles and took more than three days to complete as they continued to wind slowly across the Olympic, Cascade and Rocky Mountains, each with their incredible vistas. They picked up some speed as they crossed the vast plains that seemed to stretch forever with few stops to break the monotony. Henry passed the time reading the copy of The Seattle Times he picked up before departing cover to cover.

Since he chose the more parsimonious second-class day-coach fare and didn't fork out the extra $10 for a Pullman sleeping berth, Henry slept in fits and starts. The seat was cushioned but not comfortable for sitting such long stretches and he was beyond exhaustion by the time they rolled into Union Depot in Chicago. The earliest connecting train to New York wasn't until the morning so he set out in search of affordable lodging for the night. Despite his best efforts at frugality, he passed up the flop house on the corner as being unsuitable and opted to pay a couple of dollars per night to stay in a decent small hotel above a saloon on West Madison St., where he napped for a couple of hours and had the best damn steak he'd ever tasted.

Ironically, he was originally planning to end his trip in Chicago at try outs for the Cubs, who after winning the World Series in '08 finished in second place in the National League last season. His coach Shep Howard contacted the Cubs, sang his praises without hesitation and miraculously (from Henry's perspective) they sent him a short-term contract to facilitate a tryout appearance.

However, before he could even pack his bags, he was notified that along with fellow prospect Tony Smith (no relation) and aging veteran Bill Davidson, he was traded to the Brooklyn Superbas for pitcher Harry McIntire. Of course, being traded from the mighty Cubs to the lowly Brooklyn club which finished last year in sixth place with a record of just 55 wins and 98 losses, might be viewed as a step down but as Shep reminded him, it greatly enhanced his chances to actually make the Bigs. So, as it turned out, both his tenure as a Cub and his layover in Chicago were short- lived and he'd soon be back on the rails.

But before leaving town, Henry wanted to get his first glimpse at a Major League baseball stadium even if it was potentially "enemy turf." So, after dinner he strolled around downtown and headed for Wolcott and Polk Streets on Chicago's West Side to check out Westside Grounds, home of the National League's powerhouse Cubs. The two mile walk from Union Depot felt good after having been cooped up on the train for so long. When he arrived, he walked around the outside but since the stadium was walled on all sides, he never did get a glimpse of the field. However, the tall wooden grandstands and bleachers stood proudly and quietly in the light of the practically full moon, waiting patiently for the start of the new baseball season.

Henry stopped for a moment to imagine the roar of the crowd that would be heard when those stands were filled to capacity, holding up to 16,000 spectators. Compared to the amateur league parks he was used to playing in, Westside Grounds was downright cavernous; the outfield fence in center field was 560 feet from home plate. Of course, if he was successful in making the team in Brooklyn, he'd have several opportunities to come back and play in Chicago as a member of the visiting team. The detour to the ballpark whet his appetite for the pending adventure and he looked forward to completing his journey... so Henry made his way back to the hotel where he quickly fell into a deep slumber from exhaustion.

He awoke with a start, drenched in sweat. The dream was a variation on his usual baseball theme - this time he was sitting in the stands at Westside Grounds watching his brother Carlton, whom he hadn't seen in twenty years, debuting in the Majors rather than himself. He eventually managed to drift back to sleep and felt rested when he woke for the early morning departure to New York aboard The Pennsylvania Railroad's Pennsylvania Special.

The Bridge to the Future

Henry was weary from what should have been a five-day cross-country journey but wound up taking three times that long and looked forward to the last stretch that now lay before him. After being trapped in cramped quarters for what seemed like an eternity, his legs which usually carried him effortlessly around the base paths felt like lead as he approached the bridge.

The final leg, while a mere 800 miles as the crow flies, had taken another 20 hours. They rolled past stock yards, wheat fields, and industrial parks with time-consuming stops in Ft. Wayne, Cincinnati, Columbus, Pittsburgh, Harrisburg, and Philadelphia. There was a short delay in Hoboken, NJ to switch from the steam-fired locomotive to an electric one because steam engines weren't allowed inside the newly constructed tunnel under the Hudson River or in New York's brand new, palatial Pennsylvania Station. It was staggering for Henry to think they were traveling more than 75 ft below the surface of the river through the new tunnel which the railroad's brochure proudly proclaimed was the longest underwater tunnel in the world. After his long journey Henry had finally arrived, but somehow his mind was a step behind reality and the conductor's unceremonious "Welcome to New

Yawk! Last stop" roused him from his temporary sleepless-induced stupor.

He grabbed his suitcase and equipment bag and trudged upstairs to the main concourse but wasn't quite ready for the dream-like setting that greeted him. Pennsylvania Station's huge, 150 ft. tall, vaulted ceiling supported by pink granite Corinthian columns provided a regal framework for the mid-day sun as it sparkled through the glass and steel roof and gently reflected off motes of dust and the inlaid marble floor – the sum of which momentarily took his breath away and left him squinting. Standing in the middle of the largest indoor space in New York and one of the largest anywhere in the world, Henry was transfixed.

The voluminous interior space swallowed up the cacophony of hissing and puffing engines, screeching brakes, conductors announcing arrivals and departures, and the thousands of passengers shouting to be heard above the din. It was all spit back out as a kind of low, muffled roar that lulled the senses. The sound was so thick the huge gold Bulova clock suspended from the ceiling seemed to be ticking in slow motion. Frozen by the majestic beauty, Henry suddenly realized that the world he was about to enter was a whole lot more than 3,000 miles away from Coquille.

As he walked outside the station the noises of the city immediately became much more acute – the clanging of street cars, staccato of horses, clicking of wagon wheels on cobblestone, puttering of automobile engines punctuated by air horns to warn people and animals as they approached were layered, distinct, and dissonant. Henry had been in New York for less than twenty minutes and he'd already experienced the overture and first movements of the symphony that was modern-day urban American life. In Oregon he had taken for granted the peaceful lull of gurgling brooks, streams, and rivers that crisscrossed the area surrounding Coquille broken only by the occasional high-pitched whining of a sawmill or the low moan of a passing barge's foghorn.

Adding insult to sensory injury, the next movement of the New York Symphony he experienced was a sharp uppercut to the nose – a thick soup of acidic smoke and smell of fresh manure hung in the afternoon air burning his nostrils. Until now, his olfactory frame of reference was the crisp, pine-scented air of the Pacific Northwest interrupted only by the smell of fresh cut logs or salt air when he occasionally journeyed downriver to the harbor in Bandon.

The bombardment of his senses on multiple fronts continued as Henry walked due east from 7th Avenue to Park Avenue where he descended the steps below the street to enter yet another station. This one was entirely beneath the ground and compared to the ornate Penn Station, the Interborough Rapid Transit System subway station was all business. He purchased a five-cent token, placed it in the turnstile, and entered the long narrow tube on the downtown side. The white tiled walls glistened and reflected the string of amber electric light bulbs that illuminated the platform, offset every twenty feet with smaller decorative inlaid tiles that spelled out the name of the station, 33rd St. His excitement was building, and Henry channeled his nervous energy by pacing down to the end of the platform.

Within a few moments, the large circular headlight of the oncoming train could be seen as it came barreling into the tunnel. After it slowed to a screeching stop, Henry was amazed to see multiple sets of doors in each of the subway cars open in unison. His position on the station platform aligned him with the first car and he stepped inside. He was surprised that all the seats were already occupied so Henry put his gear down against the wall and looked for a spot to stand. Quite a few passengers were standing and holding strategically placed leather straps to steady themselves, but Henry grabbed a pole across from the small room that served as the engineer's quarters just as the massive car lurched forward to continue making its way to lower Manhattan.

The car was lighted electrically too, but as soon as they cleared the station platform, they traveled exclusively through a dark subterranean tunnel. Peering out the large circular window at the front of the car into the dark tunnel ahead was surreal. He could make out a green colored light from time to time, presumably a signal for the train's engineer but mostly they were speeding ahead into sheer darkness at what seemed a breakneck pace and in what could only be described as a leap of faith. How could you be so sure what lay ahead if you couldn't see a damn thing?

For a moment Henry felt a twinge of danger and was transported back to his childhood where he imagined fire breathing dragons lurking in the dark. That passed instantly though when he caught a glimpse of the wide-eyed boy standing beside him craning his neck up to get a better view, grinning ear to ear. Other than the two of them though, no one else in the subway car seemed to be paying any attention to what had them both engrossed. Plus, leaning through gentle curves and being thrust abruptly through the sharper ones kept Henry awkwardly on the balls of his feet, clutching firmly on the metal pole and focusing to maintain his balance. The rest of the passengers moved this way and that seemingly effortlessly and hypnotically in sync with the train car's motion.

It was eight stops away, but Henry arrived at the City Hall station in a mere twenty minutes. Its many opulent touches, including curved archways and ceilings and stained-glass skylights, marked yet another page in his magical new world.

Dragging his suitcase and equipment bag up the stairs, he exited the platform and emerged at the surface once again. He found himself across the street from the grand, U-shaped City Hall building, whose French Renaissance-style marble exterior glistened in the bright sunlight, its white marble columns reaching upward toward the large domed central tower. He stood in the lush green City Hall Park and paused for a moment to get his bearings.

Spotting the bridge out to his left he began to walk east but at the edge of the park Henry passed a vendor selling his wares from a pushcart adorned with hand-painted lettering identifying him as, "J. Russ, Purveyor of the Finest Pickled Herring and Polish Mushrooms in New York City." Mr. Russ was shouting in a heavy unfamiliar foreign accent, "Hair-ring hee-yah, Getya schmaltz hair-ring! Nickelapiece, Threefera dime!" and Henry realized he hadn't eaten anything all day.

While he'd never encountered fish sold in this particular manner, as a native of the Pacific Northwest he was certainly no stranger to all variety of fish and was eager to try some. Mr. Russ selected three choice herring from the wooden barrel on his cart and wrapped them in a copy of a newspaper, but it was not in English so Henry couldn't decipher it. He happily dug out a ten-cent piece in exchange and devoured them practically whole.

Now satiated, Henry gazed in awe at the imposing visage that stood before him. The magnificent Eighth Wonder of the World, the largest suspension bridge ever built at the time of its completion in 1883, gracefully spanned nearly 1600 feet across the East River. It connected Manhattan and Brooklyn, the newly incorporated Borough of New York and Henry's newly adopted temporary home. Beside its younger siblings the Williamsburg, which inherited the title of world's largest suspension bridge and the Manhattan Bridge, the Brooklyn

Bridge still stood out as the most majestic of the trio of lower Manhattan's East River crossings.

More symbolically, this awesome structure, which like Henry was a youthful 27 years old, represented a bridge to the challenges that lay ahead. Being the best outfielder in Southern Oregon's amateur baseball leagues was one thing; New York had dozens of amateur teams and three teams in the newly formed professional leagues – it was the epicenter of the baseball world. Being paid to play for sophisticated cranks who actually bought tickets for the privilege of sitting in the grandstands of an enclosed ballpark in the emerging, professional, National Baseball League was another matter entirely.

His self-doubts and perpetual lack of confidence were not nearly conquered – he had tried to ditch them on the West Coast and was partially successful in doing so based on the encouragement he received working out with the Seattle Giants for a couple of weeks... but somehow, they managed to stow away and join him on his journey making the bi-coastal passage all the more fitful. He was convinced this was the path he was destined for, but his parents, while proud of his accomplishments as an athlete questioned whether this was a proper way to make a living. They had felt playing ball is merely a kid's activity in which they saw no future.

He reasoned that it was in fact, a new, growing profession and was quite competitive. If he didn't give it a shot now, he'd never know whether he could have been successful. Besides, if he tried and it didn't work out, he could always come back to Oregon and follow in his dad's footsteps piloting steam ships or perhaps work the booming logging industry of the Pacific Northwest. After completing high school, he spent two years in the U.S. Navy and had learned the skills needed to earn a living at sea. In the meantime, he had worked most recently in a local shipyard, but he never outgrew his love for the game that he excelled in since his teenage years.

In the end his mom came around, "You know, Albert, Henry's right…"

"I don't know, Elizabeth, who'd want to pay hard-earned money to watch a bunch of grown men play a kid's game? Sounds pretty damn crazy to me."

"Well dear," his mom reasoned, "it's really just another form of entertainment that more and more people seem to enjoy… I read in the papers it's getting quite popular in the mid-west and out east. And if people are willing to pay money to watch them, what's wrong with that?" Albert Francis Smith was a hard-working sea captain, set in his ways - but after considerable cajoling, eventually Elizabeth got him on board and they supported Henry's decision to make his journey to Brooklyn.

He could have taken a cable car over the bridge into Brooklyn, but Henry decided to walk the final leg of about three miles since he hadn't had any real exercise in days. The butterflies in Henry's stomach were overtaken immediately by the stabbing pains in his legs he felt as he began the steep climb over the bridge with his gear in tow. He was carrying his entire wardrobe, paraphernalia, equipment, dreams, and fears in his beaten-up leather suitcase and heavy-duty khaki-colored canvas duffle bag left over from his Navy days. In some ways the pain was a relief as he was distracted from his concerns about life in the big city and whether he had what it takes to become a professional ball player.

At the crest of the bridge's boardwalk path Henry stopped to catch his breath and gaze once again at the wonder of the new world he was discovering. Behind him was Manhattan's urban landscape with its soaring buildings in place of the tall trees of the Pacific Northwest. Among them was the

Metropolitan Life Insurance building, which at 50 stories high Henry would soon learn, was the tallest in the world.

Once he crossed the summit and began his descent, the pains in his legs eased allowing his worries to re-emerge. His anxiety was driven in part, by the huge expectations he placed on himself... not wanting to disappoint his family, coach and former teammates, who (like him) had never actually even seen a professional league game played, much less competed in one. How could they possibly be so sure that Henry was destined to be a local hero? True, he was carrying an official letter of invitation and conditional contract from the Brooklyn Base Ball Club to try out for the team during their pre-season workout. But he knew there'd be plenty of other young prospects, all with similar hopes and ambitions and was not convinced he wouldn't be walking back over the bridge heading back to Oregon in a few short weeks.

While Manhattan was dominated by its urban character, Brooklyn was more of a hodgepodge landscape of urban and rural. As he scrutinized the bustling metropolis before him from the top of the bridge, he could make out distinct residential neighborhoods linked together by cobblestone and dirt streets. Horse and wagons, motorized horseless carriages, and pedestrians alike, skillfully dodged the network of wood and steel electric trolleys that crisscrossed streets and connected neighborhoods, supplementing the underground and elevated trains for the 1.6 million residents.

Signs of expanding construction were ubiquitous; industrial areas with their smokestacks sat side by side with residential neighborhoods, parks, and farms. He was too far away to hear the clanking and clamoring of his new surroundings, but he could sense the vibration and excitement even now.

Fanny's Place

F rom the top of the bridge, looking southeast beyond the meandering industrial waterway known as the Gowanus Canal, in the distance Henry could make out the grandstands of Washington Park stadium, home of the Brooklyn Superbas.

He instantly realized that with home plate looking west-northwest, during late innings in September (if he was lucky enough to still be playing), the angle of the sun could make picking up the ball from the pitcher's hand tough. But as an outfielder, he would appreciate the fact that the sun would be behind his back and not make fielding pop flies more of a challenge.

From over two miles away it didn't look very big, but he'd heard they had over 15,000 paying cranks for their season opener last year, with several thousand more watching from the free area on the grassy hill beyond the outfield. The biggest crowds assembled to watch his most exciting rivalries in Oregon paled in comparison, measuring in the mere hundreds. Henry grinned as he put it in perspective: There were more than twice as many people in the Borough of Brooklyn than the entire state of Oregon.

Once he crossed onto Brooklyn soil, Henry reached into his pocket for the directions to the boarding house where he had arranged to stay and the street map that the ball club had sent him. The Superbas had provided a list of potential housing in the area and Henry was able to reserve a fourth-floor room in a boarding house on 7th Ave. and Carroll St. in the adjoining neighborhood of Park Slope, just a ten-minute walk from the field at Washington Park. A letter to Mrs. Fanny Goldfarb had secured the room for $6.50 a week including two meals a day.

Mrs. Goldfarb was widowed – her husband Moishe was the successful proprietor of Goldfarb's Dry Goods store, which had been located on the ground floor of the building. Together they had lived with two, now-grown daughters in their multi-level apartment above the store until Moishe passed away suddenly about four years earlier. Goldfarb had done well enough. Over the years he gradually put aside the money needed to eventually purchase the building so Fanny was able to manage comfortably on the rent she received from the store (now a haberdashery) and the six boarders she took in.

Despite his intentions to get some exercise in, *schlepping* his gear up the steep incline of the bridge combined with his lack of sleep, left Henry exhausted, so he hired a horse and buggy to transport him the last few miles to Park Slope. As they traveled southeast along Flatbush Ave., just before they turned right onto 7th Ave., he saw the majestic Grand Army Plaza, with its huge Soldiers' and Sailors' Arch overlooking an ornamental fountain at the foot of the green expanse of Prospect Park and did a double take. For a moment he was transported back to Paris where he spent a week of R&R during shore leave from the Navy, and where he and his buddies enjoyed a picnic lunch at the similar but larger, Arc de Triomphe.

It was mid-afternoon when he arrived at Fanny's place at 123 7ᵗʰ Ave. and she immediately took a break in her preparations for that night's supper to greet Henry, show him to his room upstairs and make him feel welcome. She was small in stature but solidly built. With her partially graying hair, Henry placed her in her late forties – early fifties. The smell of boiled meat pervaded the house.

Fanny preferred tenants who planned to stay a while – short term itinerants, as she liked to say, "just bring me *tsuris*."[1] Speaking of trouble, Fanny briefed Henry on the house rules regarding noise, entertaining guests, when she expected payment for room and board, and so on. Several ball players had roomed with her in the past – they were good for a six-month stay before heading back to their wives, families, and "day jobs" in hometowns throughout the nation.

Baseball was quickly becoming the national pastime, but professional teams were only located in a few select cities, so the athletes often migrated back home for the off-season. The other advantage in having ball players as boarders was the fact that they are away on travel about half the time resulting in one less mouth to feed. To guarantee their rooms, the players paid the same weekly rent for their entire stay, regardless of whether they were there for meals or not.

When a member of the team was in residence, Fanny clipped the Superba's team schedule from the newspaper at the start of the season and pinned it to her kitchen cabinet to help determine how many diners would be there each night. She was also developing a love for the game and counted

-----

[1] Yiddish words appear in italics throughout the text. If their meaning is unclear, you may consult the Yiddish-English translations in the Glossary

herself among the Superbas' loyal followers. When asked about it, she'd reply, "What? Only the men should be crenks? I can get pretty crenky, let me tell you!"

Of course, the downside to having ball players in the house was their potential penchant for carousing. Grown men – mostly young – without their wives and families to assert discipline were easily distracted by the temptations of night life and there was no shortage of such temptation in Brooklyn or its sister borough of Manhattan in the newly merged City of New York, the largest in the nation.

Henry was surprised to learn that ironically, the tenant who occupied his room last season was none other than the pitcher he had been traded for, Harry "The House" McIntyre – his nickname due to his rather large frame which was continually expanding as a result of his fondness for a few pints of gat. Fanny later confided in him that McIntyre was particularly difficult – since he didn't have to perform each day, he seemed to be out late most nights, often returning in the wee hours in a less than discrete manner. The House frequently disregarded Fanny's basic ground rules of common courtesy for the other guests including maintaining quiet and banning of visitors after 11 pm despite numerous reminders. She was contemplating asking The House to find another one in which to reside this season when he was unexpectedly traded to the Cubs. Henry speculated whether McIntyre's off-the-field activities became too much of a distraction and led to the trade that brought him to Brooklyn.

Fanny was unlike any women Henry had ever met in Oregon. She was independent, smart, fluent in three languages and not hesitant to speak her mind. An avid reader, Fanny would go through several papers cover to cover each day including the New York Times and *The Forverts* also known as the Jewish Daily Forward (while he couldn't make out the words, Henry recognized this as the same paper that was used to wrap his herring and Fanny explained it was published in Yiddish). Plus, there were various political pamphlets and all sorts of books in the living room Henry passed on his way upstairs to his room. Fanny encouraged her boarders to borrow books whenever they pleased. She would often tell the boarders about the latest thing she was reading, talk about the political and social organizations she belonged to, or discuss an article in the paper that she thought was noteworthy as she served dinner or occasionally, if she sat with them for tea and dessert afterwards.

After settling in and unpacking his things into the carved wooden wardrobe cabinet in his room, Henry used the common bathroom in the hall to shower and shave before dinner. That night Fanny was serving something she called brisket, a rather well-cooked meat with boiled potatoes and cooked carrots – the smell he noticed on entering the house permeated all the way up to the fourth floor. Henry would soon learn that Fanny was a passable cook – she didn't have a large repertoire of recipes, and most were ethnic dishes he was unfamiliar with – but he always seemed to muster up an appetite to finish his meals and often asked for a second portion.

That night Fanny served her long crescent shaped *mandelbrot* cookies for dessert that were hard as a rock and needed to be dunked in the tea to avoid breaking your teeth. The after-dinner discussion was over the story that ran in the morning edition of the NY Times on Harry Houdini's latest stunt. It was quite different than his usual tricks – he wasn't chained in shackles, submerged under water or locked in a trunk – but this stunt was every bit as dangerous... a great escape of a very different variety from one of the strongest forces on earth. And it took place about as far away from his New York residence as possible.

Houdini was an amateur pilot and flew the first recorded flight over Australia in a biplane he purchased in France and had shipped down under. He defied gravity and managed to stay in the air for seven and half consecutive minutes traversing a distance of six miles at a height of about 100 ft before landing safely on terra firma. Sinead Donnelly, one of the two young women boarders worked at the Brooklyn Public Library Children's section where she frequently read stories aloud, so Fanny asked her, as she often did, to read the article in the paper to the group. "Certainly, Mrs. Goldfarb," replied Sinead. "I'll be pleased to." So, after retrieving her reading glasses that hung from a chain around her neck and carefully folding the paper the long way, she scanned the front page and found the piece halfway down the right side. Taking a sip of water to clear her throat, she began to read. The story started by quoting Houdini's reflections on his accomplishment once it was over:

> *"When I went up for the first time, I thought for a minute that I was in a tree; then I knew I was flying. The funny thing was that as soon as I was aloft, all the tension and strain left me. As soon as I was up all my muscles relaxed, and I sat back, feeling a sense of ease. Freedom and exhilaration, that's what it is."*

After she finished reading, there was some discussion back and forth about whether any of them had the courage to attempt a ride in a flying machine and if they thought they had, whether the experience would be a relaxing or a horrendously scary proposition. Someone said they'd ridden the roller coaster in Coney Island and that must evoke a similar feeling. Henry did not weigh in but thought to himself the idea of leaving the earth's surface in a flying machine (or cascading down a rickety roller coaster for that matter) made the hair on the back of his neck stand up. Fanny had the last word. "He is a very brave man, this *landsman* Erich Weiss who calls himself Mr. Harry Houdini... but he is also a little bit crazy in the head to always try such dangerous *mishegas* if you ask me!"

The other boarders including Gabriella Fiorenti, a clerk in a sewing shop, Brian Thompson, a high school science teacher, Jerome Resnick, a traveling salesman, and Frank Petrocelli, a barber were friendly enough. That first night they seemed curious about his quest to become a professional athlete, so Henry was peppered with questions which only added to his self-consciousness, but he tried to make the best of it.

Fortunately, Fanny stepped in on his behalf and said, "Henry, you must be *oysgematert*..." Henry looked confused. "*Farshteyn*? You understand? Sorry... I'm living here already almost 23 years and I still mix Yiddish *mit* English. You must be plenty tired from your travels. Maybe you should *gay shlofen*, go on up to sleep. *Oy*, there I go again!"

Henry managed a sheepish smile of relief. Admitting that he was pretty tired and had to report to the stadium early the following morning, he excused himself and made his way back upstairs to his room.

Into the Limelight

As he arrived at home plate, he felt the sweat in his palms; it was a comfortable 68 degrees on game day so he attributed the perspiration to his nerves. Before stepping into the batter's box, Happy wiped his hands on his uniform pants and continued to rub the pine tar on his bat to ensure he had a solid grip. His cap felt slightly askew, so he adjusted the brim an eighth inch to the left. He re-tucked the front of his wool jersey uniform shirt into his pants and kicked the dirt from his cleats with the end of his bat.

At this point his baseball instincts, honed by countless repetition through years of sandlot and amateur league games and endless practice drills, took over and he surveyed the field. Although he was watching closely as the inning unfolded, he reviewed in his head the critical particulars of the game as it currently stood.

Bottom of the 7th inning against the first place Cubs. Bases loaded. Two outs. One run lead but a hit or a walk brings in at least one more insurance run, maybe more. Defense playing straight away or a shade to right field. Not expecting me to pull against Three-Finger Mordechai Brown on the mound. Throws gas so I've got to be ready but has a mean changeup which he mixes in with a lights-out, off-speed overhand curve. Will pitch inside and put you on your ass just for fun. Best pitcher in the whole damn league.

He automatically glanced down to the third base coach to read the signs, although Happy knew as did everyone in the stadium, that with two outs and bases loaded he would be instructed to swing away. In fact, since the coach didn't make a move to tug on his ear, none of the animated gestures he was going through meant anything at all. Swing away kid, plain and simple.

Happy's attempt to focus was shattered by the bark of home plate ump Bill Brennan, just a few feet behind his left ear. "Hey, rookie! Haven't got all day...you gonna get in there and hit or what?"

"Yes sir!" instinctively responded Seaman Second Class, Henry Smith as he crossed the threshold into the left side batter's box.

Brennan misinterpreted this as a sarcastic response and gave Happy a dirty look. With that reaction, Happy thought he just lost the benefit of the doubt on anything close, so he'd better be prepared to swing at any pitch even remotely near the strike zone. It was never really in question, however. Major league umpires, including Brennan always gave the edge to a veteran pitcher over a rookie. That's just how things work.

Baseballs and Matzah Balls

Despite his fatigue, Henry stared at the ceiling for quite some time and soaked up the unfamiliar sounds of the city, which didn't seem to diminish in pace or volume even as the hour turned late. The alarm clock on the nightstand, which he wound before getting into bed loudly ticked off the seconds. Eventually it had a lulling, mesmerizing effect and he finally drifted off.

Next thing he heard was its jarring announcement that morning had arrived, and Henry reluctantly rolled out of bed and down the hall to the toilet. He had no recollection of getting dressed but soon found himself with his equipment bag in the dining room again. Breakfast was a simple affair of toast, *schmeared* with either a soft, white cheese Fanny called pot cheese or homemade fruit jam, and a freshly brewed pot of coffee. Then off to Washington Park for the first day of training.

On the corner of tree-lined Carroll St. heading west, Henry passed the Old First Reformed Church whose roots date back to the earliest settlements in Brooklyn (or Breukelen as the original Dutch settlers referred to it). The current impressive granite and limestone church was completed in 1891. With its tall spire and stained-glass windows, it resembled some of the churches Henry saw in his Navy days while enjoying brief shore-leave visits in Europe.   It was in fact, at 1200 ft to the top of the spire, the tallest church in Brooklyn and would prove to be a handy landmark to lead him back to Fanny's place after a night acquainting himself with the numerous taverns that dotted the neighborhood on the commercial blocks of 5th, 6th, and 7th Ave. Easter was just a few weeks away, so Henry made a mental note to attend services and get a look at the church from the inside.

The rest of Carroll St. was primarily residential with row after row of large three- and four-story brownstone houses, most occupied by well-to-do families, many of whose breadwinners commuted across the river to Manhattan to work each day.   At 4th Ave. Henry turned south and the neighborhood changed dramatically. Instead of brownstones or commercial shops stood a few factories and just a few blocks away, bordered by 1st and 3rd St., was the stadium.

The wooden grandstands towered over the streets and cast long shadows in the morning sun. As he neared the entrance, his nerves approached a gallop, and his breakfast was churning in his stomach. So rather than entering through the player's gate on the 3rd St. side he continued on and decided to walk the perimeter of the stadium as he did in Chicago, hoping to burn off some of the nervous tension he felt. Less than ten minutes later he was back at the 3rd St. gate, heart still pounding but with no excuse not to enter.

The players' entrance led straight to the clubhouse area beneath the grandstands, where he reported and was given a temporary locker to put his clothing. He was issued a uniform that was a size too big and a bit threadbare – the equipment manager explained that if he actually made the team, he'd be issued a new uniform that fit properly. The team's equipment budget didn't include shoes so Henry's old beat-up cleats he'd brought along with him would have to do. Henry promised himself that if he made the team, he'd treat himself to a new pair.

After changing, he walked with the other players through the locker room and dimly lit tunnel towards the stairs leading to the field, which were eerily illuminated by the daylight from above. The sound of dozens of metal cleats clanking on the concrete floor provided a staccato rhythm counterpoint to the catcalls and whistles from the players that echoed in the long narrow space.

When he climbed the stairs, he found himself standing in the Brooklyn dugout, which was a new experience – in the amateur leagues a bench on the sidelines was a luxury. He squinted through the bright morning sun on the broad expanse of the field and was taken aback by the bright green everywhere he looked. No sign of crabgrass, dandelions, or barren dirt in the outfield like the ones he was used to playing on. The manicured grass and clay infield was a thing of beauty. The grandstands behind the plate and extending out to both right and left field were empty, but Henry could easily imagine them filled to capacity with the roar of a sold-out crowd... He stood in the dugout for a moment daydreaming and taking it all in.

Noticing Henry's momentary trance and wide-eyed stare as he brushed by, one of the newly acquired veteran players paused on the dugout steps and grinned. "Hey kid, not bad, huh? Name's Tony." As his teammate extended his hand, Henry's reverie quickly dissolved, and he was both embarrassed and heartened at the same time. Returning the handshake was automatic but he had to swallow before any response could be uttered. "Henry" was all he could muster at the moment, but he did manage a smile in return. Yeah, it's somethin' all right he thought to himself.

This was only the second season for this third incarnation of the Superba's Washington Park stadium - it was rebuilt twice after fires had totally consumed the previous versions of wooden grandstands and Henry had heard rumors that it may be one of its last. Team owner Charles Ebbets, who took immense pride and interest in his ball club was mum on the topic. The reality was that the Brooklyn club was just scraping by financially and Ebbets was not wealthy enough to finance the construction of a new stadium on his own.

In addition to the veteran squad, the Superbas invited a rather large group of new players (36 athletes mostly from the amateur leagues all around the country) so they could whittle down the prospects to a manageable number, keeping only those with a reasonable chance of playing at a professional caliber and with a demonstrated capacity to stand up to the grilling with which they would most certainly be greeted by the regs. Eventually only five or six of those new players would be left standing as the season began. In addition to the amateurs trying to make the team, there were a handful of veterans who were new to the ball club (including Tony Smith and Bill Davidson who were included in the deal with the Cubs).

The clubhouse atmosphere in general, and the gruff demeanor of the club manager, "Bad Bill" Dahlen and his coaching staff in particular, were not unlike Henry's experience in the Navy. In retrospect, the military style approach was likely calculated to prepare the newbies for what lay ahead. But it certainly didn't ease Henry's queasiness, and he soon became acquainted with the location of the clubhouse toilets.

The first day of training was physically as well as mentally grueling. They worked exclusively on exercise and running drills which instantly brought Henry back to his basic training days in the Navy – the only difference being the uniforms on their backs and the footwear on their feet.   Exercise at the amateur level usually consisted of a few minutes of stretching and calisthenics and even Henry who was in relatively good shape struggled to keep pace.   And thus, the weeding out process began. As well as the griping:

"Still dunno why a buncha grown men like us bust our asses to compete for a chance ta play a kid's game for the poor excuse of the monthly paycheck those crooked owners dole out…"

"Oh no, here he goes again…"

"Hey Hummel, whatsamatta? Wife wantin' ya ta take 'er on vacation again?"

"Shut the fuck up, will ya? Ya know goddamn well that Ebbets got more dough'n all of us poor working stiffs combined. Plus, with the damn contracts they make us sign, them owners got us over a barrel. They last into perpetution or some shit, which is the lawyers' way a sayin' 'til hell freezes over. We got no rights to try and go work for 'nother team since them owners all stick together. Say anythin' 'bout it and they can kick your ass out of the League for good. Let's face it guys, they basically own us – not as bad as slavery or nothin', but it stinks pretty bad. "

"Calm down Johnny Boy…You's gettin' more an' more woiked up 'bout shit deez days.   Gotta let it go an jes concentrate on doin' yer best so ya make da damn team in the foist place! Ain't gonna make nothin' if y'aint even on the ball club."

"Just sayin' you ought to think about it for a minute. Workers in all kinds a jobs is getting together to demand better conditions. Why can't we?"

Henry was curious and listening intently. "Silent" John Hummel was known to be a bit of a hot head who blew off steam more often than most. But Henry had to admit what he said seemed pretty logical. Since Henry was still smitten with the idea that he just might actually make it to the professional leagues he hadn't given a moment's thought to what that might mean.

As Day Two rolled around the physical training continued but now it was broken up by hitting, fielding, and base running drills so the players could at least put their toil in perspective and begin to fantasize about meeting their goals.

Day Three saw the introduction of simulated games with live pitching and Henry was relieved to begin to have an opportunity to demonstrate his skills. But the competition was fierce – while a few players were let go in the next couple of days, most were retained and demonstrated a level of competence equivalent to or better than the all-stars Henry played with in Oregon.

As a renowned fielder, Henry was more than holding his own defensively. Batting was another matter though – while Henry was having little difficulty connecting squarely with the ball during batting practice, during simulated games against live pitching he couldn't shake his fears and wound up yielding lots of weak grounders and foul balls or worse yet, striking out an inordinate number of times. His nerves got the better of him so much they sabotaged his natural abilities. Knowing that there were just a few days to demonstrate he had what it takes only exacerbated the tension.

Henry stayed late after the third day's practice ended to get some more time in the batting cage and by the time he got back to Fanny's, showered, and changed everyone had finished dinner and the dining room was empty. Fanny was still cleaning up in the kitchen and came out to greet him with a smile and in her typically slightly sarcastic voice,

"*Nu*, how'd it go at the office today Mr. Big Shot Professional Athlete? Did you hit some house runs or get arrested for stealing the bases?"

Despite his insecurities and rocky start Henry couldn't help but laugh. "It's home runs, Fanny...and no, far from it. I didn't hit much of anything and since I didn't get on base, I didn't have a chance to steal any of them."

Fanny prided herself in being a good listener and after serving Henry a large bowl of chicken soup with matzah balls she pulled up a chair and demanded to hear all the details. It turns out she was actually a pretty knowledgeable crank and followed the box scores and accounts of the previous day's games in the newspaper, which she read religiously each morning after attending to the needs of her boarders.

Being so close to Washington Park she even attended half a dozen or so games a season – it was rather unusual to see a woman in the stands and even rarer that she'd be there without accompaniment of a male family member or suitor. But that didn't bother Fanny – as Henry was quickly learning she was feisty and didn't back down easily. Since she'd never played baseball herself, her knowledge was strictly based on what she'd observed, read in the papers, and gleaned from discussions with her ball playing boarders.

Henry recounted his lackluster hitting including as many details as he could recall – he found just talking about it with Fanny a bit cathartic. She listened intently and when he was done, she sat in silence with her eyes shut for a long while as if she was contemplating and processing all of the information. Finally, she made eye contact.

"Hmmm, I see... So your timing is all *farblunget*. You swing too late on the fastball, and too soon *mit* da curve. You know how to read, yes? You need to learn how to read the pitches, so you swing the bat at just the right time. You need to watch how the pitcher gets ready before he throws – look where he puts his hands, look how he holds the ball, look at his eyes. Pay attention to how he pitches in certain situations so you can get inside his head and think like he thinks. If you do all these things, you have better chance - less foul balls, less strike outs.

When you got everything right, hitting the baseball with the bat..." Fanny clasped her hands together and swung them from right to left.

"...is like scooping your *kneidlach* with the spoon." Continuing her gesturing she clutched an imaginary spoon and dramatically plucked a virtual matzah ball from the air and sent it flying into left field with a dramatic clap of her hands.

Henry was taken aback – of course he was well aware his timing was amiss and that pitchers often tip their hand on pitch selection. But he certainly didn't expect to hear such an informed evaluation from Fanny and he suddenly realized that he'd been so nervous he'd neglected the basics that got him here in the first place. He also realized that there was more to Fanny than meets the eye. Drifting off to sleep that night Henry smiled with the knowledge that he'd made his first, albeit unlikely friend in New York.

Wildfire of Hatred

Like so many other Jewish families in Eastern Europe and Imperial Russia, the Feinsteins were hoping to emigrate to the United States to seek a better life, but events in April 1883 changed their plans dramatically.   A series of pogroms to persecute Russian Jews had been enacted following the assassination of Czar Alexander II in 1881 and several years later, his successor, Alexander III instituted an additional series of harsh rules and penalties against Jews all across the Russian Empire.

Soon thereafter, like a wildfire of hatred, hordes of anti-Semitic drunken rioters, launched a series of nightly deadly rampages unimpeded by the Czar's troops or local police who merely stood by and watched or even encouraged the violence. Spreading quickly from village to village the unimaginable became commonplace as homes and farms went up in smoke oftentimes while the residents were asleep in the dead of night.   Once unleashed and unchallenged, the bigotry exploded into a firestorm and the merriment was brutally accented by rape and pillaging.

They'd managed to avoid the worst of it so far but many of their friends, relatives and neighbors hadn't been so fortunate and the horror was closing in on them quickly. The

Feinsteins didn't have enough rubles saved to purchase the necessary passage for all six family members to leave together and given the circumstances it would be next to impossible to liquidate their assets quickly enough to do so. Thus, her parents made the difficult decision to use what money they had managed to save to send Fanya to America on her own in the hope that they would join her later. It took several weeks to make the travel arrangements and fortunately not much longer to receive a visa – many waited up to several years to obtain permission to enter the U.S.

So on Wednesday morning May 23, 1883, 20 year-old Fanya Feinstein left her parents, two younger sisters Rachel and Gabriela, and younger brother Judah, in their shtetl on the outskirts of Kiev near the suburb of Demievka. This was Chapter One of her passage from the comforts of her family, friends and home to the world of the unknown. It had been a distant fantasy of hers that became reality without much time for contemplation. Fanya was both elated and petrified. She had never traveled beyond Kiev and only had one relative in America – her father's cousin and his family in New York to help get her established.

Her heart felt torn; she couldn't bear to leave her family and friends in this time of crisis, most especially her sisters and baby brother who just turned six years old. Their mother worked long hours as a seamstress so in addition to working part-time herself since finishing school two years earlier, the responsibility for looking after her younger siblings fell mostly on Fanya and her relationship with Rachel, Gabriela, and Judah was especially close.

While it was a huge burden to uproot her young life on such short notice Fanya didn't complain. After all, family was family, and her parents had made many sacrifices for her. For example, since Jewish girls were not permitted to attend public schools, they struggled to pay the tuition of 800 rubles per year so Fanya could attend a private religious school and could receive a balanced and progressive education. Despite the cost and the fact that they could have used the additional income if Fanya went to work at an early age as most girls did, they made sure she continued to stay in school to complete a high school education.

She was proud that her parents felt she was worthy and mature enough to take on this monumental responsibility. She was also old enough to understand their predicament. Her parents' decision was both an act of love for Fanya and vote of confidence in her capabilities... but at the same time it was a desperate hope that somehow, they could elude danger long enough for her to establish herself in America and earn enough money to send for the rest of them to reunite the family.

That dark reality and challenge did not faze her. In fact, Fanya had no doubt that she would accomplish her task and continue to make her parents proud. Filled with despair at having to leave and set out on her own, especially under these desperate circumstances, Fanya was at the same time, thrilled at the prospect of discovering a new world for herself and with all that lay ahead.

The Task at Hand

Now in the batter's box, he assumed his offensive stance which placed him just off the inside corner in a vertically straight position. One tap of the outside edge of the plate with his bat, which he then raised high above his shoulders and held relatively steady. Happy preferred to position himself in the box, get comfortable, and concentrate on the task at hand. Absent were any extraneous motions like bouncing while in a crouch or swinging the bat back and forth, techniques that were popular with many players.

As he stepped up and positioned himself, he got an earful from Cubs catcher Noisy Kling in an attempt to distract him and break his concentration. Noisy's approach usually began with disarmament via friendly banter which could easily progress to the more insulting variety.

"Hey kid, dying for a pastrami sandwich after the game. You know where I can get a good one?" Happy glanced back and gave him a smirk but didn't respond. "S'matter kid? You a mute? My wife's cousin's one of 'em. Can't speak a word. She can see ok, though... not like that Helen Keller lady who's deaf, dumb AND blind. Course, most players might as well be blind as good as they hit ol' Three-Finger, know what I mean?"

Happy knew of course, just what Noisy was up to and wished for a moment that he were deaf so he wouldn't have to put up with the non-stop chatter coming from behind the plate but without thinking he fell into his trap anyway.

Coincidently Fanny had just taken a copy of Helen Keller's newly released autobiography "The World I Live In" out of the Brooklyn Public Library and was talking about it at dinner just the night before so his mind started to wander for a fraction of a second. She had read the chapter entitled, "The Hands of Others" aloud and he recalled thinking what it must be like to rely solely on one's hands to see, hear, and feel the world around you. Doing so, he subconsciously tightened his own hands gripping the bat. He imagined Helen Keller would appreciate the fact that like her, Mordechai Brown has been able to overcome his handicap, finding a way to turn his disability into an asset.

Not only was his mind about a hundred miles away from baseball, but the tension in his hands radiated through his arms and shoulders as if he were about to go flying down the Dips and Drops roller coaster at Coney Island that Tex never stopped talking about. All of the advice he had ever received from baseball coaches and mentors on successful hitting (which could be summarized by the mantra: stay loose, eliminate extraneous thoughts, keep your eyes on the ball, swing smoothly and make solid contact) was out the window.

Smith stared straight ahead. Still fixated on hands, he noticed Three-Finger gripping the ball in his throwing hand which he dangled loosely on his right thigh as he stared down to pick up Kling's sign for the first pitch. Most pitchers keep their throwing hand behind their back before they start their windup, but Brown liked to show off his deformity to try and get an additional edge on the hitter. The pointer finger on his right hand was severed below the knuckle in a farm machine accident and the remaining stump helped him get extra spin on the ball that caused his pitches to have lots of action so they would drop and dive unexpectedly.

Brown had picked up the sign from Kling but before he began his windup he paused, made eye contact with Happy and gave him a devilish grin. Welcome to the big leagues kid.

Fanya's Journey

S he'd never been on an overnight train and once under way, with the teary-eyed parting behind her, Fanya was transfixed by the new sights rolling by. The first leg of her journey by rail from Kiev due south to Odessa departed at 7 am and took 28 hours. There were numerous stops of the combined passenger and freight train to load and unload goods and livestock along the way. During a two-hour layover in Uman, the approximate halfway point to Odessa she was able to get off and take a walk around the small city. As more than half its citizens were *landsmen,* Fanya felt at home strolling about the streets and the Sofievka, the large, wooded park on the outskirts of town. Here she passed a band of musicians playing traditional Klezmer music whose familiar melancholy sound both warmed her heart and reminded her of all she was leaving behind.

On the way back to the train she was overwhelmed with the smell of freshly cooked blintzes prepared at an outdoor stand adjacent to the rail station. She realized it was past her usual dinner time and she'd only had a few snacks since leaving, so without hesitation, she gladly paid the one ruble for a cheese blintz served with a familiar cucumber tomato salad. She savored her first meal on her own and returned satiated to resume her travels.

With a full stomach and not much to distract her, she drifted off to sleep as soon as the train was back under way, dreaming of what it will be like to be on her own for the first time. By the time she awoke, the train was pulling into Odessa for another short four-hour stopover.

Her first lesson in making it on her own was trying to stretch the food and the small amount of money she had with her as long as possible. No telling when she'd be able to get a job or what she'd be able to earn in New York. Fanya got off the train and had a small late-morning picnic meal in the sunny park across from the Odessa rail station with some of the provisions her mom had carefully selected and packed for her. She cut off a few slices from the salami which she ate on crackers washed down with water from the public fountain. The brief change of pace and opportunity to stretch her legs was well appreciated.

Some of her fellow travelers were disembarking here to board steam powered ships heading west directly from the port of Odessa but her dad was able to negotiate a considerably lower-cost ticket for the transatlantic voyage by having her depart from Athens. So, Fanya would continue by rail another 14 hours southwest to the Romanian port city of Constanta, and board a sail powered fishing boat bound for Athens to deliver its catch. It sailed through the Bosphorus Strait, the waterway connecting the Black Sea and the Sea of Marmara which separates Asia from Europe, then through the Dardanelles Strait where it joins the Aegean Sea, and due southwest on to Athens.

Despite the fact that it added an extra few days to her travels, Fanya was thrilled because the Romanian fishing boat would be stopping overnight in Istanbul before continuing on to its final destination. Even though she wouldn't stay long in either Istanbul or Athens, the idea of including these exotic destinations in her itinerary made her journey feel all the more magical.

When not taking in the scenery out the train's windows, Fanya had several books to read and a journal she was keeping of her adventure. She didn't get much more sleep on the next leg but worked out a routine to keep her interest in world and public affairs stoked by collecting and reading discarded newspapers left behind by departing passengers.

On May 25, for example, the headline in the Kiev Daily Times "Eighth Wonder of the World Opens Today" caught her eye and she grabbed the abandoned paper to read about this miraculous engineering feat in her soon-to-be new home. The immense size and beauty of the bridge spanning the sister cities of Brooklyn and New York was amazing and she couldn't believe she would soon be able to see it with her own eyes.

In that same paper, she read of a new traveling entertainment show, which was giving their initial performance in the Western U.S. but was soon scheduled to appear throughout the country with stops in both Brooklyn and Staten Island in the New York area. It was founded by a gentleman by the name of William F. Cody, but the show went by his nickname, Buffalo Bill Cody's Wild West Show and included an assorted collection of animals, cowboys, and Indians, in a kind of Western Frontier circus. Surely anything was possible in her new land of opportunity.

In world news, she read about a series of memorials that were being planned in Paris, London, New York, Madrid, Frankfurt, and St. Petersburg to commemorate Karl Marx who died in London two months earlier. Organizers were former members of the now defunct International Workingman's Association (also known as the First International) and were disciples of Marx and his political ally Frederick Engels.

Since Marx was from an Ashkenazi Jewish background, his story was well known within The Pale of Settlement in Russia and Fanya had studied some of his works in school. She was a member of the debate club in her senior year of secondary school, and as a practice exercise the club re-enacted the debates between Marx and Mikhail Bakunin, his anarchist rival in the First International. Fanya's friend Elena represented Bakunin's views in which he preached complete abstention from all centralized government in favor of more utopian decentralized worker control while she argued Marx's premise that radical change would require a more iterative process and ultimately it would be necessary for the state to change the economic structure.

A story from The Dutch East Indies described volcanic activity at the Perboewatan crater on the Island of Krakatoa. Starting on May 20, 1883, steam was observed to be venting and eruptions of ash reached as high as 6 km. Explosions from the island were heard as far away as Batavia, located 160 km from the volcano. The activity has reportedly settled down, but scientists have expressed concerns that a much more powerful eruption may be imminent.

There was a story too, about the famous statue being built in France as a gift to the United States that once completed, will be the tallest sculpture in America. The project was conceived by French abolitionist, Edouard de Laboulaye, as a gift from France to the United States to celebrate the end of the Civil War and liberation of the slaves. The overall design was by sculptor Frédéric Bartholdi in collaboration with the French engineer Gustave Eiffel, who designed its framework. It was originally planned for completion by 1876, in time for the centennial celebration of the American Revolution, but lack of funding and other issues created significant delays. Construction finally got underway earlier this year and Lady

Liberty's 17 ft. head was now on display in the Champ de Mars at the Exposition Universelle in Paris, while the remainder of the statue was being completed. The United States is responsible for constructing the statue's pedestal and apparently is planning to install it in the middle of New York Harbor so she can welcome future immigrants seeking liberty. Even though she would arrive well before the statue, Fanya was pleased that Libertas, the Roman goddess of freedom was selected for this important job, symbolizing that in America, women can play an important role in the democratic process.

After two solid days of riding the rails, they arrived in the Black Sea port of Constanta and despite her fatigue from insufficient sleep, the excitement of the pending voyage at sea rejuvenated her. It was about two kilometers from the railway station to the port where her boat was docked so Fanya surveyed the landscape for assistance to *schlep* her suitcase to the dock. There were several horse-drawn carriages available for hire right outside the station located in the historic Peninsula District but those seemed way too extravagant, so she kept walking. Before reaching the end of the long avenue which hosted the main inter-city rail hub and was also a major stop for several inner-city trolley lines, she spotted a line of ponies and mules for hire parked and tied to the street posts provided for them. The drivers were enthusiastically hawking their services to anyone in need, each boasting they offered the very lowest fares and signaling the price was quite negotiable. This made Fanya nervous until she spotted a driver who was standing beside his pony quietly above the fray, smoking a pipe. She decided he looked trustworthy and made a bee line towards him. Although her knowledge of Romanian was limited, she managed to convey her destination, and he merely nodded to affirm he understood. The driver quickly secured her suitcase, assisted her into the saddle, and walked alongside for the 25-minute ride to the docks.

The commercial docks in Constanta were packed in so tightly it took the driver a few minutes to locate the Greek fishing trawler Gávros (Anchovy). It was a typical commercial fishing boat with most of the available space on deck cluttered with lines, nets, tools, tanks, etc. The living quarters below deck were barely big enough for their crew of 12 sailors and fishermen but to bring in extra cash, the captain sold passage to an equal number of paying passengers. With twice the number of people on board, Fanya felt like she had entered a floating can of sardines. Four sets of sleeping berths were stacked three high with barely enough room to sit up; the rest of the galley was filled with a table and chairs for meals or to sit and read or play cards. During periodic lulls in fishing activities, the passengers were permitted short turns on deck to get some fresh air and sunlight. Fanya would come to relish those moments of relief from the stale stench of fish combined with the odors of a dozen sweaty sailors badly in need of a bath.

Fanya was only one of two women on board – the other being as old as her grandmother. From the moment she boarded she immediately felt uncomfortable and vulnerable under the leering glares and coarse banter of the crew, made all the worse because she could only imagine what they were saying about her. She recalled the crash course in self-defense her father gave her shortly before departing and as she passed through the galley, she spied a knife on the counter and slipped it into her jacket pocket just in case she needed to defend herself.

Sure enough, during her first night, one of the sailors whose body odor was overpowered only by the pungent smell of rum on his breath stumbled noisily into the cabin and began to climb into her berth. She was not sure if he was motivated by lust or was just too drunk to remember which was his bunk but she wasn't going to wait to find out. Fanya reached for the knife and shrieked as loud as she could manage.

The drunken sailor who was caught totally off-guard yelped in response as he leapt back and smashed his head on the bed frame and fell in a heap. Fanya's scream and the thud of a 125-kilogram hulk hitting the floor were loud enough to be heard on deck. Within moments the captain came and retrieved the unruly sailor, and in halting, broken Russian offered apologies to Fanya with assurances that it would not happen again.

Other than the unwelcome advance and fetid tight quarters, the remainder of the passage to Athens was unremarkable. There was some queasiness the first night as she adjusted to being at sea and they experienced occasional choppiness, but overall, the weather was relatively calm. Despite the fact that their overnight stay in Istanbul was short – they arrived just before dark and set sail at the crack of dawn - it was every bit the exciting diversionary adventure she had envisioned.

During their brief time ashore, Fanya took a walk through a large crowded open-air market. The aromas of grilled meats and fresh brewed coffee, mixed with the pungent smoke of hookahs wafting from open-air cafes, smelled like heaven... a welcome contrast to the cabin on board the Gávros. Two passengers departed in Istanbul, but their places were filled by a couple of French archeologists who were traveling to Cannakale Turkey to participate in a recent restoration of the Doric Temple of Athena that dates back to 530 BC.

Every few meters was another merchant selling everything from spices and grains to vegetables and fish right alongside silk scarves and handmade rugs. The cacophony of commerce filled the air as customers and shopkeepers shouted above the din to be heard, bargaining and bartering as if their lives depended on it. Even though many of the fine goods caught her eye, other than a small piece of halvah she purchased as a special treat, Fanya was content to soak up the ambience and resisted the temptation to buy more things. It occurred to Fanya that despite the modern times she was living in at the dawn of the twentieth century, what she was experiencing at the market in Istanbul has probably been going on pretty much unchanged for hundreds if not thousands of years.

Back aboard the Grávos, she fell asleep to the sound of the sea lapping against the wooden hull and didn't wake until after the ship was already under way. The Sea of Marmara was considerably calmer than the Black Sea and they reached Cannakale at the mouth of the Dardanelles Strait where it joins the Aegean by the following afternoon. The two archeologists disembarked there and Fanya was able to clearly see the towers of the Greek temple overlooking the mouth of the Aegean Sea. Another stark reminder that Fanya wasn't in Demievka any longer. One final long day's sail landed them in the Athens port of Piraeus where they unloaded both cargo and passengers.

Ball One

Happy felt the tension in his muscles ratchet up yet another notch and radiate through his abdomen straight down to his cleats. He might as well have been a granite statue.

Finally, Three-Finger completed his windup, paused before continuing, kicked his leg high and let the first pitch fly. Happy was instantly aware it was a fastball, and his brain put out the signal to his body: Incoming! For an instant he was Seaman First Class Henry Smith again...All hands on deck. Prepare to strike!

The sun, low in the western sky, was shining in his eyes and giving Three-Finger yet another advantage. For a fraction of a second Happy recalled when he crossed the Brooklyn Bridge and got his first glimpse of Washington Park, thinking about the impact of the sun's glare on the hitter's ability to pick up the ball. That was only five months earlier but having experienced the better part of a full major league season it seemed like ages ago. His prediction was spot on, and he now found himself squinting as he awaited the arrival of the ball.

OK, in order to connect with the fastball, he'd need to begin his swing on the early side... but how early was the question? Turns out it was moot, because the pitch was way inside and would prove to be unhittable.

An inside fastball "purpose pitch" to brush Happy back off the plate and establish the inside corner as Brown's own territory was not a total surprise. He'd seen him use the same approach with Silent John. The challenge now was staying out of the way to avoid getting beaned. Of course, if he was hit by the pitch, it would get him a free pass to first and score a run.

But taking one for the team from a Three-Finger Brown fastball was a whole 'nother matter compared with an errant off-speed pitch. At best, it would bring on a hematoma and associated achiness and swelling of his arm, shoulder, hand or thigh, whichever was the lucky body part to be struck. At worst, it could mean a cracked rib or skull, the kind of serious injury you don't get up and walk away from. His wool baseball cap wasn't much protection against a major league fastball. He'd seen a player in Oregon get beaned in the noggin by a hard-throwing but wild pitcher that put him in a coma for weeks and put an end to his baseball days. All these thoughts were swirling through his head in the split second before the ball was upon him after leaving the pitcher's hand.

Before his brain could process the information and make a rational decision on what to do, however, his legs took matters into their own hands and went AWOL. Next thing he realized, Happy was picking himself off the dirt and heard Noisy chuckling.

"Nice bailout, kid. They teach you that shit in the Navy? Man overboard! But believe me kid, Three-Finger wanted to bean you, you're beaned."

Brennan motioned nonchalantly to nobody in particular that the ball was out of the strike zone.

Speedy Punishment

Henry soon learned Fanny was in a league of her own... she was on the governing board of the Women's Trade Union League (WTUL), a partnership between progressive middle-class and working women dedicated to raising wages and improving the conditions for working women. They usually met monthly to discuss topical issues or hear lectures about history or current events and because Fanny had more space than many of the members' cramped apartments, that's where they usually gathered. Attendance was limited to the members of the organization but since it was at Fanny's house, her boarders were invited and encouraged to listen in.

The topic for this month's meeting was sobering: a discussion of the recent upswing in lynchings of Black men. Ida B. Wells-Barrett was their guest lecturer. A former slave, Wells-Barrett co-founded the National Association for the Advancement of Colored People (NAACP) in 1909, but its leadership was soon taken over by liberal whites and those Blacks who were on the board of directors didn't want to rock the boat. Because the board considered her too radical and they didn't agree on political strategy, Wells-Barrett moved on. She recently helped found and became president of the Negro Fellowship League, which established a settlement house in Chicago to aid Blacks relocating from the Deep South.

Wells-Barrett was also a well-respected investigative journalist and expert on Negro history, especially on the topic of lynching. She was a frequent lecturer and published extensively on this subject.[2]

After a short introduction, Ida read directly from numerous newspaper accounts that told, in stark detail, of a recent incident in Dallas, Texas in which Allen Brooks, a 59-year-old Black handyman was on trial for allegedly molesting a young white girl. Ida's previous research showed that oftentimes such charges were pure fabrication or resulted from consensual liaisons. An angry mob estimated to be as many as 10,000 people gathered outside the courthouse demanding the accused be turned over to them for immediate "justice." Law enforcement officials tried half-heartedly to calm the restless crowd and keep them outside the building. Before long though, a group of a few hundred stormed the courthouse steps and pushed their way past the fifty or so police whose job was to keep order.

When the intruders found Brooks cowering in a second-floor room, they called to the crowd below for a rope which they tied around his neck. A group of men on the ground then began to pull and Brooks came crashing through to the ground, landing on his head. He was then dragged through the streets which ripped the clothes from his body until someone suggested stringing him up. A ready volunteer

---

[2] Some of the books Ida B. Wells-Barrett published: On Lynching: Southern Horrors (1892), Tabulated Statistics and Alleged Causes of Lynchings in America (1895), Lynch Law in Georgia (1899), and Mob Rule in New Orleans (1900).

scaled the metal spikes used to climb a wooden utility pole and secured the rope while others on the ground hoisted his limp body, so it hung from the pole for all to see. Finally, after someone cut the rope, the local Sheriff stepped in to retrieve the body for burial.

Most of the group in Fanny's living room sat speechless, staring straight ahead while Ida read. Henry was extremely uncomfortable as he felt his heart race and beat so loudly he was sure it could be heard throughout the room over the silence. He had difficulty sitting still and began to fidget nervously. In Oregon, he'd had little interaction with Blacks; he'd certainly heard about racial discrimination but never anything quite so graphically brutal, so sickening as this account. It was not clear whether the suspect was guilty of the heinous crime he was charged with, but Henry knew in his heart it couldn't possibly justify the reprehensible actions of these citizens of Dallas who took the law into their own hands. The Dallas Morning News reported the story in a cold, factual manner and tipped their hand of complacency with a sub-heading that read: "Speedy Punishment Comes to Negro For His Crime."

"Unfortunately, this abhorrent behavior is not isolated or unique. In fact, when hatred goes unchecked, it breeds faster than fruit flies. Case in point are the horrendous and indiscriminate mass murders that happened just last week in the East Texas town of Slocum. Groups of white citizens from half a dozen to several hundred in number went on the war path shooting their rifles at any Black person they saw. The word spread quickly in the Black community and people began to flee for their lives. Many were gunned down in the back as they tried to escape through the woods. The New York Times interviewed Sheriff William H. Black, of Palestine, Texas about the massacre. He said, and I quote,

> *'Men were going about killing Negroes as fast as they could find them. These Negroes have done no wrong that I can discover. I don't know how many were in the mob, but there may have been 200 or 300. They hunted the Negroes down like sheep.'*

"The Sheriff is not even sure how many people were killed. He went on to say, 'it will be difficult to find out just how many... because they were scattered all over the woods.'"

Ida challenged the group to question what they would have said or done if they came face to face with any of these irrational, hate-mongering mobs. Would they have had the courage to speak up, to challenge the psychology and power of an unbridled hateful throng? If they worked as law enforcement officers stationed at the scene, would they have used their power (and weapon if necessary) to ensure the prisoner in Dallas was given his constitutional right to a trial or to keep the peace in Slocum?

There was an uncomfortable silence for several moments while the guests tried to imagine themselves engulfed by the rabid fury of hatred in Dallas or Slocum. Eleanor Hayes, raised in a family with strong abolitionist ties was the first to break the ice.

"Well, I just can't imagine how those Southern bigots can stand to look at themselves in the mirror after behaving like that! Nothing short of disgraceful. It's just not civilized. That kind of behavior would not be tolerated up North."

"Well, you are certainly correct to characterize these acts as disgraceful and uncivilized, even barbaric..." responded Ida. "But unfortunately, this deplorable behavior is *not* isolated geographically or limited solely to the South. Let us not forget, just two short years ago in the home city of our esteemed President Abraham Lincoln, in the capital of the great Northern state of Illinois... hundreds of miles north of the Mason-Dixon line, thousands of white residents of Springfield rioted, destroyed homes and businesses in the Black sections of the city and brutally lynched several Negros following several crimes that were allegedly committed by Black men."

"The only difference between the events in Springfield and those in Dallas or Slocum is that the authorities in Springfield responded by quickly transferring the prisoners away from the local jail to prevent their abduction. But the blood thirsty mob in Springfield would not be deterred and grabbed the first two Black men they saw on the street who had nothing to do with the case - a barber and a local businessman for the public hangings."

The discussion that followed connected the dots. Ida made a convincing case that these lynchings and massacres were not isolated incidents, but rather a symptom of persistent, lingering, blatant and ubiquitous racism.

"They say time heals all wounds but the wounds of slavery and the civil war it precipitated are still deep and festering some forty-five years later. Sometimes hatred lurks from beneath anonymous hoods under the cover of darkness, or under the thin veil of gospel preached in the name of God in houses of worship. But all too often, it oozes like putrid puss in the light of day and cannot be ignored. It may be especially acute in the South following Reconstruction but can happen anywhere."

To further her point that racial hatred knows no boundaries, Ida then asked Fanny to talk of the anti-Semitism she lived through in Russia. Fanny described life under the pogroms throughout the Russian Empire which limited what Jews could and could not do and led to state-sanctioned mob violence in which thousands of Jews were massacred. Henry knew that she had immigrated to the U.S. to escape a hard life in Russia but had no idea of the extent of the oppression under which they lived. It was just not something she dwelled on. But to hear her speak of it, he realized just how difficult it must be for her to recall and recount her personal tragedy.

The parallels of how hatred can breed and flourish based on ignorance and mistrust were evident. As difficult as it was for Fanny to discuss those painful memories, they gave her the strength and conviction to speak out and confront racism in her adopted home. Fanny added that the difference was that in America, she was at least free to speak her mind and encourage discussion of the subject.

At the end of the forum, Henry returned to his room with thoughts swirling through his head. The evening was another eye-opener for him. Racism was no longer an abstract concept. He was beginning to see beyond the bubble that was his world in Coquille, to one that was more complex and far from the idyllic vision he harbored in his sheltered life there.

Henry's Transformation

W hether it was Fanny's advice or just that he needed time to adjust from his journey and the rigorous routine of major league baseball, by Day Five Henry began to relax at the plate and connect with the ball, consistently driving hard line drives to all fields. He was never a power hitter, and his hits were usually solid singles, but he felt comfortable stepping into the batter's box and his self-confidence was beginning to return. His turnaround was not lost on the coaching staff and even Bad Bill, a man of few words managed a "way to hustle, son" when he legged out an infield hit during practice.

His teammate Tony Smith also took an interest in Henry and provided lots of encouragement when he noticed that he was starting to turn the corner. Even though Henry had tremendous respect for his Oregon coach, having an actual big leaguer express confidence in his abilities was a boost to his self-assurance. Since he was also new to Brooklyn, Tony made an effort to reach out and get to know Henry. Several years his senior, he served as both a role model and friend.

Two weeks of daily drills, workouts, and simulated games passed quickly by. Henry enjoyed the routine – it was hard work, but it provided a rhythm and focus for his new life. He would soon learn whether he'd just be having a cup of coffee or sticking around to enjoy a full five-course major league experience.

Somehow when Dahlen announced that the final team roster would be posted at the end of that day's practice, Henry didn't feel nervous. He wasn't sure if his performance would be considered as big-league caliber, but he felt he'd given it his best shot and was comfortable with the knowledge that whether he made the ball club or not, he had been able (in part, thanks to Fanny's coaching) to demonstrate what he could do.

Before even ambling over to see the posting, several of his teammates came by, slapped him on the back, and offered their congratulations. He gently squeezed through the crowd to get close enough to read for himself the manager's handwritten list tacked to the bulletin board to confirm his good fortune in making the team. It was a whole different level of course, but the feeling of acceptance was similar to how he felt as a boy in Oregon when he was asked to join a sandlot team of boys several years his senior.

After the crowd thinned out, Tony came over, tousled his hair and said "Way to go kid! Knew you had what it takes for the Bigs."

Just then, a well-dressed gentleman in a grey pinstriped suit and bowler hat walked over. "Charles H. Ebbets, welcome to the ball club boys. Just want to say, I've been watching you during Spring Training and like what I saw. Lotta hustle." Ebbets gave them each a firm handshake. "Tony, we're counting on you to be a critical spark this season..." and turning to Henry, with a wink he said, "Hang in there son, stay loose and keep your head in the game – never know when Big Bad Bill's going to call on you." He then tipped his hat and moved on to greet some of the other players.

"Damn," said Tony, "You sure are lookin' a whole lot happier now than you've been for weeks... think we're gonna have to start callin' you Happy from now on. Suits you fine."

The Crossing

In ancient Greece, Piraeus, which has been inhabited since the 26th century BC served as the main seaport for Athens, approximately nine kilometers to the north. Fanya had several days before her departure for New York, so she took in a few of the local sites including The Archaeological Museum. Many of the statues depicted Athena, Greek goddess of wisdom, courage, inspiration, civilization, law and justice, just warfare, mathematics, strength, strategy, the arts, crafts, and skill. Fanya had studied ancient Greek and Roman history and wondered how women in these cultures could be so revered as goddesses in mythology, while living subservient lives to their male counterparts in reality.

On June 2, Fanya boarded the steam-powered freighter SS Kairos bound for New York. When she saw the name painted on the stern she smiled, recalling from her studies that Kairos was a Greek god of opportunity. Hopefully this was a good omen.

That feeling was short-lived however, once she boarded and descended below to the steerage section of the ship.

Incredibly, the accommodations on the fishing boat now seemed like first-class compared to the conditions in steerage on the freighter. The SS Kairos was returning from delivering bananas from Brazil and was now being filled with barrels of Greek olives and olive oil bound for America. From there it will deliver wheat to South America and start the cycle over again.

The below-deck quarters were cramped, dark, stale, and smelly. Little time or effort was devoted to cleaning out the hold between runs so the accumulation of detritus and ground-in cargo was ripe, providing free first-class board for the stowaway, well-traveled rodents. Little effort was made to afford much comfort or dignity to the human cargo, however.

Dirty straw mattresses stacked in bunks from floor to ceiling of the hold. They were separated into make-shift "rooms" every few meters by surplus tattered burlap bags no longer useful for holding cargo that were stitched together and suspended from ropes. There were only two temporary toilet facilities in steerage, right next to their sleeping quarters which contained chamber pots that were dumped into a large tank after each use. Once each day the crew would dump the contents overboard but didn't bother to clean them out much, so the stench permeated the entire storage deck.

Cargo was the primary commercial driver for these ships. The income from the hundred or so passengers they carried was supplemental but quite profitable. When Fanya heard the ticket for steerage class cost more than 2,000 rubles, she was shocked but when she now saw the absolutely abhorrent conditions that exorbitant sum had procured, she was beyond disbelief. She knew the only way the shipping companies could get away with those prices was to capitalize on the huge discrepancy between the demand for transatlantic transport and the supply of available seaworthy vessels. The stream of immigrants fleeing oppression and seeking opportunity in America seemed endless.

Fanya did the math. A triple bunk to "house" three passengers took up three cubic meters of cargo floor space, displacing six barrels of olive oil. Converting to U.S. dollars in her head for practice, at $50/ticket minus $7 food and $3 insurance the passengers represented $4000 in revenue for the journey. The 100 passengers displaced 198 barrels of olive oil, which at a shipping fee of $2.50 each amounted to only $495 in revenue. They also needed one less dock worker to load and unload the smaller cargo load which amounted to another $5 savings. So the net gain from hauling people rather than merchandise was about $3510 each trip, enabling the shipping company to approximately double its revenue. It was easy to see why this practice was attractive enough to offset the additional risks associated with hauling live passengers.

The crew was busy with its sailing duties, so except for the very modest meals which were prepared by the ship's cook and one assistant, passengers were left to fend for themselves. Most suffered from seasickness at some point on the journey. Worse, poor health conditions and various illnesses from head lice to influenza were passed and shared by the passengers who were in close contact during the voyage. Those who landed with observable illness or disease and failed the medical exam, were refused entry and turned back to the country of origin at the expense of the shipping company.

So, even though she was young and in good health Fanya was concerned about this last portion of her journey. Food was limited to small portions of canned sardines, dried salt cod, Greek olives, rice, crackers and rationed fresh water. For the first several days she didn't eat much more than the plain, dry crackers as her equilibrium adjusted to the rolling seas.

Perhaps the hardest part for Fanya was the lack of suitable light to read and write – there wasn't much room for passengers on the deck and the inclement weather they had for a good deal of the journey limited their opportunities to get fresh air. Thoughts of her prospects for the future kept her focused and got her through the ordeal.

Time slowed to a crawl as each day at sea looked and felt like all the rest. On the trains and even the trawler to Athens, there was much to see and many opportunities to break the monotony. But the nine-day journey in the belly of the iron hulled freighter seemed like an eternity. Even when the weather permitted them to go topside for a few hours a day there wasn't much relief as the 360-degree view of rolling seas to the horizon was much the same no matter what day or time you looked.

Many of the passengers were like Fanya, from eastern Russia, Poland, Latvia, Lithuania, and the Ukraine - displaced Jews fleeing oppression in Czarist Russia. But many were non-Jews from Italy, Poland, and Ireland also seeking a fresh start in America. There were numerous single men of various ages traveling alone presumably like Fanya to get a job and make enough money to send for their families. But as far as she could tell, Fanya was the only woman traveling unaccompanied.

A few families managed to scrape together their life savings and relocate all at once. Several "berths" down from where Fanya was assigned, an Italian family with two children about the same ages as her sister and brother were camped out. Seeing them when she first boarded reminded Fanya of the separation from her own family, and she was instantly struck with heartbreak. But even though they couldn't communicate verbally Fanya established a rapport with the younger kids- undoubtedly, they admired her independence –

and their father kept an eye out to protect Fanya against unwanted male advances.

On the morning of the ninth day, every passenger crammed onto the deck despite the lack of space, to witness their entry into U.S. territorial waters and shortly thereafter into the New York Harbor. It was an overcast gray day so visibility was poor, and she could barely make out the skyline but unmistakably off to her right spanning the East River was the new bridge she read about days earlier. It was an inspiring sight that accentuated the end of her long journey and the start of her new life and uncontrollably brought tears to her eyes.

The SS Kairos was met by the border security patrol while they anchored outside the harbor to do a routine passenger pre-screening and cursory medical examination – fortunately none of the passengers were turned away. From there, they headed for and docked at the Castle Garden immigration center in Battery Park at the southernmost tip of Manhattan where they set foot on American soil for the first time. As soon as the last of the passengers and their luggage made it off the ship, the gang plank was stowed, and the Kairos continued up the Hudson River to offload the rest of its cargo at a commercial pier.

The broad, brick Castle Garden facility was built at the turn of the 19th Century as a fortress to stave off the British Navy during the War of 1812. In 1824 it was converted to a public resort and restaurant and several years later, hot saltwater baths were added. In 1845 a cupola-style roof was installed to enclose the grounds so it could serve as an opera house and theater until most recently when it was re-purposed in 1854 as the official New York State immigration processing center.

Some natural light filtered down from the windows in the roof but since it was a cloudy day there wasn't much light to be had. The gas-lit chandeliers remaining from its opera house days tried their best to illuminate the large open space but were only of minimal help, in the end providing only accent marks in the dark and gloomy rotunda. The air felt damp and smelled of mold, smoot from the chandeliers, and the pungent aroma of hundreds of immigrants in need of a bath. Despite the bleak ambiance and having to stand in line for processing for over four hours, Fanya was focused on her new life and maintained a cheerful spirit.

Hours later, Fanya emerged from Castle Gardens and was met in Battery Park by her cousin Miriam Feinstein who had been waiting for her all day with a sign bearing her name. She brought along a wagon to carry Fanya's suitcase as they walked the cobblestone streets for more than two miles to her new home at their apartment located at 97 Orchard St. between Delancey and Broome Streets.

Flash

The day after the final team roster was posted they broke up into smaller groups to work on fundamentals. Each group worked with a coach to hone their skills in bunting, hit and run plays, situational base running, sliding, stealing bases, etc. During the sliding drill Happy slid hard into second base and twisted his ankle sending a sharp pain shooting up his right leg. His will was commanding him to jump up, take a few steps and shake it off but his body had other ideas. After just making the team, to be injured before ever seeing a major league game was Happy's worst nightmare. But as he lay writhing in pain, he realized he wasn't going to be able to just suck it up.

The pain muffled the sounds of baseball being played all around him. It overrode his sense of time so it seemed as if the actions on the field were slipping through an hourglass one grain at a time. In reality, the coaching staff and several players were on the scene to assist him within seconds and helped him to an upright position. Unable to put much weight on his right leg Happy resembled a stork standing solely on his left leg with his right leg bent at the knee. Several coaches helped him hobble and hop off the field where Flash, their equipment manager came to his aid for the remainder of the walk back to the clubhouse.

"Hey Kid, first casualty of the day. What happened to you?" Flash reached around to place Happy's arm across his shoulder for support.

"Spike caught... corner of the bag... durin' the slidin' drill," Happy managed to reply between winces.

Happy had only met Flash briefly when the uniforms were being passed out. "I suppose a formal introduction is in order... Samuel P. Jones, but most folks just call me Flash," he explained. "Glad to make your acquaintance," reaching out with a firm handshake. "Wear two hats: graduated from University of Michigan with a degree in nursing so I help keep the team healthy when I'm not dealing with the equipment. You prefer Henry, or is Happy ok?"

"Happy's fine with me. That's what all the guys are callin' me now so I'm kinda gettin' used to it."

"Swell. So let's get that shoe off and have a closer look at your ankle...Geez, from the looks of that bent up cleat you really twisted it pretty good. We'll have to get that straightened out too, but first things first. Let me know if it hurts when I move it."

Flash gently rotated his ankle ever so slightly to the left and then the right. "How's that feel?"

"Well, it kinda hurts just sitting there but not much more when you move it either way."

"OK, that's good news – looks like nothing's busted, just twisted is all. It's pretty swollen already so we'll ice it for a while and then tape it up to give you support. I'll get you some Bayer's Aspirin powder for the pain and swelling, too. With a little rest and a bit of luck you can probably be back out there tomorrow or the day after."

Happy sighed with relief that he hadn't prematurely sabotaged his shot at playing in the Bigs.

Flash smiled, "Know how you feel...dodged quite a few bullets during my playing career too. Here's the Bayer's powder – I mixed it in a spoonful of Fox's U-Bet chocolate syrup so it doesn't taste so nasty; just swallow it down and take a drink of water."

"Where'd you play ball?" inquired Happy before quickly downing the syrup. Flash wrapped the ankle in a towel filled with ice from the ice box which quickly took some of the edge off the pain.

"Well, I got started in college, playing in Michigan – was the starting shortstop on the team that Moses Fleetwood Walker was catcher. Our coach was kind of open minded and wanted to put the best team out there so he didn't think twice about putting two Black players on the field. Caught a bunch of crap for it too but he stood up for us every time. After we graduated, I got picked up by a Negro League team called, the Page Fence Giants, out of Adrian, MI. Had to switch to third base because Home Run Johnson was on that team and he had shortstop locked up. He hit 60 home runs that first year."

"60 home runs? Are you serious? Nobody in the majors has ever come close to that. This guy must've been something to see!"

"You got that right. Ned Williams from the old Chicago White Stockings has the Major League record at 27 homers in a single season back in '84, less than half what HR hit that magical season... I wound up playing four years on that team and then another four years in total for the Chicago Unions, the Chicago Columbia Giants, and the New York Gothams barnstorming the country playing whoever was willing to take the field against us..."

"Let's get that leg elevated a bit more – it'll reduce the swelling...After I met my wife and we had a couple a kids, I got real tired of that life... so when I heard that Brooklyn was looking for a new equipment manager I sold them on the idea that not only was I thoroughly familiar with the game and could easily handle those responsibilities but with my degree in nursing, I could provide medical support and serve as their physical trainer, too. Lean back, these pillows under your leg will keep it elevated... So, Mr. Ebbets interviewed me and I think he was surprised to meet a Black man with my level of formal education. He's a shrewd businessman and realized having someone who could help with physical conditioning and tend to injuries would protect his investments in the players. Plus, getting two for one was a good deal. Hired me on the spot..."

"...But Fleet was the big story. As you may have heard, he was an exceptionally talented player. Right after graduation he got drafted by the minor league Toledo Blue Stockings in the Northwestern League and quickly became their starting catcher. The next year, in '84 they joined the major league American Association so that's how he got to be the first Black man to play in the Bigs. Course, what we experienced playing for Michigan wasn't nothing compared to the shit storm Fleet had to deal with on the Blue Stockings. Couldn't sleep or eat with the team on the road in many of the cities they played like Louisville, St. Louis, Cincinnati, Baltimore and Richmond. Got beer bottles thrown at his head if the on-deck circle was anywhere close to the stands. Players on the other teams calling him nigger and refusing to play on the field with him. Was pretty tough on him until he got injured that year - only played a half season but batted a respectable .263. After that year he was back in the minors playing for the Syracuse Stars. Then both the American Association and the National League agreed to extend Jim Crow to baseball and unofficially ban us Black players. Rest is history as they say."

"Wow…" Happy was at a loss for words. He'd never thought much about racial segregation in baseball and was getting a real-world education from someone who lived it first-hand. Black players had demonstrated they could play the game as well or better than their white counterparts and it was simple racial bigotry that kept them out of the Major Leagues. Flash had been an accomplished ball player and yet never got the chance that Happy was enjoying now. He recalled the words of Ida B. Wells-Barrett about the lives of Black Americans forty-five years since the end of the Civil War, realizing that America's pastime reflected just how far the nation itself has to go.

Wanting to keep the conversation going, Happy asked Flash about his nickname.

"Well, I was pretty damn fast back in the day. Played on Michigan's Track and Field team too. Could run the 100-yard dash in under 12 seconds and was on the 4 x 100 relay team. Had lots of fun trying to steal as many bases as possible – when I stole 32 bases in my senior year, they joked that I was fast as a flash o' lightning. Started calling me Flash and it kind of stuck. Fleet got his nickname on account of Fleetwood being his middle name but with the wear and tear on his knees as a catcher he was anything but fleet on the base paths. So we were Fleet and Flash but only one of us had any speed."

"Hell, we could use that kind of speed on the Superbas…Think you might have made it in the Majors if not for Jim Crow?"

"Hard to say. In addition to my speed I could hit for average – lifetime I was something like .290 or thereabouts and was considerably better than that in the earlier to middle part of my playing days. Got on base plenty and could spark a rally by grabbing the extra base on slow rollers or gappers, advancing on run and hit plays or just plain old stealing. There's lots of very talented Black ballplayers so the competition in the Negro leagues is considerable..."

"Certainly wasn't a superstar like HR or Fleet but I could play some – guess I could've held my own with the likes of lots of the players on our club today... Yeah, reckon I could have been a Big Leaguer. But seeing what Fleet Walker had to put up with, there's no way I'd have the constitution to deal with that shit. Someday that'll all change but it won't come easy or anytime soon..."

Flood

Washington Park, June 19, 1910: In today's rubber game of the first series of the season between Chicago's Cubs and the Brooklyn National League Baseball Club at Washington Park, the Superbas were battling a force much more powerful than the former World Champs.

The game began under ideal weather conditions with clear skies and plenty of sun – a bit hotter than usual but a perfect day for a day at the baseball park. Both hurlers were tossing well, and the game was a scoreless tie. Then as Brooklyn was batting in the bottom of the third, the wind suddenly picked up and grabbed everyone's attention, surrounding the stadium with menacing-looking dark gray clouds. Rain began to fall, slowly at first but gradually steadier and with more force. Despite the inclement conditions, the game continued and was so engrossing that very few fans left to take cover at this stage.

Before long, however, the sky turned dark as night, save when illuminated by streaks of lightning that periodically lit the sky. These were followed quickly by the powerful low rumble of nearby thunder that shook the very foundation of the grandstands. Reluctantly the cranks began to seek shelter – considering how the day started off, very few were equipped with umbrellas or protective rain gear. Even those who paid for premium grandstand seating with a roof over their heads were not afforded much protection from the monsoon.

At this point it was clear Mother Nature, the ultimate World Champion, had the upper hand and was delivering damaging blows at will. Home plate umpire and crew chief, Oliver Johnstone had no choice but to step in and stop the action in the interest of protecting the safety of the players and fans.

Both teams and the entire assembled crowd of more than 18,000 at the stadium ran for cover or the exits. It was fortunate that no one was trampled or injured during the mad rush that ensued. Manager Bill Dahlen opened the home and visiting clubhouses to women and children, and many availed themselves of the temporary respite provided by a safe and dry shelter.

The field was covered in a swirl of soggy paper programs, hot dog wrappers and pages from this and other local newspapers. There were even unconfirmed reports of a small tornado touching down just beyond the outfield fence. The groundskeeping crew made a valiant effort but tried in vain to cover the pitching mound and area around home plate but eventually surrendered in defeat. As Mother Nature continued her assault with wave upon wave of pummeling rain and intense winds that whipped the waterproof canvas tarpaulins like old glory flapping in the breeze, it was clear to all in attendance that if this were a boxing match the referee would promptly declare a TKO. Johnstone followed Major League Baseball protocol however, and waited 30 minutes before officially postponing the game. During that time, so much rain fell it could not be absorbed by the turf and the outfield resembled Prospect Park Lake.

As it turns out, the action at Washington Park was merely an undercard for the main event that was unfolding across the city. Hailstones, lightning, and winds measured at over 60 mph were observed throughout the metropolitan New York area.

The storm travelling from the south was no surprise to the Weather Bureau. However, the fury of the squall, the most severe on record for many years, was quite unexpected. In a few short hours it wreaked havoc and even turned deadly. At least a dozen people were killed and scores more injured by lightning strikes. Collapsed wooden residences and felled trees scattered the city's landscape. Small craft were capsized in the harbor like children's toys in a bathtub. Property damage is estimated in the hundreds of thousands of dollars and counting (See Deadly Storms, Page 1).

The baseball game at Washington Park was not the only local sporting event impacted. The fury of the storm hit smack in the middle of the annual 24-man yacht race in Gravesend Bay sponsored by the New York Canoe Club, capsizing four boats and beaching two others. Fortunately, all contestants returned safely or were rescued from the tumultuous waters (See Racing Yacht Negotiates Gale Force Winds, Page 58).

The Brooklyn Baseball Club owner's son, Charles Ebbets, Jr. serves as the team Treasurer and as such is tasked with handling the logistics of issuing rain checks. When baseball adopted the practice of allowing fans to return for another game in the event of rain-induced postponements about 30 years ago, separate paper tickets were issued allowing re-entry to the ballpark. Ebbets recently streamlined the process to economize on printing costs by a new innovation of incorporating the rain check as a portion of the original ticket.

However, the Superbas did not anticipate the demand for tickets to today's game and only printed 8,000, far short of the 18,000 needed due to the large number of fans who did not purchase tickets in advance and arrived at the last moment. To meet the demand, the Brooklyn Ball Club issued leftover tickets from previous home games which will create a potential bookkeeping challenge because of the date stamped on the ticket and many of the fans expressed their concerns. In a press release, Ebbets assured cranks that the team recorded the serial numbers of all issued tickets and promised that every person would be guaranteed re-entry to a future home game of their choice.

Unfortunately, Mother Nature grabbed the headlines and imposed an early ending to what was proving to be an exciting baseball contest. Each of the previous hard-fought games of the series had been decided in extra innings with Brooklyn taking the first game 3-2 and Chicago coming back to win the next, 1-0. So naturally there was much electricity in the stadium long before the first lightning bolt struck.

With a scoreless tie through three innings, today's game was proving to be an equally close and well-played pitcher's duel. Brooklyn hurler George Bell was demonstrating his Houdini-like talent as an escapist artist, managing to get himself out of several tight jams. In the top of the first, after giving up a base on balls to Evers and a wild pitch which advanced a runner to scoring position, several failed bunts and a strikeout ended the Cubs early threat.

In the second he yielded a two-out, two-bagger to Tinker but got former Superba Jimmy Sheckard trying to bunt his way on with a weak dribbler in front of the plate which was easily handled by Tex Irwin. Settling in, Bell made quick work of the Chicagoans in the top of third retiring their batsmen in order.

With Brooklyn's debut of highly touted outfielder Jack Dalton, who arrived last night as a result of a trade with the Western League's Des Moines ball club, there is much anticipation that the Superbas are finally assembling the necessary pieces for a winning club. He was traded for Frank Schneiberg and a cash consideration. Not many cranks will take issue with this deal; in his only appearance for the Superbas several weeks ago Schneiberg lasted only one inning, giving up four walks and seven earned runs for a bloated ERA of 63.

The eager Superba crowd welcomed Dalton with a standing ovation as he stepped to the plate for the first time to lead off the bottom of the first. It's too early to tell whether Jack Dalton has what it takes to excel in the National League, but one thing is for certain. He is not intimidated by Major League pitching and proved himself by holding his ground against the Cub's starting pitcher.

Rube Kroh started off without his best control and his third pitch was high and inside, hitting Dalton in the upper arm. He advanced to second on a sacrifice bunt by Jake Dauber but was put out at third attempting to tag up on Zac Wheat's fly ball to right field. Dalton demonstrated good speed on the base path arriving there just ahead of the strong throw from Wildfire Schulte, but the momentum of his aggressive slide took him beyond the bag and was thus vulnerable to the tag applied by third baseman Harry Steinfeldt.

Kroh found his rhythm in the second and retired Brooklyn's offense in order. But the Superbas mounted a potential scoring threat in the third inning. Tony Smith singled to right, moving to second on Tex Erwin's sacrifice and advancing to third as Bell grounded weakly to Kroh. As the rain began to fall in earnest, Dalton walked on four pitches, perhaps because the baseball was too wet to grip properly. With first and third and two outs, the skies opened, precluding the continuation of play.

Brooklyn has yet to reschedule the rainout, but it can be expected to be added to the schedule as a double-header during Chicago's next and last visit to Washington Park in September.

The Wager

Just three weeks into the season, the Superbas packed their bags for their first extended western road trip that would take them to Pittsburgh, Cincinnati, Chicago and St. Louis. Happy was excited to be back on the Pennsylvania Special, the same train that took him on the final leg of his eastern journey, relieved however that it was as an official member of the Brooklyn Base Ball Club and not a quick return trip to Oregon after having failed to accomplish his dream.

There were lots of other ways in which this journey contrasted with his earlier trip, of course. This time he was accompanied by a carload of his friends and teammates. They had already been on brief excursions to Philadelphia and Boston but this was their first extended trip and as such, the anticipation was palpable and spirits were high. A plentiful assortment of bottled beer was waiting for them on ice in a cooler chest to help in that regard and it didn't take long before the sound of caps popping and bottles clanking filled the air. Shortly thereafter, the decibel level in the train car increased with each new empty glass bottle added to the pile.

Charles Ebbets Jr., who also served as the Superbas Road Manager, kept a close eye on the bottom line and took pride in his frugality. Thus, the accommodations were not first-class, but since they commissioned a private car which they had to themselves, there was lots more room to stretch out and relax. Buffet meals were provided for the team in the club car.

Several of his teammates were amateur musicians and took turns leading small groups in song to pass the time. Irvin "Kaiser" Wilhelm played the squeeze box and he and fellow pitcher Elmer "the Baron" Knetzer (both born in the U.S. but with strong ancestral ties to their families' homeland) taught their teammates German beer garden drinking songs. Later, catcher Emil "Tex" Irwin played some guitar and serenaded anyone willing to listen, with his cowboy ballads.

Happy played numerous rounds of gin rummy in between reading the newspaper and assorted magazines and taking a nap. The more serious gamblers kept several games of poker going non-stop.

Happy was sitting next to infielder Pryor "Humpty" McElveen who was taking a breather after having lost big at the poker marathon. He came across an article in the paper about the upcoming appearance of Halley's Comet that piqued his interest.

"Hey Hump, says here that that Halley's Comet'll be here in a couple of weeks. First time in 75 years and then won't be seen again by anyone on this planet 'til 1986. The earth is supposed to pass through the comet's tail on May 18 and it'll last about six hours. Says here:

> *"...There has been much speculation on the part of both scientists and the public on whether any tangible evidence would be observed or felt as a result of the collision."*

Humpty smirked but before he could reply, reserve outfielder "Judge" Harry Lumley sitting just behind them piped in, "Yeah," "the pastor of our church has been preachin' about it for a coupla' months. He believes it may signal the end of days and the second coming of our Lord Jesus Christ. The scientists discovered some kinda poison comin' from the comet so they're sayin' we need to stay inside and seal the doors, windows and keyholes to keep the poison from comin' in."

Humpty felt compelled to establish his position on the matter, "I figger we're all doomed anyhow so may as well live it up, pray for forgiveness and go out in a blaze a glory!"

"Well," said Happy playing the role of mediator and continuing to reference the newspaper, "the article says lots of people have been pretty riled up after the New York Times reported that a French astronomer – a guy named Camille somebody – said poisonous gas was detected that would *'impregnate the atmosphere and possibly snuff out all life on the planet...'"*

In fact, a British scientist named Sir William Huggins had recently detected the presence of cyanogen gas within the comet's tail using a new technique called spectroscopy that reveals an element's composition by analyzing the light reflecting off it. Frenchman Camille Flammarion, in noting that *"a mere grain of its potassium [cyanide] salt touched to the tongue, being sufficient to cause instant death"* further theorized cataclysmic consequences when the earth's orbit coincides with the comet's 24-million-mile-long tail.

"...But most scientists aren't taking much stock in that doomsday stuff and don't think there's any risk at all. Seein' as how Halley's has been a regular visitor for as far back as anyone can tell and we're all still here, makes me think there's nothin' to worry about. You may want to reconsider runnin' up your gamblin' debts like there's no tomorrow cause in all likelihood, we're all gonna wake up same as usual the day after."

"Five bucks says we all die!"

"Uh Humpty, let's just say you're right…how you planning on collecting your winnins'?

"Well, guess you got a point there Hap, but in the meanwhile, may as well have some fun. Screw it all."

"For the record," offered Judge Lemley, "I'll be at mass on May 18 praying for forgiveness just in case."

Judgement Day

On Wednesday, May 18 the Superbas were in Chicago to play the Cubs and complete their long road trip. They'd lost four of seven thus far and their spirits were eager for something to shake things up. That evening Happy joined several of his teammates and headed to Lake Michigan to try and observe the approach of Halley's Comet, whose long-anticipated arrival was finally here. Humpty McElveen and several other teammates gathered at their hotel for one last high stakes gambling blowout. Judge Lemley played his cards considerably more conservatively and attended confession and service at the Hyde Park Presbyterian Church, which had just celebrated its 50th anniversary golden jubilee. Unlike the pastor at his home church, Reverend Joseph A. Vance took a somewhat more positive viewpoint with a sermon entitled, "The Church for the Future."

Back at Fanny's place in Brooklyn, the imminent approach of the comet was all anyone was talking about at dinner. Many New Yorkers were planning outdoor comet-watching parties on building tops, parks, and along the shoreline to try and get a better view. Some were genuinely curious to witness firsthand a rare astronomical occurrence. Others were only looking for an excuse to celebrate and this seemed like an appropriate event.

Still others however (like the pastor of Judge Lemley's church), were convinced the comet would wreak havoc and were preparing to witness the Armageddon. Some were busy sealing their homes and apartments against poison gas as a precaution. Hucksters and unscrupulous merchants were taking advantage of the mania to turn an easy profit selling bogus anti-comet pills and elixirs, even bottles of oxygen. Houses of worship were mobbed as many attended special services to receive spiritual guidance and have one last confessional. Similarly, the police reported an increase in confessions to unsolved crimes, in an attempt by criminals to absolve themselves before it was too late.

Brian Thompson, one of Happy's neighbors on the fourth floor and science teacher at Erasmus High School, reassured the other boarders at Fanny's that while we still lack detailed scientific information about the composition of comets and their tails, the likelihood of any kind of cataclysmic episode was virtually nil. He was joining some of his colleagues who were planning an excursion to observe the sky with a telescope. Brian explained the need to get away from the bright lights of the city to get a good glimpse of the nighttime sky, so they were taking the Ocean Electric Railway trolley operated by the Long Island Railroad out to its terminus in Rockaway Beach.

The beach along this spit of land off the main coast of Long Island was considerably more remote than closer alternatives like Coney Island, where the arcade and city lights would likely interfere with a clear viewing of the transient and infrequent visitor. The last trolley back to Brooklyn was at 1 a.m. so he and his colleagues were planning to stay the remainder of the night with Brian's aunt and uncle who had a summer bungalow on Beach 89th St. just several blocks from the ocean. Fanny volunteered to pack him a snack to tide them over during the long evening.

First thing Thursday morning Fanny perused the papers for news of the comet. Brian had not yet returned from Rockaway, but from what she read it was doubtful they had any luck. It turns out that not much was seen by professional or amateur astronomers, even those using the most advanced telescopes stationed high atop mountains across the globe.

In the Brooklyn Daily Eagle, she read that Professor E. Jerome McCaffery of the Navy Street Observatory had another idea:

> *"It was just as I had expected and have predicted from the beginning. When the inexpressibly etherealized appendage of the comet came into immediate contact with the immensely superior density of a circumambient atmosphere of the terrestrial orb which we inhabit the tail took the ten count and dropped out of the ring."*

There were no reports of anyone dying from cyanide poisoning. But the predictions for mass gatherings of citizenry were fully realized, even exceeding expectations. An estimated ten thousand souls gathered in the East New York section of Brooklyn. Inquisitive believers and skeptics assembled together - old and young alike, families with children in tow resembled a pilgrimage on their way to Mecca as they crept slowly up Force Tube Ave. towards Reservoir Hill in Highland Park. You could tell at first glance which camp people were associated with by their attire. Those anticipating the apocalypse were dressed in black and the revelers in everything but. While they were not treated to any extraterrestrial excitement, in the end most made the best of it, staying at the park late into the night.

Walter Budzinski, who was going on fourteen years old begged his parents to let him and his friend Billy Labriola come along and stay up late to watch the comet. He said his teacher assigned it as homework which was a bit of a fib. They had discussed it in class and were encouraged to observe the comet but were not actually required to do so. Walter wasn't sure how his parents would feel about it so he embellished the story so as not to take any chances. Realizing the historic significance, his parents were more than willing to oblige and even though Brooklyn was a large metropolis he'd never seen so many people in one place, except perhaps at a sold-out ballgame.

Flash Jones' wife Florence had spent the day shopping for art supplies in the Brooklyn neighborhood of East New York. Since her husband was out of town for the week on the team's road trip, she and their daughter Josephine decided to meet there for a light dinner and then join the comet watching festivities before heading home to Bedford Stuyvesant. An event such as this, be it the celestial fireworks production itself or the momentous crowds that gathered to watch, could prove inspiring for her next work in oils on canvas.

Kevin and Dorothy Kearney celebrated Halley's arrival over a few pints of stout and a fish and chips dinner at O'Malley's Tavern in Red Hook before catching the elevated Broadway spur of the BMT Canarsie Line over to the Cypress Hills station in East New York. Back at street level again, they stopped into George Distler's Hotel and Brewery on Jamaica Turnpike for a nightcap and then the nearby Haarmann's Casino and Hotel for another before catching up with the tail end of the crowd floating their way up the steep hill at Cypress Hills St. to Highland Park. However, they were not the only ones who had a bit to drink that night.

Mr. and Mrs. Frederick H. Whitin drove by in their chauffeur-driven black Russell Knight automobile with gold plated trim. They were not there to picnic with the masses, of course. The Whitins had been invited to an exclusive black-tie comet-watching ball sponsored by J.P. Morgan in a section of the park cordoned off and provided by Brooklyn's borough president McAneny. They were dressed appropriately for a night on the town – Mr. Whitin in top hat, tuxedo, and white bow tie and Mrs. Whitin in a gold metallic floral embroidered tulle, black and white silk A-line evening gown trimmed with a simple golden velvet rosette. This was a solid working-class section of Brooklyn, unaccustomed to fully decked out socialites in their limousines and their presence turned heads and brought fingers pointing in their direction. Likewise, from the luxurious comfort of their mobile cocoon, the assembly of commoners was a curious site, and the driver was instructed to proceed slowly so they could take it all in as they made their way toward the ball.

Pranksters took full advantage of the circumstances. In one case, Fanny read of a large ball of fire which was observed moving across the skies above the Erie Basin Park in Brooklyn's Red Hook section and was thought by many to be the arrival of the comet. It turned out to be just a fire balloon released in the vicinity by a practical joker.

In a possibly related development, Fanny read a somewhat sarcastic piece in the Brooklyn Eagle in which comet fever likely played a supporting role. Fanny smiled to herself and was relieved that she'd decided to retire early last night to avoid all the tumult:

MORE TANGIBLE THAN THE TAIL

Louis Kalb's Horse Sought to Make an Investigation on Ocean Parkway.

As twilight was fast deepening into night a bay horse attached to a light wagon, driven by Louis Kalb of 16 Henderson street, might have been seen pursuing a northwestward course last night on Ocean parkway. Kalb was wrapped in deep cogitation over the possible effect of a plunge into the comet's tail. Likewise, possibly, the horse. Suddenly from out the fringe of trees bordering the boulevard a bright white light gleamed forth.

"The comet!" gasped Kalb, clutching wildly at the reins.

Whether or not his excitement infected the horse or whether that sagacious beast merely wanted to conduct a scientific investigation on his own account is a matter of speculation, but straight toward the light the animal dashed, and Kalb, after a vague sensation of unimpeded flight through the air, awoke a few minutes later to find himself lying on the roadway and to observe the horse, still attached to the remnants of what was once a light wagon, trying vainly to scale a nearby electric light pole. Mounted Patrolman McGilvey galloped up just then and helped to straighten out matters. It was found that, with the exception of a few bruises, Kalb was all right, but the damage to the wagon amounted to about $50.

Reprinted from The Brooklyn Daily Eagle, May 19, 1910. The driver is presumably the author's great uncle.

Cranks Get Cranky

After picking himself up off the dirt and dusting off his pride as well as his uniform, Happy stepped out of the batter's box to get a moment to recompose himself.

"Hey rookie, that pitch wasn't all that close. Quit bein' a prima donna and get back in there," snapped home plate ump Brennan. "We gotta a ballgame to play."

But the Brooklyn fans had seen enough of Three-Finger's aggressive approach, repeatedly putting their players at risk with his "purpose pitches" that came dangerously close to potentially lethal beanballs. They spontaneously burst into a sustained chorus of boos. Thousands of fingers went up throughout the stadium in salute of Three-Finger, followed by a series of epithets directed personally at Brown. Once the verbal assault got under way it rapidly grew in intensity and was punctuated by an ocean of trash showering the field.

At that point Brennan had to acknowledge the circumstances and called a temporary time out to cool things down and allow the grounds crew to pick up the trash. Unfortunately, a particularly loyal and most likely inebriated angry fan, took the opportunity to jump the rail of the left field grandstands and started to rush toward the mound. Brooklyn's security guards and the two NYPD officers in attendance immediately reacted to intercept the out-of-control fan and escort him off the field.

Frank Chance, Chicago's Player/Manager had a temper of his own and raced over to try and take matters into his own hands. He exchanged a few choice words up close and personal with the fan which quickly escalated into a shoving match that was about to come to blows when the police interceded and broke it up. They escorted the fan off the field to a standing ovation while even more trash was showered in Chances' direction. He stooped down to pick up a beer bottle that landed near his feet and as he walked back to first base, he tossed the bottle back toward the stands over his shoulder with one hand and flipped the fans the bird with the other.

Happy's butt was a bit sore having taken the full weight of his fall as his legs had gone straight out from under him, but his ego took the bigger pounding. He was angry at Three-Finger for the dusting, angry at Brennan for making light of it and angry at Chance for unsportsmanlike conduct. He couldn't believe his appearance as a pinch hitter was the cause of such a big hullaballoo from the fans. His heart was racing and he felt a bit lightheaded.

Coney Island Mardi Gras

On Friday night, September 9, the Superbas returned home from a short, less than successful road trip to Philadelphia, having dropped three of four to the Phillies. Next afternoon, back in the friendly surroundings of Washington Park in Brooklyn, they bounced back and swept a double header from the Phillies, 7-1 and 7-2, to continue their away and home series. So, despite a long day on the field, a bunch of the Superbas were heading down to check out the Coney Island "Mardi Gras" to celebrate. Happy was confused. Mardis Gras? Really? In September? In Brooklyn?

However, with mass participation parades and unthrottled partying fueled by large amounts of alcohol, it resembled the look and feel of its southern namesake.

Happy was in an upbeat mood and when his teammates asked if he'd join them, he didn't hesitate. The event sounded like fun, but he was just as eager to finally get to Coney Island and check out the amusement parks, arcades, and beachfront he'd heard so much about. They walked from the stadium down 3rd Ave and caught a trolley heading south down Coney Island Ave. all the way to its terminus in Coney Island and in 30 minutes were joining the throngs of people that were beginning to gather for the evening's festivities.

Somehow, even though he'd been in Brooklyn for over five months, Happy had not yet laid eyes on the Atlantic Ocean so that was the first stop on the evening's agenda. As soon as they hopped off the streetcar, the familiar smell of salt and seaweed was in the air. In the distance were the carnival-like sounds of a calliope emanating from the lavish and newly installed El Dorado carousel just down Surf Avenue outside the Dreamland Amusement Park.

Within a block of the beach, he could hear the low roar of the sea punctuated by the rhythmic staccato of the waves breaking on the shore at high tide. Without thinking, Happy broke into a sprint down the remainder of Stillwell Ave. to get his first glimpse of the sea. Like a bunch of 10-year-old buddies, the other Superbas all joined in to see who could make it to the beach first. Happy won easily and didn't stop until he reached a bench where he could remove his shoes and socks. His teammates followed suit and they walked to the water's edge to put their feet in the water and soak it all in.

The visceral feeling of the cool ocean water on his feet, its spray in his nostrils, and the sounds of the surf pounding the shoreline were reminiscent of the Pacific Northwest and brought on a brief moment of homesickness. This faded quickly when a large splash of cold water landed on his back and soaked his shirt. He turned to find Tex cracking up and retreating quickly after his surprise sneak attack with a child's pail left behind after a family excursion.

Back on Surf Ave. they walked up the ramp leading to the long wooden boardwalk that ran in parallel with the shoreline. They passed the rows of smaller indoor arcades, rides and amusements that despite their proximity to the three major amusement parks (Luna Park, Dreamland and Steeplechase), were brimming with customers eager for entertaining and amusing ways to part with their money.

One of the latest varieties, a recent import from Philadelphia, was a kind of miniature bowling alley known as Skee-Ball, where for a nickel, you got to roll nine wooden balls up a ramp into a series of concentric rings and you got points based on how close to the center you could get your balls to land. The points were paid out in Skee-Ball script redeemable for prizes big and small.

Tony had one of the most accurate throwing arms in baseball and could roll a Skee-Ball bull's eye practically with his eyes closed. Since the most difficult roll netted 50 points, a perfect score in Skee-Ball was 450, similar to rolling a 300 in bowling. In three consecutive games, Tony rolled a 420, 450, and 440 while Happy's best score was a mere 380. Tony's unusually high scores created quite a bit of attention and when the word quickly spread that the mysterious Skee-Ball master was none other than the Superba star shortstop, the crowd gathered around quadrupled in size. The arcade manager was thrilled as it was a lot more successful bringing customers in than the barker he hired but the players took this as a signal to move on so they could return to the luxury of just having some fun on their own.

Greyhound Racer was a competitive game where you sat on a stool and pushed on a lever that flipped a rubber ball into the air. When it landed in one of the adjacent holes it would advance a replica of a greyhound on a racetrack. The distance and speed your dog advanced depended on how quickly and which hole the ball landed in. You competed against up to nine others to see whose dog crossed the finish line first. Customers were entitled to cheap trinkets (or *tchotchkes* as Fanny would say) for winning their race and were eligible for a more substantial prize if they got their dog to finish in less than one minute, which was very difficult to do. Perhaps because they were tired of calling attention to themselves, none of the Superbas took top honors in several rounds of the Greyhound Racer.

One of the star attractions was the Sea Lion's Shoot-the-Chutes water slide. The line was around the block so they decided to skip it, but Happy and his teammates walked across the bridge that overlooked the lagoon into which the flat-bottomed boats splashed at the ride's conclusion to get a closer look. They stopped for a few minutes and watched one of the boats filled with ten passengers plus an attendant as it began its steep, slow ascent to the top of the man-made platform high above Luna Park. Happy watched the passengers at the bow nervously anticipating their adventure close at hand and was transported back to his dad's boat as he departed on his own adventure just a few short months ago. At the apex, the boat made a U-turn, so it faced the downward slope and after a brief suspenseful pause, was released. The boat glided along its rails in a gravity-induced slide, increasing in speed until it splashed into the man-made lagoon below.

Coney Island had plenty of options for eating and drinking of course, ranging from Feltman's Hot Dogs and Seafood Pavilion, to Izzie's Brooklyn Knishes, New York Pizza, Helga's German beer garden and Oscar's Oyster and Clam Bar. Gazing at all these tempting food establishments reminded the teammates they hadn't eaten since the morning – most players skipped lunch on game days. So, when Silent John said, "Don't know 'bout you guys but I'm gettin' sumpin' ta eat," they quickly set off in pursuit of the nearest culinary option.

Several of the saloons, including Oscar's fronted on Surf Avenue and had long bars where you could order a cold draft and appetizers without even setting foot inside, so they wandered over. Happy had a hankering for shellfish – back home, fresh shellfish of all kinds were ubiquitous, but he hadn't had much since coming east. At the end of the regular bar at Oscar's, two workers at the raw bar were shucking a mile a minute huge buckets of fresh local oysters and clams on the half shell from the south shore of Long Island. At a dollar a dozen or ten cents apiece, Happy and his teammates tried their best to keep up with them. It was futile of course, because after downing every oyster or clam a swig of beer was in order, which naturally slowed them down. The shuckers caught on and got into the competitive spirit by turning up their shucking speed a notch or two and left the Superbas in the dust.

Happy inquired about the origins of the Blue Point oysters and Littleneck clams they were serving. They told him to keep up with demand, the big oyster companies like Sealshipt Oyster System imported seed oysters from Connecticut and Huntington and Northport Harbors on the Long Island Sound – large schooners brought seed oysters to the South Shore's Great South Bay in the spring so they'd be ready for harvest in the fall and early winter. The season for local oysters was limited to months that contain the letter "r" (September through April). The hard clams originated just west of Nicholl's Point and they were easiest to catch in the summer months so their season was just about to end. September was the rare month both varieties of local shellfish were abundant. They were serving Littleneck clams but they explained that Littlenecks (smallest), Cherry Stones, Top Necks, and Quohogs (used in chowder) are all various sizes of the same variety of hard shell Quohog clams based on their age.

As a native of the Pacific Northwest, Happy considered himself a fresh shellfish aficionado and both the oysters and clams surpassed even his high standards for sweet taste and smooth consistency. But he discovered that Brooklynites had their own technique when it came to how to eat raw shellfish:

a squirt of lemon and a generous helping of fresh horseradish complimented the oysters and a tobasco-laced cocktail sauce was served with the clams. His first bites went down quickly but lit a small bonfire in the back of his throat that burned clear through his nose en route to the top of his head, causing his eyes to tear and the top of his scalp perspire... Happy quickly reached for a fire extinguisher in the form of his tall mug of cold beer. He was currently sampling Brooklyn's own locally brewed Excelsior Brewing Company Ale but for the next round switched to an "imported" brew from the Rubsam and Hormann Brewing Co. of Staten Island.

The sun was beginning to set off to the west, illuminating the partly cloudy sky in a purple haze. Slowly but steadily Mardi Gras revelers, dressed in outlandish costumes, began to wander by and even though the parade wasn't starting for several hours, the level of ambient noise was steadily growing.

Tex insisted that a trip to Coney Island was not complete without checking out at least one of the numerous roller coasters and steered them over to his favorite, the Drop the Dips coaster on the corner of Bowery and W. 15th St. It created quite a stir when it was first built in 1907 and was still the premier ride in all of Coney Island. After a fire destroyed it just one month after it opened, owner Chris Feucht rebuilt it with even sharper curves and steeper drops but added some safety features including a mandatory lap bar and safety wheels to keep the cars from going airborne.

As they approached the gate to enter, the teenager taking tickets just about crapped his pants when he recognized them. "Geez, I don't believe it! The Brooklyn Superbas Smith Brothers, Tex Irwin, and Silent John Hummel! Holy shit... Welcome to Drop the Dips guys!" He could barely get his words out. "I'm a real fanna youse guys – got the whole team's trading cards at home! My dad says they'll be worth a whole lot someday…Can-I-getchyas autographs?" Tony laughed and said, "Sure, kid" and they each scribbled their names in pencil on the kid's log sheet attached to a clip board that was used to record the number of customers every running cycle. Tony then reached for his ticket but the kid insisted that at Drop the Dips the Superbas ride for free.

The monstrous wooden roller coaster was bigger than Happy imagined especially when standing right beneath it and while he wouldn't admit it to his teammates and didn't want to make a scene in front of the ticket kid, Happy was nervous as hell about getting on board. Too late now he figured – he'll just have to suck it up. The kid pulled on the brake lever to slow the cars approaching the entry gate and after a final shrill squeal of the metal wheels on the steel rails, the passengers in the group of six cars got up to exit. Most of the adults stood up slowly, their legs a bit wobbly as if they'd just disembarked from an ocean voyage. The younger riders leaped out of the cars with enthusiasm and practically danced their way down the wooden platform to exit on the opposite side, many eager to return for another round.

The Smith "brothers" walked up to the first empty car and climbed in, pulling the safety bar across their laps, while Irwin and Hummel settled into the next car. "OK, you can do this" thought Happy trying to convince himself. The wait to fill the cars was less than a minute but once he was aboard, it seemed a lot longer than that as he worried about how he'd react once they were underway.

Tony was making small talk as they waited but Happy was recalling Harry Houdini's recent Australian adventure and wasn't really listening. He wondered whether Houdini ever got as nervous as he felt right now. Finally, the cars were loaded. "Enjoy the coaster!" the kid shouted as he pulled on the lever and the cars jerked forward and began to roll slowly away from the platform.

Now that they were underway Tony turned to Happy and burst out laughing. "Hey kid, you're not scared of this thing, are ya?" The pallor of his face must have been pretty obvious and given him away.

"A helluva lot more than my first at bat in the Bigs" admitted Happy sheepishly as he figured no point in trying to bullshit his buddy, especially if the queasiness in his stomach got the better of him.

"May not feel like it but yer a million times safer here than in the box against a pitcher whose control is a bit wild with nothin' but a stick in your hand to protect ya!" Tony assured him.

At that point they turned the corner for the first slow upwards climb. As they gained elevation, the spectacular view penetrated Happy's fear and provided a pleasant distraction. They cleared the top of the red Drop the Dips entry sign and off to his right all of Coney Island began to come into view. The click-clack, click-clack sound of the car's safety bar being dragged across the sawtooth anti-rollback device affixed to the tracks began to dominate as they advanced slowly upwards on the steel rails and the background sounds of the calliope and the large crowds below faded into the distance. Happy became aware that the rest of the passengers on the ride had quieted too, an eerie calm before the storm as they took in the surroundings and prepared themselves for what lay ahead.

The wooden supports of the coaster superstructure and rail supports gave out an occasional groan as the weight of the cars shifted the load on its shoulders. The first climb was not Drop the Dips' steepest or longest. Since it preceded all the mayhem soon to follow, it allowed the riders to truly enjoy the sights below them. Happy now had a clear panorama of the ocean, its peaceful rhythmic waves illuminated by the setting sun.

"Now that's something'" he said, and Tony just grinned back. As he looked down he thought to himself that Coney Island would make an ideal location for a baseball stadium.

His peaceful interlude was short-lived as they soon reached the first peak with no more track in front of them. The car swung sharply around a full 180 degrees and Happy could feel his stomach clench involuntarily. And then, without further warning, the bottom dropped out and they began what felt like a free fall. Happy was speechless but Tony let loose a primal scream which seemed to spur on many of the riders behind them who did the same. The wind in their faces blew Happy's Superba cap back on his head but his white knuckled grip on the lap bar wouldn't loosen for an instant to allow him to reach up and secure it.

The bottom of the first drop sent them into a steep banked curve and Happy could feel his weight shifting to the left as his hands gripped the bar even harder so he wouldn't wind up sitting in Tony's lap. And then like a one-two punch in a prize fight they hit a series of smaller but sequential drops and dips that threw their heads back quickly.

The last motion was the straw that broke free Happy's cap and he heard Tony explode with glee as it flew off his head and floated off into the labyrinth of the coaster's superstructure below. His teammates behind them saw the whole event unfold before them and joined Tony in uproarious laughter. The combination of having survived his first roller coaster challenge, and the infectious laughter around him lit Happy's face into a broad grin.

The next phase of the ride was more of the same with dips and drops just a bit steeper, and curves a bit sharper. In the same way that he survived his first major league brush back fastball, Happy could feel his self-confidence return. A weight lifted from his shoulders and his grip on the lap bar relaxed, allowing him to stare down the coaster and think to himself, "OK, show me what you got." He thought to himself this is just what Houdini was talking about when he described the sensation of flying.

Before he knew it, they completed the final twist and coasted back to "home plate". They advanced slowly to the ramp where another eager group of riders awaited their turn "on deck." They climbed out slowly and Happy felt a bit wobbly. He realized just as if he were returning from an extended voyage at sea, it would take a moment to regain his land legs.

The kid was there eager to ask his famous customers how they enjoyed their ride. An older gentleman was there too, who beat him to the punch and reached out to shake their hands, "Honored and glad to make your acquaintance! What did you like best about the Drop the Dips coaster?" he asked. Tony laughed and responded, "Gettin' to ride for free!" whereupon the kid turned bright red as he introduced the anonymous admirer as his boss and owner Chris Feucht.

Realizing his faux pas and trying to make sure the kid was not in jeopardy of losing his job, Tony quickly reached for his wallet and presented them two free player passes to Washington Park for any Suberbas home game. As it turned out Feucht was not in the least bit upset since he was a big fan of baseball and would have done the same if he were collecting tickets. In fact, to show all was forgiven he told the kid to take the two passes himself since he could better afford to pay his own way. "Geez, Mr. Feucht, that's awful swell of ya" he beamed and after more handshakes all around Happy and his teammates headed off.

Next stop they walked over a couple of blocks to Feltman's Seafood Pavilion Restaurant on W. 10th St. and Surf Ave. Charles Feltman, who emigrated in 1857 entered the restaurant business after the wild success of his pushcart food wagon business where he introduced for the first time in America a type of German sausage. The profits on his ten cent "hot dogs" as they came to be known were sufficient to enable him to gradually expand his establishment into one of the largest restaurants in the world employing 1,200 waiters who could serve up to five million diners a year.

The teammates grabbed an outdoor table under an umbrella. They ordered another round of beers and the house specialty platter of hot dogs with spicy mustard and mounds of sauerkraut to get them started. They each followed with a three-course shore dinner of clam chowder, lobster, fresh corn on the cob, baked potato, and cherry pie for dessert. Sunset over New York harbor was the entertainment over dinner and twilight had snuck in before they finished desert. A strong sea breeze accompanied the exit of the sun and introduced an even more pungent aroma of salt water and seaweed in the air.

When they were done eating and totally stuffed, Happy recalled his queasiness a few hours earlier and laughed, "Good thing we did the coaster ride before dinner!"

"To conquering all fear!" added Tony and they clinked their beer mugs in unison.

Just then a loud deep thumping noise accompanied by women's voices shouting in unison pierced the din of the clanking plates and conversations in the packed restaurant courtyard. As they looked up a group of several dozen women in full length white gowns carrying poster board signs (and one with a bass drum which accounted for the thumping they heard) appeared rounding the corner onto Surf Ave.

Amidst the din it wasn't clear right away what they were yelling, especially because their sudden presence captured everyone's' attention simultaneously and people began pointing and shouting back in their direction. The Superbas jumped out of their chairs to get a better look and once they could make out the writing on their hand-carried signs they realized it was a march of pro-temperance women protesting the Mardi Gras parade.

Their signs read "Lips that Touch Liquor Will Not Touch Ours," "Women's Christian Temperance Union," "Anti-Saloon League," "Liquor means Alcohol, Alcohol means Poison...Why Drink Poison?" But the one the players quickly voted as the most-original was captioned "Devil's Toboggan Slide, Death & Co. Proprietors" and showed a drawing of men descending down an amusement park slide (similar to some of those available in Coney Island) past various sections labeled, "Popular Hotel, Saloon, Doggery, Gambling Hall, Corruption", and ending up at the bottom of the slide which was marked, "Drunkard's Grave."

Silent John couldn't contain himself and pierced the air with a shrill whistle to get the attention of the woman carrying that sign and shouted "Looks like fun! Where's the entrance to that ride?" Tex, raised his mug and shouted, "We'll drink to that!" while Happy poured another round from the pitcher of J. Ruppert's Lager beer for the occasion.

As they headed back out, the streets were now thick with Mardi Gras revelers, well-primed for a long night of public partying. The temperance demonstrators, outnumbered several hundred to one, had made a hasty retreat and disappeared. A marching band of Negro musicians called the Beale Street Brass Band emerged in their place followed by officials of the Coney Island Chamber of Commerce carrying a broad banner emblazoned with "Welcome to Coney Island, Brooklyn NY."

Dancing to the rhythms closely behind were a couple of clowns in purple, yellow and green silk costumes with matching colored ribbon-laced hats and wearing traditional Mardi Gras masks of comedy and tragedy. One was juggling three baseballs which caught Tony's attention. "Maybe we should get him to shore up our infield!"

Next came a slow-moving procession of horse drawn wagons and a few gasoline-powered flatbed trucks – many were decorated in nautical or beach themes in salute to summertime in Coney Island. Tony poked Happy with his elbow and pointed to a float decorated in a mermaid theme that carried a curvaceous bathing beauty in a golden swimming suit and jeweled tiara atop her blond hair with a sign declaring her the "Queen of Mermaid Avenue." Many of the parade floats were sponsored by local businesses and were packed with dozens of celebrants in masks and/or hats tossing candies and beads to the surrounding and cheering crowds.

As they continued to imbibe the readily available beer sold on the street (by unlicensed vendors who avoided police harassment by supplying them with free beer), Happy's vision and memory became cloudier and next thing he knew they were stretched out in the trolley screeching and rumbling northward back to the Slope in the wee hours. Somehow, he managed to find his key and quietly open the front door, careful not to wake Fanny and call attention to the fact that he was, for the first time, breaking curfew. Fortunately, there was no game scheduled for Sunday so Happy was able to sleep in and nurse his hangover. Despite the day of rest, the Superba's performance for the final game of the series against the Phillies the next day was uninspired and they were easily shut out by a score of 3 - 0.

From Shtetl to Ghetto

Fanya was made welcome in the tenement apartment of her father's cousin's family, Sheldon and Rose Feinstein on Manhattan's Lower East Side and was able to share a room with Miriam and her teenage sister Rebecca. Ironically, she had considerably less space in New York than their tiny home in the Ukrainian shtetl but considering the conditions of her travels, Fanya was used to squeezing into tight quarters. And if not roomy, the apartment was comfortable and clean – Rose took pride in keeping the place spotless. Fanya spent the next several weeks eagerly getting acquainted with her new city and there was lots to explore.

On the Sunday following her arrival, Fanya and Miriam walked to and then over the Brooklyn Bridge – it was every bit as majestic as described in the newspaper. The fact that the bridge opened in time for her arrival in New York felt like a symbol that she was crossing over into a new life.

In the six weeks after coming to America she received four letters from her family and replied promptly to each one. They didn't contain much news about how things were going – mostly just small talk about the weather, how her sisters and brother were doing in school, plans for the holidays, and the two new suits her dad was preparing at his tailor shop for the Rabbi and his son who was soon to marry one of Fanya's classmates. She would have been invited to the wedding if she hadn't left for America.

Fanya knew her family's letters were self-censored so as not to upset her or cause her to worry any more than she already was. They were mostly filled with questions focusing on how she was adjusting to her new life and wanting to know the smallest details. In her replies, Fanya tried to capture the enormity of the changes she was experiencing daily but she too, tried to stay upbeat and didn't dwell on how much she missed her family.

But suddenly the letters stopped coming. Sheldon heard news from friends in Kiev that as bad as they were before Fanya left, things had gotten much worse. Reports were that most of the Jews from Fanya's area had either fled or perished in the latest round of pogroms. As hard as they tried to get more information, accurate reports were hard to come by and they were left to speculate and hope for the best. And while they couldn't get absolute confirmation, Sheldon feared the worst... it was doubtful her family survived.

Fanya was devastated – she wished she'd never left and couldn't live with the guilt of being the lone survivor. Her dreams of finding employment and then working hard to save enough to help reunite her family were now probably moot. Her hopes for starting over in the land of opportunity rang hollow if it was at the expense of her whole family. And even though the circumstantial evidence led them to believe the Feinsteins perished in Ukraine, the lack of definitive news made it all the more painful to accept this unthinkable turn of events.

In her young life, Fanya had experienced plenty of hard times but nothing that compared with the cavernous sorrow into which she now plummeted. She survived her rough journey on the vast high seas only to drown in sadness within the confines of a Lower East Side tenement. She didn't leave the apartment for weeks – in fact she barely left the 10 x 12 ft. bedroom she shared with her two cousins. The tiny room was quickly overflowing with her feelings of despair, snuffing out any positive hopes for the future she had been kindling.

Rose brought her meals to her but she barely touched the food. Fanya's sorrow clung tightly for weeks as she began to wither both physically and emotionally. It was an all-consuming, impenetrable grief; she appeared distant, disengaged. The sadness was highly contagious in such cramped quarters, but Sheldon and Rose were patient and supportive. They tried, in vain, whatever they could think of to get her to grab one of the many lifelines they cast her.

After what seemed an eternity of helpless flailing, Sheldon found an opening. He arranged to get her piece-work at home cutting fabric for the Isadore Kaufman and Sons coat factory on Mott St. and coaxed Fanya to give it a try as a means of alleviating her grief. She agreed, reluctantly at first, but slowly Fanya began to focus on the work and gradually felt the burden of her despair dissipating. With it, Fanya's spirit of hope could once again be rekindled, albeit in a much more somber context.

One of the first things she uttered in weeks was a request for a *Yahrzeit* candle that she could light in memory of her family. Neither Fanya's family nor her cousin's family were particularly observant, but at a time such as this, her request seemed appropriate. Finally, the Feinsteins had Fanya clinging to a life preserver and began to bring her back to safety.

As she began to surface, Fanya was grateful to her new family for rescuing her. She began to help Rose with chores around the apartment while the others were gone at work. She started to regain an appetite – Rose was a better than average cook and the smells in the tiny tenement apartment were enticing. Like an Indian snake charmer, they lifted her spirits and drew her in; for the first time in her life, she started to spend time in the kitchen, both helping to prepare meals and cleaning up afterwards.

Rose was relieved to see Fanya's recovery and very pleased to have her companionship. She began to teach her the family recipes and it was here that Fanya learned to cook classic Jewish cuisine: chicken soup with matzah balls, *flanken,* several varieties of *kugel,* kasha *varnishkes*, blintzes with homemade farmer cheese, and later potato *latkes* at Chanukah. Rose was also proud of her baking and made fresh *challah* and apple cake, *rugelach*, and *hamantashen* for dessert – they made the usual *mohn* and prune varieties but Fanya's favorite was apricot.

Fanya learned some cooking tips from Sheldon too. Unlike her father who never stepped foot in the kitchen, he took over for Sunday morning breakfast and specialized in recipes that used leftover foods before they spoiled. For example, he might pan fry last night's cooked potatoes, a stray onion from the cupboard and possibly a piece of salami together with some fresh eggs to create a sumptuous feast. He took stale bread, spread it with butter and cut a round hole in the middle into which he placed an egg and fried it, thus transforming it into something special. Or he soaked stale *challah* in egg to make French Toast and at Passover the unleavened equivalent, *matzah brie*. Fanya's favorite though was something Sheldon called *schmudda*, which was farmer cheese that had sat in the ice box a bit too long and was on the verge of spoiling. Rather than discard it, he melted the cheese in a frying pan on the stove and served it on toast. Fanya was amazed that it didn't taste at all "off" and she liked it so much she begged Sheldon to start making it from fresh cheese and he happily obliged.

The work was repetitive and mindless but required attention – she was cutting and sewing fabric and the required concentration helped her get her mind off her grief. She quickly became proficient and within a month the company offered Fanya a position on the factory floor. Getting out of the apartment, even just to trade for 10 – 12 hours in another cramped environment, making a pittance of a salary was a step in a positive direction. Her dreams were not the same as when she departed her homeland but now more focused on building a new life for herself and her future.

The Smell of Newly Mowed Grass

After relieving himself at the Men's Comfort Station trough urinal, Kevin Kearney rejoined his brother Michael, their work buddies and the rest of the cranks in the left field sideline bleachers who hadn't sat down after the 7th inning stretch and finally had something to cheer about. The Superbas were more than holding their own in this day's battle against the mighty Cubs.

Usually by this time in the game they were out of it and players and fans alike were just going through the motions. But standing in several inches of spent peanut shells he and his fellow longshoreman had devoured, they knocked down bottle after bottle of Ballentine's Ale from the "Be-Ah He-Ah" guy and were feeling pretty good. Starting before the crack of dawn they had worked the early shift on the docks of Red Hook in Brooklyn overlooking NY harbor, so they could hustle over to Washington Park after work and get there by the second inning of that afternoon's game.

This week they were unloading fifty-pound sacks of green Colombian coffee beans from the seemingly endless hold of a large freighter. They'd haul the sacks from the dark bowels of the ship and load them onto carts which they'd push up a series of ramps that wind up on the dock and then load them into trucks bound for the roasters. Back and forth from dark to light and back again; monotonous, physically grueling, toil. The newer diesel-powered ships were being equipped with mechanical lifts and conveyor belts to speed up the process. Eventually this will mean fewer jobs for the likes of the Kearneys, but that's a struggle for another day. Considering New York is the largest importer of green coffee beans in the world, averaging more than 675 million pounds per year, the work is plentiful.

And at least for part of the time they are working in the fresh air with a beautiful view of New York harbor at their feet and not cooped up in some sweatshop. On each pass they got a glimpse of the Statue of Liberty as she stood watch to the south, the mighty Brooklyn Bridge leading to the metropolis of Manhattan to the north, and Governor's Island just ahead to the west. One-year earlier Kearney was able to witness Wilbur Wright take off from the island in his airplane to make his historic first flight over American waters as he circled the skies over Lady Liberty.

"Shite! Did you see that for Christ's sake?" screamed Kearney, "Brown is `throwin' right for Silent John's noggin'! And that SOB thinks it's a big joke! Someone oughta bust his feckin' cranium!"

Apparently Three-Finger's indiscreet smirk did not go unnoticed among the fans at large and a spontaneous chorus of boos began to rumble through the stands.   Hummel's strikeout several pitches later and subsequent ejection added gale force winds to the mix, causing an escalation into a full-fledged thunderstorm of wild jeering throughout the stadium.

"Hey Ump, take the balls outta yer eyes and get yer head outta yer arse, ya feckin' shoibag!" sugggested Kearney. And turning his wrath to Brown, "Hey Mordecai, you caffler[3] ... your mum's fanny's like a billposters bucket![4] Did ya face[5] her last night?"   He was on a roll now... "Hey Mordecai, you wonker,[6] we'll give ya More-ta-cry about!" And in a mocking sing-song tone, "Morta-cry!"

His brother and a few of the fans nearby immediately joined the chant so that other cranks several sections away could hear and Kearney fed off the positive feedback. Brooklyn's rally turned the fans' attention in a more positive direction however, and soon the boos were replaced with cheers for their hapless heroes. A bona fide rally was a rare event and the fans were basking in its ephemeral euphoria.

When Happy Smith stepped out of the dugout as the pinch hitter there was a bit of a hush in the stands as the fans tried to figure out just who was coming to bat.   Since substitutions were allowed and even adopted as part of the strategy of the game these days, you couldn't assume who the player was just because of the position he was playing or where he appeared in the batting order. Kevin wondered why they didn't put the player's names or perhaps a number on their jersey so the fans would easily recognize them.   Or perhaps have a system of megaphones to make announcements to the crowd and relay it throughout the stadium.

So much for his futuristic visions... in today's world, knowledgeable fans close enough to see, identified the player and would pass the word along so that before long everyone in the stadium knew who it was. In Happy's case, the news

---

[3] [asshole]

[4] [rather promiscuous woman]

[5] [have sex with her]

[6] [masturbator]

was slightly delayed because with only 36 at bats under his belt the whole season, his name wasn't exactly at the tip of anyone's tongue and required consultation with the player listing in the official scorecard along with a process of elimination.

And once his identity was discovered, there was lots of speculation over what Dahlen was thinking. Was he really going with a player this green in such a game-critical situation? But Brooklyn fans tended to be optimists and Smith was given the benefit of the doubt along with a cordial reception as he took his warmup swings in the on-deck circle and finally approached the plate. Rooting for the underdog came naturally to Kevin and he was back on his feet to enthusiastically welcome this most unlikely choice.

Brown's brush-back pitch against Hummel had stoked the anger of the crowd but when his first pitch to Smith, an untested rookie, sailed toward his head they'd seen enough. Like a mother goose defending her nest the fans leaped to Happy's defense. Kevin started a reprise of his taunt once again and this time it quickly gained momentum.

Realizing he was on to something he could capitalize on, Kearney jumped up, motioned for everyone to get on their feet, turned to the crowd behind him raising both hands over his head to lead the chorus of fans in the left field sideline bleachers, "Morta-cry, Morta-cry, Morta-cry!" As the chanting picked up steam, he then ran down the aisle leading toward the field level seats stopping every few rows to encourage more fans to join in and in no time, half the stadium was mocking Three-Finger Mordecai Brown and his aggressive tactics.

A few of the angry fans near the field level then started throwing trash and beer bottles onto the field. Caught up in the growing pandemonium and drunk on his ad hoc role as rabble rouser-in-chief, in addition to the countless Ballentine Ales he'd consumed, Kevin continued cheerleading as he raced down toward the field.

As he approached the field level railing with a head of steam he grabbed the top with both hands, catapulted his feet over sideways and kept on going with a flying leap straight onto the field. Once he landed on the field he gazed around for a moment and was frozen in time as he tried to comprehend what he'd done and figure out what the hell to do next.

Of course, his action caught the attention of most of the fans and those hands that weren't already busy saluting Three-Finger with one of their own were now pointing in Kearney's direction. His momentary hesitation gave the security guards and NYPD cops assigned to patrol the game a head start in corralling him and he spotted four figures running in his direction from the dugout area. Without further contemplation, Kearney instinctively sprinted across the field towards the first base side to avoid capture.

As he approached first base, he was surprised to see one of the Cubs not only holding his ground but barreling towards him. It was Cubs manager/first baseman Frank Chance who was screaming, "Come on buddy, let's have a go." His six-foot four-inch 210 pound stature earned him the nickname Husk but his behavior on the field led many of his teammates and Cubs' reporters to dub him their "peerless leader."

Throwing his first baseman's mitt to the field, Chance continued shouting, "Think you got a pair a balls comin' out here? Let's see how fucking tough you really are!" And with that he lunged toward Kearney with both hands straight out throwing him off balance and back several feet. No easy feat as Kearney was no slouch himself – a couple of inches shy of six feet but with a longshoreman's solid muscular physique.

At this point the catcalls, whistles, and general roar of the crowd in his defense added a layer of drama to this surreal moment in Kevin Kearney's life. He recovered and instinctively returned the shove but with less effect. The momentary altercation with Chance gave his pursuers the time they needed to surround him and before he realized it, they had him wrestled to the ground and a knee was pressing him into the grass in foul territory.

A moment later, a billy club was pressing his face into the turf and another was applied across his legs so he was firmly pinned. The smell of the newly mowed grass and moist earth was an odd, pleasant juxtaposition to the shooting pains he felt from the bony knee pressing into his kidney and the cool wooden stick on his skull. And the roar of the crowd in his defense temporarily buffeted the pain until he felt a bolt through his shoulders as his arms were twisted behind his back in pretzel-like fashion and his hands were locked in place with a pair of cool metal hand cuffs.

Their coordinated movements gave the impression the security detail had done this once or twice before. Without wasting a second, he was unceremoniously lifted to his feet and with a solid whack with one of their night sticks commanded to start walking off the field. He was no longer playing the hero or self-consciously resisting but his reaction wasn't rapid enough to suit the NYPD and now joined by two additional patrolmen on horseback to usher him off the field, he received another solid whack and was told to move along.

Fanya's Transformation

There were over a hundred women of all ages working at the Isadore Kaufman and Sons coat factory on Orchard and East Houston Streets and it provided Fanya with an opportunity to make numerous acquaintances and several friends. It was here she met Ethel Goldfarb and Luisa Del Fiore, fellow immigrants from Poland and Italy, respectively and the three young women quickly bonded. Ethel's family had emigrated to the U.S. from Bialystok, Poland when she was five years old, so she felt and acted like a typical New Yorker. Luisa was just a babe in her mother's arms when her family moved to New York from Southern Italy, so this world was all she knew. They both lived within a few blocks of the Feinsteins' tenement on Delancy St.

They didn't have much free time on the shop floor to socialize – even stopping to chat for a brief moment could bring a harsh rebuke from the tyrannical managers whose job it was to keep the workers on task at all times. But the young women began walking back and forth to work together which gave them an opportunity to bond and get to know one another. Ethel spoke Yiddish, Polish, and her English was flawless, spoken with a typical New York accent. English was Luisa's primary language although she was also fluent in Italian as that was what her parents and extended family spoke. Fanya told her friends she was jealous because while she spoke Yiddish and Russian fluently, her English which she learned in school, was still spotty and spoken with the heavy accent of a recent immigrant.

"On that note," Ethel told her, "If you want to blend in and not advertise that you're just off the boat, you might want to change your name to something a bit more American sounding."

"Yeah," Luisa piped in, "You got a middle name you can use?"

"Yes, but..."

"*Nu*?" said Ethel, "out with it!"

"*Lieb*...it's for love" she added for Luisa's benefit.

"Well, that's lovely," said Luisa... "but not exactly your typical American name."

"Yes, no good for making me American. I need some ting more betta."

"Better, not 'more better'... Hey, I've got one... how about Fanny? I read about this great lady named Fanny Wright in the last issue of the Ladies' Garment Worker newsletter. Said she was an immigrant who came here about a hundred years ago and was a real freethinker... believed in equal rights for women and worked to free the slaves. She gave speeches, wrote pamphlets, and even started a utopian socialist commune – that's where a bunch of people live together in..."

"I know from communes! I like Marx and study him in school... *Nu*, Fanny Feinstein! I like it. Sounds like how I feel in my new country, in America. And, it's honor for me to be named for such a person as this Fanny Wright. Tank you Luisa!"

"My pleasure Fanny, now we just need to work on your English," she said with a grin. "Maybe we should sign you up for the Union's English literacy class."

Ice Cream Sundae

As Happy returned to the batter's box after being decked he was having a hard time focusing. Perhaps it was due to the lightheadedness he was feeling, exacerbated by the deep-rooted instinctual fear that was beginning to dominate no matter how hard he fought it...but suddenly his mind took him back in time to a much earlier baseball experience where fear was the common denominator.

There was just one out remaining in the last inning of the championship game and Smith's team was leading 3-2 but their opponents were threatening with runners at first and third and their hottest hitter at the plate. Henry decided to play deeper in right field – a single could tie it but anything over his head could result in a walk-off game winning hit so he backed up a good five steps. Other than a weak dribbler that snuck between the first and second basemen back in the second inning, not a single ball had been hit to him all game.

Henry was fine with that – traditionally at this level in baseball the fewest balls were hit to right and that's where the player with the least skills was sent to languish and where after dutifully reciting the Hippocratic Oath, he would attempt to do the least harm. In one of life's ironies, he was listed as Team Captain in the League schedule but that was only because his name appeared last on the roster and nobody realized that was where the captain's name was supposed to go. So even though his team adopted the name The Echoes (in honor of the steamship that his dad piloted and the fact that he graciously purchased matching baseball caps for the entire team) and their opponents The Oysters, the schedule listed the game as Smith vs. Immerhoff.

At 12 years old "Captain" Henry was small for his age; his teammates were all bigger, more coordinated, and more athletic than he was. He felt fortunate that despite his limitations his friends had even included him on the team roster and the fact that he was the official captain was kind of an inside joke. Henry was two years from his first growth spurt that more than evened the score physically with his classmates and eventually allowed him to develop the skills to excel in the game he loved so much and reach a level that he only dreamed about. He'd never played on a championship team in any sport and was now one out away from his first trophy and a hot fudge sundae – the team planned to head for the local ice cream parlor to celebrate if they won.

Henry's daydream about ice cream sundaes was interrupted by the loud pinging sound of a solidly hit baseball. The right-handed batter got around on an off-speed pitch and pulled a hard line drive down the third base line. Henry breathed one sigh of relief as he realized the ball was not hit to the opposite field (i.e., nowhere near him) followed by a second one when he saw it sail over the third base bag and land just inches over the white chalk line in foul territory. The home plate umpire confirmed that it was foul and the runner on second, who had already rounded third, had to trot back out to start all over again.

Instinctively, Henry had taken a few steps towards left and had to turn around and retrace his movements in deep right field to get set for the next pitch. As he did, he took in the whole scene. The championship game was being played on the Southern Oregon region's semi-pro field which was much better groomed than any other he'd played on. The infield was just dirt and the outfield grass was a bit patchy but as Henry looked around him he admired the real bases, freshly applied bright white chalk foul lines, bleacher seating on both sides of the field and even a "scoreboard" which consisted of a portable schoolhouse chalk board that a volunteer used to update the score each inning.

A couple of pitches outside the strike zone and a swing and a miss put victory a mere strike away. Henry pounded his mitt nervously, adjusted his cap, and assumed his semi-crouching defensive position, with his glove and throwing hand resting on his knees to await the next pitch. His pitcher was feeling the pressure too, as it seemed to be taking a lot longer than normal in between pitches. Finally, he delivered, and this time let loose a fastball high and tight that the batter managed to connect on, in an "inside out" swing, driving it the other way.

Henry noticed right away that the ball was going to the right side of the field and that it was hit in the air. He was still playing deep and because it wasn't well hit, it didn't seem like it had the power to go over his head. But it wasn't immediately clear how far it would travel and whether it would be fielded by an infielder going back or was going to be his responsibility.

At that point his senses went into slow motion and the butterflies in his stomach took flight. From the corner of his eye, he saw the runner on second take off as soon as the ball was hit (as expected with two outs). For the slightest instant he froze. Was the ball hit well enough to reach him in deep right field or did he need to charge? Something within instructed him to take the latter approach and he began to move in. Would the ball have enough hang time to allow him to complete the play or would it drop in to tie the game or worse? As he ran toward the infield, he heard his name being shouted by one of his teammates which pretty much sealed the fact that all eyes were on Henry. It was his play to make, and he hastened his run.

For a moment he envisioned overrunning the ball only to have it land embarrassingly over his head. But he now saw that the ball had reached its apex and was beginning its descent. It was not at all clear however, whether he'd get to the ball before it landed in which case, he'd have to field it quickly and get ready to throw the ball in for a play at the plate... or if it would remain airborne long enough for him to catch it for the final out.

He accelerated his approach to a full throttle sprint. Next thing he knew the ball was upon him and he threw up both hands for the catch – no time for any fancy stuff. He instinctively squeezed as the ball hit his mitt with a solid thwack and miraculously it stayed put within the confines of his leather mitt. His momentum carried him forward to the infield where he was met with a hero's welcome as gloves and hats were tossed in the air. "Attah boy, Henry!" "Way to go, kid." It was one of those random moments in life in which you're in the right place at the right time and you get the trophy and the ice cream sundae. Could easily have gone a different way but didn't.

Ironically it was the catcher's chatter that brought Happy back to the present and the realization that he was at bat in the major leagues. "Hey kid, what the hell you smiling about?"

The Fifth Kashe

Ethel's family was more observant than Fanny's – as a Rabbi's daughter she was expected to attend *shule* each Sabbath, and did so dutifully but without conviction. She saw herself as a modern girl and her family's traditions part of an archaic past, disconnected to how she felt growing up as a New Yorker, as an American. It wasn't that she was ashamed of her heritage or that she was ignorant of her peoples' history and culture. She certainly read in the papers of the current struggles that Jews in Eastern Europe were facing and the pain and suffering that her new friend described firsthand were not lost on her. She relished Jewish culture but was unmoved by what she interpreted as antiquated, unthinking reverence to primitive beliefs. Ethel realized that nothing in her life came close to Fanny's narrow escape from oppression and the devastation of her entire family – none of which was enough to convince Fanny to find salvation in a rededicated devotion to Judaism.

She and Fanny shared a vision of the next generation of Jews in America; proud and aware of their Jewish heritage but not slaves to repressive and regressive thinking. They identified not only as Jews but as modern, intelligent and strong women, part of the burgeoning new progressive social and political movement of the twentieth century. The two had much in common, and their friendship quickly blossomed. During their short breaks at work and their walks back and forth to the coat factory, they talked of many things. In addition to the usual topics including eligible men, dating, clothing, etc., they had spirited discussions about politics and cultural events.

So, Ethel was thrilled when Fanny accepted her invitation to join her family for the first night of their Passover *Seder*. Fanny asked her aunt and uncle if they would mind if she shared the holiday with Ethel's family. They were so pleased that she was making new friends, they did not hesitate in giving their blessing. This would be the first Passover for Fanny in her new homeland and more significantly, her first Passover since losing her family. While her background was much more secular than religious, Fanny recalled her fond memories of this holiday. For her, more than any other holiday, it was a time that provided a connection to her heritage and what it meant to be a Jew.

This year however, in addition to the usual Four *Kashes*, she would be asking, "Why must this Passover be different than any other?" It was no longer a parable of tragic events that happened to faceless victims long ago - from this year forward, it would have an even deeper impact as the story of her own family's oppression gave new relevance to the message being remembered.

Perhaps a bit selfishly, Ethel also felt it would be fun to have someone she could talk to, albeit in a hushed whisper while hiding behind their *Haggadahs*, as her grandfather, father and uncles droned on in Hebrew for the two-hour ceremony. Did it have to be so boring, in a language that few barely spoke? Why not translate the story into English or Yiddish and get everyone to participate? Wasn't that the whole point of the holiday anyway? She felt similarly about the weekly service read from the Torah, not to mention the fact that women had to sit in the balcony of the synagogue and were not really welcome to participate in the first place.

Truth be told, Ethel also had another ulterior motive inviting Fanny to the family Seder... her brother Moishe, just three years her elder was a bit shy around women and she was hoping to play *shadchanis*, introduce them and light a spark. Moishe was in the entertainment business – he was a second-tier performer in the Yiddish Theater which meant that he was part actor, singer, dancer, and comedian. He was not a headliner but rather a journeyman able to get small roles in short-running productions and was either looking for work or auditioning for new roles as often as he was actually performing. Ethel considered Fanny a dear friend and believed she would make the perfect sister-in-law.

She didn't utter a peep about her plans to Fanny and managed to keep Moishe totally in the dark lest she put the *kanehura* on the whole thing. She sat to Fanny's left and was successful in getting Moishe to sit next to Fanny on her right, but at the end of the evening she hadn't counted more than a dozen words exchanged between them. While Moishe didn't have an ounce of stage fright performing in front of hundreds of strangers, when it came to talking to a young, attractive woman, his tongue was tied in knots.

Disappointed that her clandestine plan had fizzled, Ethel took consolation in the fact that she helped Fanny navigate through a difficult time. Two weeks later however, Moishe scared up the nerve to ask Fanny out for a date – well not a date, exactly... he asked if she'd like a complimentary ticket to see him perform in *Dos Meydl Fun der Gehto* in which he played several small roles.

After the show they went to Murray's Dairy Restaurant on Hester Street for blintzes and coffee. Seeing the play was difficult for Fanny since it was reminiscent of the life and her family she left behind but talking about it was cathartic and Moishe was a good listener. Since Fanny was willing to bare her feelings, he began to open up. He discussed his love for the theater but talked of how difficult it was to earn a living as an actor. He confided his fears that he will soon need to find a more sustainable vocation, especially if he met the right girl with whom to "settle down." Fanny blushed and was grateful when the conversation turned to baseball, for which they both shared a passion.

Six months later, Moishe proposed and a few months after their wedding he got a job working for a cousin in the dry goods business. Initially he worked behind the scenes ordering supplies and stocking the shelves but gradually he learned the business and took on greater responsibilities managing the register and finally in sales.

Once he overcame his shyness, Moishe realized the sales business was not so different from performing on stage. He excelled and was promoted to the position of store manager in just two years. His cousin was busy expanding his business and opening several more stores, so in another couple of years he offered to sell the store along with the real estate on which it stood to Moishe for very attractive terms. Giving up a potential life in show business wasn't as difficult as he expected – besides he never managed a big enough role to warrant getting his name on the marquee and now he had a huge sign with three-foot block letters spelling out Goldfarb's Dry Goods Store on one of the busiest avenues in Park Slope.

The Blink of an Eye

Happy tried to stay focused but his close encounter with Brown's beanball followed by the crowd's spontaneous reaction and the shenanigans of the inebriated crank swirled through his head and combined to create a circus-like atmosphere. Earlier in the season he attended the P.T. Barnum and Bailey's Greatest Show on Earth show at New York's Madison Square Garden while on his first date in New York and as he blinked and scanned the infield, it was transformed into a three-ring extravaganza.

Frank Chance was tapping his big floppy shoes while juggling four baseballs on first, Johnny Evers with his cap turned backwards clowned by doing backflips on second and on the left side of the infield Joe Tinker and Harry Steinfeldt were performing an aerial duet between second and third. Headlining in the center of the infield of course was none other than Ringmaster Wild Mordecai Brown, tipping his top hat to the crowd as he paraded around the infield on horseback with his outstretched arm shooting blanks from a six-shooter into the air. Aptly named for his role as circus barker, Noisy Kling beckoned the crowd through his megaphone, shouting, "Step right up…"

"…To the plate there, rookie!" he continued, bringing Happy back to earth with a shake of his head to clear his thoughts. Got to concentrate.

Following the high and inside brush-back fastball, Happy figured they would go with a low fastball on the outside corner. Rather than accede to Brown's intimidation, however, Happy moved an inch closer to the plate to improve his ability to reach out and poke the ball to the opposite field. But how could he be sure?

He then remembered the tutorial he received from Seattle Giants' skipper Mike Lynch and quickly motioned to the ump for a time out and began to step out of the batter's box while he rubbed his eye in an attempt to remove an imaginary piece of dirt. He barely turned his head toward Kling and shot him a quick glance hoping he'd catch him flashing his sign to Brown.

Observing his little acting job, Noisy just chuckled and piped up, "Nice try kid, save that actin' shit for yer Broadway audition. But hey, I'll make it easy for ya…Yer gettin' the hook on the next pitch an' no way in hell ya gonna come anywhere close."

Of course, Happy figured this was just another of Kling's attempts at deception to throw him off and mess with his confidence – he wasn't sure what Three-Finger would toss, but he was pretty certain it *wouldn't* be a curve ball. Maintaining his stance, he dug his heels in and reached across the plate with his bat tapping the dirt just beyond the edge of the outside corner to make sure he was positioned properly.

Brown took the sign with a slight tilt of his head and barely perceptible knowing grin. He took the exact same windup as the initial pitch, affirming Happy's premonition that another heater was on its way. His exaggerated motion and high leg kick were yet additional signs that Brown was reaching back for some extra gas. Three-Finger's fastball had been clocked at a mere 0.46 seconds to travel the 60 ft. 6 in. to home plate. That's equivalent to 132 ft./sec or 90 mph, twice as fast as a thoroughbred racehorse, literally just slightly longer than the blink of an eye – not much time to make a decision. Happy tried to blink his eyes right before the pitch was released so he wouldn't lose sight of it on its way home and would be ready to start his swing early to catch up with Brown's fastball.

Three-Finger completed his release and launched the ball in Happy's direction. Somewhere on its trip between the pitcher's mound and home plate, about a quarter of a second later, Happy noticed several things. Rather than approaching like a speeding bullet, the ball appeared to be in slow motion. Its trajectory was well above the strike zone – not low and outside as he anticipated. Instead of starting his swing early to get around on Brown's fastball, his arms froze as he waited for its arrival and the umpire's signal of two balls and no strikes.

But just as it was about to cross home plate, the motion of the ball mysteriously and abruptly changed. It fell from a height well above his shoulders right across the plate, belt high. His knees buckled and all Happy could do was watch as the ball floated down and landed in Kling's over-sized mitt. A classic and perfectly thrown overhand curve ball just as Noisy had warned. A collective sympathetic groan quickly rolled across Washington Park from the dedicated Brooklyn cranks who couldn't believe what they just saw. Brennan seemed to appreciate the beauty in the masterfully thrown pitch and practically sang out "Steeerike One."

"Oughta make that one illegal" smirked Kling.

Muttering to himself, Happy asked the ump for time out again and stepped out of the batter's box to collect his thoughts.

"S'matta kid? Can't say I didn't warn ya!" Happy didn't look back but he could hear Brennan chuckling at Kling's sarcastic comment.

Happy tried to convince himself that at one ball, one strike, it was still early in the count and anything was possible. He did not want to complete the at bat without taking a swing but that pitch was unhittable. If Three-Finger continued to throw the hook that well, he was dead meat.

The Uprising of the 20,000

Last year, following a series of ad hoc strikes in the garment industry, labor leaders organized a large open strategy meeting at Cooper Union to discuss how best to respond to the horrific working conditions that are ubiquitous in the industry. It was held in the Great Hall where Lincoln presented his speech outlining his anti-slavery platform prior to his nomination in 1860. The hall was packed to capacity with about 900 workers, activists and union leaders in attendance. While no longer a garment worker herself, Fanny attended as a member of the Women's Trade Union League (WTUL).

Speech after tired speech was delivered by the senior, all-male union leadership despite the fact that the garment workers were mostly women and the issues being debated impacted their working lives directly. They called for patience and many openly doubted whether women workers had what it took to withstand the difficult conditions imposed by a long strike – loss of income, physical reprisals by police and company-hired goons, and even arrest and jail time.

Finally, after listening to several hours of fruitless oration and bickering over minutiae from the male union leaders, a slight young lady in the audience rose to her feet, and approached the podium. Clara Lemlich, a young organizer for the International Ladies Garment Workers Union (ILGWU) had heard enough.   Head of the American Federation of Labor (AFL) Samuel Gompers had just finished an appeal for patience and was yielding the floor to a colleague when a loud, high-pitched voice pierced the air.

"*Genug,* enough already! *Hak mir nisht keyn chaynik!* So much hollow noise, like the clanging and banging of an empty teakettle signifying nothing! Let *me* speak! I want to say a few words on behalf of the women!" At first, a shocked silence rolled across the floor of the Great Hall in response to Clara's auacity.

Just three years earlier, she'd helped form Local 25, which unlike the national union, featured meaningful participation by women workers. She led several short-lived walkouts over specific working conditions and was quietly gaining the respect of her fellow workers. The male union leaders on the other hand were skeptical at best, many were cynical that women could play a meaningful role or had the stamina for a protracted struggle.

Quickly the silence of disbelief gave way to murmuring of the crowd. "Who's that one?"

"I don't know, but it's about time!"

"Whoever it is, she's got *chutzpah!*"

Then as the word spread that this was Clara Lemlich the new firebrand ILGWU organizer, the murmuring turned to a rumble.

"Atta girl, Clara!"

"You tell those chickenshit bureaucrats!"

Considering Clara's' tenacity and the crowd's response, the speaker Jacob Panken, ILGWU organizer and attorney, stepped down and yielded the floor. He didn't really have much choice.   Then Lemlich delivered an impassioned address in both English and Yiddish that culminated in a call to action:

"I went to work two weeks after landing in this country. We work from sunrise to sunset seven days a week... Those who work on machines have to carry the machines on their back both to and from work...The shops we work in have no central heating, no electric power... And the bosses! They hire such people to drive you! For talking shop, girls are immediately fired. At the conclusion of the day's work the girls are searched like thieves. The hissing of the machines, the yelling of the foreman, makes life unbearable. Not only your hands and your time but your mind is sold. It's a regular slave factory!"

"Ikh bin eyner fun yene vas suffers fun di abiusiz diskreybd do ... I have no further patience for talks as I am one of those who suffers from the abuses described here... *Un ikh makh az mir geyn oyf a general shlogn...* and I move that we go on a general strike!"

Her powerful words sliced through the hours of tiresome bureaucratic rhetoric and immediately galvanized the audience. They rose to their feet and cheered. A spontaneous chant of "Strike! Shlogn! Strike!" erupted across the auditorium and the union leadership was reluctantly forced to call a vote. History was about to be made once again within the walls of the Cooper Union Great Hall.

The workers overwhelmingly voted in favor of a strike and over the next several weeks, tens of thousands of women walked off their jobs in the garment industry in what was soon characterized in the press as "the Uprising of the 20,000."

The strike quickly picked up momentum as garment workers for the first time began to believe that together they could force greedy factory owners to end intolerant conditions such as wages that barely fed their families, the 60+ hour work week, forced overtime, no time off for holidays, unsafe and uncomfortable work environments, lack of benefits if they get hurt or sick, and retribution if they attempted to organize to bring about change. Supporters, including the WTUL, raised money and collected food and clothing to aid the striking workers.

Fanny was very active in this campaign – from her time in the sweatshops as a new immigrant years ago, she had first-hand experience and knew these pent-up demands were long overdue. She organized a benefit at her house to raise funds for the striking workers. Her guests were fellow activists in the WTUL, friends, neighbors, and of course her boarders. She invited Clara Lemlich who took the subway from the City to come talk about the working conditions the strikers encountered daily and discuss the specific goals and demands of the strike.

Afterwards, Clara stayed to help Fanny clean up and the two had an opportunity to talk. Like Fanny, Clara was also a Russian immigrant, albeit a more recent one having arrived in the U.S. in 1905 at the age of 19. She worked in many of the same types of Lower East Side sweatshops that Fanny had worked in before she met Moishe and left to raise her family. Clara was among the new wave of so-called *"farbrente Yidishe meydelech."* Despite their difference in age, Fanny felt a special bond with Clara. She appreciated Clara's ideals and carefree determination to fight for what she believed was right. They shared a love of literature and culture and were both active in the women's suffrage movement. They quickly became good friends.

Fanny's Call Up

Fanny was excited about the debate on women's suffrage that was being co-sponsored by her organization (the Women's Trade Union League) and The Town Hall on August 12, 1910. The event was attracting significant attention in the newspapers as it included several notable female political activists including the leading anarchist Emma Goldman and the WTUL co-founder Ida Raugh. The other two scheduled speakers were Josephine Marshall Jewell Dodge president of the National Association Opposed to Woman Suffrage (NAOWS) which had formed in New York the previous year, and Fanny's new friend and ILGWU organizer Clara Lemlich.

The Town Hall was founded in 1895 by a group of suffragists known as The League for Political Education to "continue the struggle for women's rights by raising political consciousness" through political and cultural events. As a WTUL volunteer, Fanny had helped organize the event, coordinating with The Town Hall staff and handing out leaflets.

Unbelievably, on the day of the debate Raugh developed laryngitis and was literally unable to speak. The inner circle of the WTUL and Town Hall staff held an emergency meeting to try and figure out what to do. Panic struck quickly when they realized other notable WTUL and Town Hall leaders who might have easily filled in were not in New York at the time.

Mary Elisabeth Drier who led the New York branch of WTUL and chaired the New York City Women's Suffrage Party was in Lowell, MA assisting textile workers organize their union. Adele M. Fielde, prominent author and one of the original founders of the League for Political Education in 1894 was back visiting China after spending ten years there studying and publishing works on the life of Chinese women. Rose Schneiderman and Pauline Newman, two other veteran organizers of the 1909 Uprising were in Lawrence, MA providing striking workers there with financial and logistical support. In fact, Fannie had read about them in the paper just that morning where Schneiderman was quoted as saying, "The worker must have bread, but she must have roses, too" making the point that not only were fair wages needed for survival but issues related to worker dignity, political equality, and quality of life (including the right to vote) were every bit a part of the overall struggle, too. Fanny thought these were the simple but eloquent words needed for winning a debate.

Emma Goldman was the big attraction and her engagement schedule was booked solid a year in advance, so postponing the debate was not an option. She was also an experienced and talented public speaker, so the organizers were feeling pressured to ensure that strong arguments in favor of women's suffrage were presented to counter the anarchists' position.

At one point during a lull in the discussion, Clara looked over at Fanny. Making eye contact she smiled as one of those new-fangled light bulbs was illuminated in her mind. "I know who can do this and she's in this very room right now!" she exclaimed.

"Fanny Goldfarb is an outspoken and active WTUL supporter both with her time and money. She organizes and runs lectures on many progressive issues including women's suffrage and is an eloquent spokesperson for the movement and for women rights in general." There was a momentary hush in the room as Clara's suggestion sank in. It's safe to say that nobody had anticipated this name as a replacement for Ida Raugh, but no one was more shocked than Fanny. She started to object but was too stunned to speak. That's not a good trait for a debater she thought.

Before she could verbalize her objections however, her old friend Luisa Del Fiore, who now worked part-time as an administrator for the Town Hall took the floor to second the nomination and said, "I've known Fanny since we were both twenty years old working in the coat factory together. As a recent immigrant she was eager for knowledge about life in America... but boy, is she smart and such a quick learner. In just a few years we were all going to Fanny for advice on political issues. She may not be well known but I'll put my faith in her ability to tell things as they are... in plain language that all can comprehend. And there's not one among us who is more dedicated to the cause of equal rights for women!"

Anna Artlidge from the executive board of WTUL knew Fanny casually from her work for the League but didn't know much about her background. Frankly she was skeptical about her abilities to speak before a large audience and asked, "Well what sort of experience does she have as a debater? It's not enough to just believe in the issue. Looking in her direction, "Fanny, have you ever been in a formal debate?"

While she wasn't at all comfortable with the idea of taking the stage that night, she was matter of fact in her response. "Well, I did like debating when I was in high school and was a member of our school's debate team... but I'm sure that was nothing compared to..."

Clara cut her off and chose to argue for the glass half full. "There, you see? She's articulate *and* experienced. What more can we ask for?" After what Fanny thought was way too brief a discussion of her qualifications, there was a voice vote. Mostly for lack of a more qualified candidate with just four hours to go before the debate was scheduled to begin, Fanny was unanimously approved as their backup debate team substitute.

It was quite an honor of course, but Fanny knew full well it was a lack of depth on the bench that precipitated the move to bring her in as a pinch-hitter. She was not a seasoned public orator and even when she had debated back in high school it was never in front of hundreds of people which made her extremely anxious...and then there was the challenge of doing so in English. Even though she had made tremendous strides, and her vocabulary was now much better than when she first arrived in New York, she had not been able to lose her strong Yiddish-tinged accent which made her self-conscious.

Her old friends Ethel and Luisa provided encouragement, but it was Clara who finally convinced her to accept.

"Accent, schmakcent... This is the city of immigrants and nobody cares about that. What, I don't have an accent thick like yours? You know I'm more comfortable speaking Yiddish and I have to remind myself all the time to talk in English. Tell you what, I'll stand next to you on the podium and if either of us starts talking in Yiddish we can give a *zetz*!"

Fanny laughed, and said, "But..." when Clara cut her off with, "But nothing! You may not realize it but some of us think you are in Ida's league. Besides, you know honey," she said with a wink knowing of Fanny's passion for baseball, "when the manager calls your name you step up to the plate and keep your eye on the ball."

So, with that, it was decided. Fanny would be the fourth speaker in the debate and had just a few hours to collect her thoughts and prepare.

The Wink

With the two pitches he'd seen thus far, Happy was feeling severely over-matched, and stepped out of the box again to re-set his focus. He couldn't stop wondering why Dahlen called on him in this critical portion of the game when other teammates were clearly more qualified. Was this a kind of test to see if he could play under pressure? Was his fate as a Brooklyn Superba or even perhaps a major league baseball player on the line? Or was it something else?

He moved his head in a circular motion to loosen up his neck. Next he placed the bat behind his neck, resting it lightly on his shoulders while grabbing it at each end with palms facing out. He then slowly twisted his back at the hips to relieve tension. As he rotated his body, his gaze for the first time picked up individual faces in the crowd sitting in field level seats on the right side of the field. Many eyes were fixed on his every move. They were all anonymous, some shouting words of encouragement, others just sizing him up. He was pretty sure she was at the game but fortunately Josie was nowhere to be seen.

His teammates were all off the bench rooting him on. A bonefide Brooklyn offensive rally was a rare occurrence and when executed against a team like the Cubs, rarer still. His quick glance picked up Bill Bergen, Jake Daubert, Tex Erwin, and Pryor McElveen all crouched on one knee on the Brooklyn dugout steps.

Someone shouted, "Atta boy, Happy! Keep your eye on the ball!"

Fresh from his tour of the base paths to score the go-ahead run, Tony Smith joined Dolly Stark, Tommy McMillan, and Bob Coulson who were on their feet beside the others. More of a wishful thought than accurate assessment, one of them was shouting at Three-Finger, "Nooooo pitcher, no pitcher, no pitcher!"

Silent John Hummel had his hands cupped to his mouth in a makeshift megaphone that made his unmistakable booming voice easily heard over all others, "Heeeey, Hap, Hap, Hap, Hap Hap! Wait for your pitch now, wait for your pitch!" Sage advice from the guy who has struck out in each of his plate appearances so far today. Easier said than done, thought Happy. Recently expelled and the chip on his shoulder still smarting, Silent John couldn't help direct some additional commentary at home plate ump Bill Brennan. In return Brennan shot Hummel a glance as if to say, why the hell are you still on the bench? And, keep it up and I'll have you arrested.

Doc Scanlon, now out of the game, was standing with his fellow starting pitchers Nap Rucker, George Bell, Cy Barger, and Elmer Knetzer. With a win hanging in the balance if the Superbas offense can blow the game open and/or the relievers Kaiser Wilhelm and Rube Dessau can contain the Cub batters for two more innings, Doc had a vested personal interest in the outcome. He stood on the top dugout step so he could be seen by the fans and directed his emotions toward rousing the crowd, waving his arms wildly like Walter Damrosch conducting the New York Symphony Orchestra at Carnegie Hall. His orchestrations were simple but effective and a groundswell of voices in unison grew louder and louder. Just two notes alternating on each syllable: "Let's Go, *Brook*-lyn, Let's Go, *Brook*-lyn!"

Continuing his panoramic glance, Happy picked out a face he recognized just to the right of the dugout. Dressed in his usual grey suit and bowler hat was the team's owner. He was sitting with a number of other equally well-dressed gentlemen and one woman who were absorbed with their hot dogs and beer. In that moment Ebbets didn't seem to be paying attention to his guests and returned Happy's glance with a wink and a simple tip of his hat. It was subtle but unmistakable. What could this mean? He recalled the only two encounters he'd ever had with Ebbets.

The first was right after he'd made the team and Ebbets advised him to stay loose, keep his head in the game, and always be ready. More recently though was the tense clubhouse meeting that had Happy nervous about his future with the team. Was he being set up for failure so Ebbets could let him go without calling attention to the "scandal"? Or was this some kind of late season, last chance trial by fire to see whether he was talented enough to extend his contract with the Superbas?

A broad mischievous grin on Ebbets' face convinced Happy he was getting warmer. But either way, he realized worrying about it was not conducive to a successful at bat. He shook his head quickly as if to vanquish these demons from his thoughts before placing his bat across the plate to ready himself for the next pitch.

Fanny On Deck

T ime evaporated in the blink of an eye and before she knew it, Fanny was standing backstage gazing out into the theater as people gathered and took their seats. The Town Hall was temporarily located at the Grand Theater on Grand and Chrystie Streets in Manhattan's Yiddish Theater district while the new, dedicated building uptown was under final design prior to construction. She panned the vast interior replete with rococo-style rounded ornamental plaster scrollwork that accented and surrounded each level of the multi-tiered auditorium. The newly installed electric light chandeliers brightly illuminated the hall and the light from its many individual hanging crystals glistened off the ceiling's ornate gold painted carvings and hand-painted murals as the sold-out crowd of almost 1,500 people filtered into their orchestra, mezzanine and balcony seats.

Like a batter in the on-deck circle, Fanny tried to relax and focus to get herself prepared. But as she peered out from her darkened vantage point backstage into the lights of the hall, she was transfixed. She gazed through the crowd for familiar faces. She knew there'd be dozens of people she knew, including the boarders in her rooming house, but it was all a blur.

She did notice a phalanx of officers from the NYPD strategically placed throughout the perimeter of the hall and recalled this was typical for large public gatherings that Emma Goldman or other popular anarchists addressed. She had read just the other day in the Brooklyn Daily Eagle that at a local lecture to commemorate the first anniversary of Spanish anarchist Francisco Ferrer's execution by Spanish authorities,

> *"[Goldman] extolled Ferrer as a martyr, preached anarchy in a diplomatic and unlibelous way, and had the police guessing as to whether they should stop her lectures or let them go on."*

NYPD even deployed stenographers at her speech to record her every word, presumably to potentially be used in future prosecution against her. The paper reported:

> *"Although the police have not seriously interfered with Emma Goldman in Brooklyn, they nevertheless keep very close tabs on anything in which she might be expected as having the slightest interest."*

It was likely that they'd be recording Goldman's words here tonight too, and Fanny felt a twinge of nervous anxiety when she realized that perhaps her words also would be recorded for posterity by the police. Ironically however, since tonight Emma Goldman would be arguing against granting women the right to vote, it was unlikely the political establishment would make any attempts to get in her way. In the words of Mark Twain's friend, Charles Dudley Warner, politics do indeed make the strangest of bedfellows.

On stage were four plain wooden folding chairs, two on either side of the speaker's podium. Fanny noticed there was a wooden stool hidden under the podium so even though she was barely five feet tall she'd be able to see and be seen while speaking.

Unlike in America's favorite pastime and Fanny's favorite sport, where the fans expect changes and substitutions in the lineup during the course of the game, substitutions in a debate were highly unusual and Fanny could hear the buzz of the crowd after seeing her name on the one-page program that was quickly re-printed just hours before. Who is this rookie, Fanny Goldfarb and how could she possibly stand her ground against the experienced all-stars assembled on stage? The crowd noise continued to grow, roaring like a tumultuous sea in Fanny's ears but she wasn't sure how much was due to a heightened acuity resulting from her anxiety.

Charley's Vision

B rooklyn Baseball Club owner, Charles Hercules Ebbets was holding court in his usual front row seat beside the Superba dugout, where he had both an excellent view of the field and ready access to club manager Bill Dahlen, if he felt compelled to relay his opinion on baseball strategy (as he was known to do on occasion). Ebbets had worked his way up through the ranks having sold scorecards, held various jobs in the "front office," and gradually invested his earnings in the team until he eventually became majority owner. He even tried his hand at managing the team on the field in 1898, but with a record of 38 wins and 68 losses he decided his talents were better suited to managing the duties as team President and he traded his baseball cap for a stylish black bowler.

From his vantage point, Ebbets slowly looked out across the whole stadium and took in the crowded wooden grandstands of Washington Park, overflowing with eager cranks rooting for their hometown team against the first place Cubs. But as he stared, the trained architect in Ebbets' mind's eye saw a very different image.

Washington Park's wooden superstructure which had already experienced two devastating fires emerged as a grand, modern, fire-resistant steel and concrete baseball palace. The entrance lobby was airy and covered in a marble floor and a huge electric chandelier featuring large, illuminated baseballs hung from the lobby ceiling. The worn-out bench seating was replaced by comfortable new individual folding seats that allowed for three times as many paying customers to luxuriate with back support as they cheered on their favorite bums. Not to mention the convenient, sanitary indoor public restrooms and parking facilities in which an internal communication system would be used to have your car or carriage delivered to the front curb.

Beyond Ebbets' architectural apparition, his vision was also based on business strategy. The Superbas hadn't had much success of late and certainly weren't selling out games against lesser rivals. The Brooklyn players and manager were often criticized by the newspaper sports writers, but they always seemed to be able to keep the games competitive and despite consistent derision, the loyalty of their fan base was second to none. Ebbets felt if the amenities of the stadium were improved and it was considerably larger, they could significantly improve ticket sales at the gate and finally begin to make a healthy profit.

"Hey, you guys hungry? I brought some hotdogs with lots of sauerkraut and extra mustard and some brew to wash it down."

Ebbets' 32-year-old son, Charles, Jr., was recently promoted to Treasurer and was being groomed to take over the reins when his father retired, but in the meanwhile he too, wore many hats, including sometimes waiter.

"Thanks, Junior" responded Ebbets as he passed a portion of the lunch to his distinguished guest. Joining them on this day was Alfred E. Steers, Brooklyn Borough President, who was born and raised on Flatbush Ave. and was a loyal and devoted Superbas supporter. Steers, accompanied by his wife, had thrown out the ceremonial first pitch as he never missed an opportunity to gain political visibility. Since Brooklyn's recent merger with New York and the relinquishing of its status as an independent city, his was now largely a ceremonial position; Steers never turned down a ribbon cutting ceremony, Grand Marshal position in a parade, or in this case, a free day at the ballpark for what was quickly becoming America's favorite pastime.

"Thanks Charley, doesn't get better than this! An afternoon of professional baseball for me and the missus right here in the Slope, accompanied by an authentic Feltman's Coney Island hot dog and Trommer's Pilsner beer from Bushwick. A complete Brooklyn experience! By the way, don't know if you heard the sad news, but my old buddy Charles Feltman passed just yesterday.

"Yes, so sorry to read about Mr. Feltman's passing in the paper this morning, Al. 'Spose I'll be seeing you at the services tomorrow ... and as a matter of fact we are planning a Buy-One, Get-One-Free special on all frankfurters at Washington Park during tomorrow's game in his honor."

"He was certainly one of Brooklyn's great visionaries — conceived and facilitated the development of Coney Island as a resort and amusement park like no other in America. He was also a pioneer in the restaurant world," continued Steers. "Real American success story - went from inventing the modern-day hot dog and making a killing selling them from pushcarts and street stands to operating the largest restaurant in Brooklyn and maybe the entire country. I'd like to raise a beer in his memory...to one of our great prestigious civic leaders, and a real Brooklynite, he'll be remembered for many years to come."

"Here, here! To Charles Feltman and the Coney Island Hot Dog!"

After the third inning the group was also joined by Ebbets' attorney and real estate associate, Barney York who had been out looking at properties on the eastern side of Prospect Park. For the past two years, Ebbets was quietly purchasing adjacent lots in an undeveloped "swamp" area currently used as a garbage dump called Pigtown located between Flatbush and Crown Heights. The land purchases were made under a dummy corporate holding company so as not to draw attention and thus drive up the cost of the properties, which considering their location are not prime real estate. If successful in getting all the necessary property, this would be the site where Ebbets was planning to implement his vision of a state-of-the-art baseball stadium. He already owned 25 contiguous lots and needed about five more to have sufficient room to build his dream. Although it was just two miles due east, he'd be taking a risk on an obviously less desirable section of Brooklyn. But Ebbets was confident that his new baseball palace would attract baseball cranks via subway or trolley from throughout Brooklyn and perhaps the entire city.

Ebbets knew that getting his vision realized would be an uphill battle. He was not a poor man but compared to some of his fellow owners like Connie Mack and Ben Shibe (Philadelphia Phillies), Barney Dreyfuss (Pittsburgh Pirates), and Charles Comisky (Chicago White Sox) who all successfully financed and built big new stadiums using much of their own fortunes, Ebbets will require considerable external financial and political assistance.

He'll need other assistance too. Despite being trained as an architect himself, Ebbets realized he'd be in over his head and hired renowned architect Clarence Randall Van Buskirk, who had already assisted him with renovations to Washington

Park. Van Buskirk was excited to take on the challenge of making Ebbets' fantasy stadium a monument to the game of baseball, as solid as concrete and steel.

Part of his reason for inviting Steers to the game today was to share his vision for the stadium, seek his counsel on getting necessary city permits and begin discussion about purchase of a piece of adjacent property owned by the city, known as "Old Clove Road." This was a bit delicate however, because as much as he needed Steers' assistance, he did not want to go public with his plans.

Ebbets trusted Steers' loyalty to the team and what it meant to Brooklyn, so he decided to confide his plans and discuss the proposition while spending a relaxing day at the ballpark. It was a sun-drenched baseball afternoon, the Superbas and powerhouse Cubs were tied at one into the home seventh and they were enjoying a lunch of hot dogs and beer. Ebbets felt he couldn't have asked for better circumstances to hold the talks.

Extremely adept at multi-tasking, he never took his eye off the field however and was ever cognizant of the details of the game, recording them neatly in baseball shorthand on his scorecard. When Tony Smith lined his blooper to left to get on with the potential go-ahead run, Ebbets punched the air with his fist and broke into a grin ear to ear.

Not missing a beat in his well-orchestrated sales pitch, he continued, "So, as I was saying... a new, modern stadium will boost player and fan morale, increase ticket sales and team revenues, and be a big fat feather in Brooklyn's cap." He tapped his black bowler hat for emphasis. "We'll have one of the best damn baseball parks in America!"

At that point the crowd throughout Washington Park began to shout "Egg-ie!" as Ed Lennox stepped up to plate and Ebbets had to shout to be heard above the din. "I don't have to tell *you* what that would mean for the business community and the economy of our great borough!"

As hoped, Steers was very receptive to the idea of building the new stadium – in fact he was downright ecstatic. "Damn, right Charley! About time we showed Philly, Pittsburgh, and Chicago that Brooklyn rules. We'll be the envy of the whole goddamned League. And you can bet your ass that John Brush is scheming to rebuild that ramshackle Polo Grounds for his Giants just as soon as he can and I sure don't want to face Manhattan Borough President McAneny if they beat us to the punch." On a personal level, Steers envisioned access to prime seats in which he could entertain and impress his political and business cronies.

Mrs. Steers, who couldn't care less about all the business wheeling and dealing talk, was perplexed with the crowd's chant and elbowed her husband in the ribs to get his attention. "Hey Honey, how'd this guy get the nickname Eggie?" she asked. He explained that of course, it was partly because it sounds like Eddie, but the main reason was that his family owns a chicken farm east of Astoria Queens and Lennox managed the business in the off-season.

The Honorable Borough President promised Ebbets he'd do whatever he could to assist and expedite the process and ensure a permanent home for baseball in Brooklyn. In practice, that would likely mean typical political favors like greasing the skids for the land purchase from the city, talking with officials in the Department of Buildings and helping to use his influence to expedite the huge expansion of subway and streetcar service. Easy transportation to the park from most parts of Brooklyn and New York would greatly facilitate fan access to the new stadium complex on the eastern side of Prospect Park. Such challenges were just the sort of pitch Steers loved to tee off on; the foundation of his political success was based on his knowledge of which gears needed to be oiled, when, and with how much lubrication.

As soon as Steers and Ebbets shook hands to consummate their little quid pro quo arrangement, Lennox successfully got the bunt down moving Smith into scoring position and the cranks were on their feet. With Kling's wild throw to second on the double steal which allowed Tony Smith to score the go ahead run, the stadium exploded in pandemonium. While ecstatic over his team's good fortune, Ebbets felt a twinge of concern when the grandstands literally shook under the force of thousands of jumping and stomping fans. He then thought about the sturdy structures Van Buskirk was proposing for his future ballpark's design and breathed a sigh of relief.

When Chicago decided to intentionally walk eighth place hitter Jack Dalton, Ebbets took out a business card from his wallet and scribbled something on the back. For emphasis, he used the fountain pen from his suit jacket rather than the stubby pencil he had for his scorecard. He then folded the card in half and summoned the teenager in full team regalia who was sitting on a stool next to the dugout about five feet to their right. Ralph the bat boy came scurrying over to the owner's box and practically saluted. "Yes, sir, Mr. Ebbets, at your service- what can I do for you?"

"Hey kid, take this card over to the dugout and give it to Manager Dahlen, would ya?"

"You bettcha sir!"

Dahlen opened the note and climbed the dugout steps to peer around to the owner's box. The two locked eyes for a brief moment. Dahlen's stare was steely and incredulous. Ebbets responded with the slightest simple stoic nod of the head, invisible to his guests. Dahlen shook his head and retreated. After a short delay, Happy Smith emerged from the dugout and made his way over to the on-deck circle.

The Debate

At precisely eight minutes past the hour the moderator took the stage, the house lights were dimmed, and magically the loud murmur of the crowd was silenced as if it was wired into the same circuit that powered the electric lighting. The moderator welcomed the debaters onto the stage; Emma Goldman and Josephine Dodge to the left of the podium and Fanny Goldfarb and Clara Lemlich to the right. After welcoming everyone on behalf of the WTUL and Town Hall he remarked that while the sponsors have a clear position in favor of women's suffrage, they believe it is critical to hear all sides on the issue and make informed choices and thus decided to hold the debate to address this important issue. He also pointed out that,

> "Although we will be hearing very different views on this issue tonight, they are all coming from women who are deeply committed to the cause of women's equality so please treat everyone with respect."

The moderator then introduced each speaker with a short biographical summary including their credentials in representing their position for and against. He began with Emma Goldman:

"We are fortunate to have with us tonight, the writer and renowned lecturer on anarchist philosophy, the labor movement, women's rights, free speech, and social issues, Emma Goldman..."

Isolated cheers and whistles erupted from the audience.

"Emma is no stranger to controversy and has championed the cause of freedom for all, organizing against unjust government policies and laws and refusing to be silenced even when it meant arrest and imprisonment. She has published numerous pamphlets, newspaper and journal articles and founded and edits the journal Mother Earth. Despite her unwavering support in favor of women's rights, Emma will be arguing against the cause of women's suffrage..."

Sporadic gasps, murmuring and hissing once again interrupted the moderator.

"Ladies and gentleman, I remind you this is a debate and we ask you to please respect the speakers and refrain from expressing your views or distracting from the proceedings. Thank you."

He continued,

"Speaking in favor of enacting federal legislation to grant all women the right to vote, our next speaker is Fanny Feinstein Goldfarb. As you know she is filling in for Ida Raugh, who unfortunately took ill and could not participate. Fanny is on the Women's Trade Union League governing board and has been an active supporter of the labor movement and the struggle for equal rights for women from the time she arrived in America 27 years ago.

Most recently Fanny helped coordinate the League's efforts in support of the "Uprising of the 20,000," an event many feel may very well be remembered as one of the turning points in American labor history. We especially appreciate her willingness to step in on such short notice."

Fanny heard her name mentioned and understood she was being introduced but was still grappling with the enormity of her circumstance and heard little else. She sensed the audience focusing on her but tried to concentrate on breathing deeply and not give in to her nervousness. Finally, a brief round of polite applause signaled the announcer was moving on.

"Our third speaker representing the National Association Opposed to Woman Suffrage is co-founder and president, Josephine Marshall Jewell Dodge. Headquartered here in New York, the NAOWS is active on the state and federal level. They have established a newsletter, Woman's Protest, which is a leading outlet for anti-suffrage opinions. Josephine has been an outspoken proponent of the day nursery movement and is a sponsor of the Virginia Day Nursery and the Jewell Day Nursery to care for and educate children of working mothers here on the Lower East Side."

"Our final speaker is Clara Lemlich, a labor organizer for the International Ladies Garment Workers Union here in New York..."

The audience was well-stocked with union supporters and the spontaneous response to Clara's name was every bit as enthusiastic as the one Emma Goldman received. The announcer simply stopped for a moment to wait for the enthusiastic response to subside before continuing.

> "Despite her young age, Clara has played a major role in fighting for better wages and against the deplorable working conditions in the sweatshops of the garment industry. She has recognized the need to include women in the leadership of labor's struggles and helped to organize several union locals. Clara's role as a catalyst for the "Uprising of the 20,000" is well recognized and quickly gained her an important voice in both the labor movement and struggle for women's equality."

Happy was pleased that the Superbas were playing a series at home against the Pirates this week so he could attend the debate and have an opportunity to reciprocate some of the support that Fanny provided him in spades. They lost a close game that afternoon (final score 3-2) but as usual Happy rode the bench so he wasn't too tired to sit through the debate. He bought a ticket for 50 cents to sit in the upper balcony and watch Fanny (all proceeds benefited WTUL's political action committee). He was as impressed with the glamour of this prestigious hall as he was when he first stepped foot into Washington Park.

As the house began to fill Henry closed his eyes and realized the noise of the crowd was familiar and comforting. After the debaters took the stage and the introductions were being made, he watched Fanny sitting nervously with the other three speakers, looking around anxiously. It was a familiar feeling.

He waved but of course she couldn't see him in the blur of the crowd. When he had asked her earlier about Emma Goldman, Fanny explained that while they share a common vision for the future there are strong differences between the various factions of the so-called progressive movement and these debates on how best to achieve their ends are intellectual wrestling matches that are oftentimes heated. That was the context through which Happy filtered the thoughts expressed by Emma Goldman as she was the first to step up to the podium to present her views with self-assurance:

> "Good evening, ladies and gentlemen. Today, we boast of the age of advancement of science and technical progress. All over the world these advancements are rapidly changing how we live as we begin to harness new electric powers to shed light all around us and steam to power our ships, trains, and carriages. Is it not strange, then, that we still believe in fetish worship? True, our fetishes have different form and substance, yet in their power over the human mind they are still as disastrous as were those of old.

> Our current, modern fetish is universal suffrage. Those who have not yet achieved that goal fight bloody revolutions to obtain it, and those who have enjoyed its reign bring heavy sacrifice to the altar of this omnipotent deity. Woe to the heretic who dare question that divinity!"

A number of her supporters nodded in agreement, and a few could not help let out shouts of "Yes, sister!" and "She speaks the truth!" as if they were at a Baptist revival meeting while opponents rustled uneasily and tried to restrain themselves.

"Woman, even more than man, is a fetish worshipper, and though her idols may change, she is ever on her knees, ever holding up her hands, ever blind to the fact that her god has feet of clay. Thus, woman has been the greatest supporter of all deities from time immemorial. Thus, too, she has had to pay the price that only gods can exact: her freedom, her heart's blood, her very life!

Woman's demand for equal suffrage is based largely on the contention that woman must have the equal right in all affairs of society. No one could possibly refute that... *if* suffrage were a right. Alas, for the ignorance of the human mind, which can see a right in an imposition. Or is it not the most brutal imposition for one set of people to make laws that another set is coerced by force to obey? Yet woman clamors for that "golden opportunity" that has wrought so much misery in the world, and robbed man of his integrity and self-reliance; an imposition which has thoroughly corrupted the people, and made them absolute prey in the hands of unscrupulous politicians.

Needless to say, I am not opposed to woman suffrage on the conventional ground that she is not equal to it. I see neither physical, psychological, nor mental reasons why woman should not have the equal right to vote with man."

With those remarks, there were several outbursts from members of the audience in support of women's suffrage who were becoming increasingly agitated. Goldman realized she shouldn't have paused at that moment and quickly continued, having to raise her voice to be heard until the crowd quieted back down...

"But that cannot possibly blind me to the *absurd* notion that woman will accomplish that wherein man has failed! As if women have not sold their votes, as if women politicians cannot be bought! If she would not make things worse, she certainly could not make them better. To assume, therefore, that she would succeed in purifying something *which is not susceptible of purification*, is to credit her with supernatural powers!"

After her minor misstep, Goldman was using her experience in public speaking to great advantage. Not unlike a Baptist preacher who captures the spirit of the audience and herds them carefully towards the security of his fenced in corral, she worked her points towards a rising crescendo...

"Since woman's greatest misfortune has been that she was looked upon as either angel or devil, her true salvation lies in being placed on earth; namely, in being considered human, and therefore subject to all human follies and mistakes. Are we then to believe *that two errors will make a right?* Are we to assume that the *poison already inherent in politics* will be decreased, if women were to enter the political arena? The most ardent suffragists would hardly maintain such a folly!"

The women of Australia and New Zealand can vote, and help make the laws. Are the labor conditions better there than they are in England, where the suffragettes are making such a heroic struggle? Does there exist a greater motherhood, happier and freer children than in England? Is woman there no longer considered a mere sex commodity? Has she emancipated herself from the Puritanical double standard of morality for men and women? Certainly none but the ordinary female stump politician will dare answer these questions in the affirmative. If that be so, it seems ridiculous to point to Australia and New Zealand as the Mecca of equal suffrage accomplishments. And we have no reason whatsoever, to assume things would be any different here in the United States!"

There was a mixture of enthusiastic applause from Emma's admirers and even very subdued, polite applause from her opponents in the audience who recognized her oratory skills. Happy was no expert but got the sense that Emma was playing long ball and struck first for the early lead.

Fanny was up next and she rose slowly, looking straight ahead and ambled reluctantly to the podium. She stepped on the stool, gazed across the auditorium, adjusted her reading glasses, rustled her notes, and cleared her throat nervously several times. As Happy watched Fanny apprehensively approach the podium, enter the glow of the spotlight, and attempt to calm her nerves, he sensed the same knot in his stomach as he felt when stepping up to the plate for his first major league at bat. At least she didn't have a condescending umpire or wise-ass catcher whispering in her ear but the next several seconds of silence caused a rumble of anxiety to roll through the auditorium.

"Thank you. Very much. Let me begin, by saying...concerning the comments... expressed by my distinguished... and learned sister in struggle... I am pleased to hear we share common ground... on many of the points..."

It was a nervous and halting start and her supporters were wondering whether it was wise to take a deferential approach and play "small ball" rather than come out swinging for the fences. Then another pause and Henry worried that Fanny was dazed, paralyzed by the bright lights and attention bearing down on her. But in reality, she was attempting to formulate a rebuttal on the fly, buying some time, almost like a batter adjusting his cap or taking a practice swing before entering the box.

Then suddenly an idea occurred to her out of the blue. Henry thought he saw a twinkle in her eye and the faintest hint of a smile on her face. Fanny found herself transported back in time to the stage in her school where she argued against the anarchist view that all governments are evil and reform is counterproductive. In order to bring about change, workers have to fight *within* the boundaries of existing political systems for incremental as well as fundamental change. That's the hook she had been searching for and Fanny forged on.

"Certainly, the contention that woman must have equal rights in all affairs of society, is indeed one on which, no one can disagree. Likewise, there is no dispute that working conditions must improve and we must free ourselves of Puritanical double standards regarding appropriate conduct. And I dare say, that Emma Goldman and I are also on common ground, with respect to a vision for a Utopian society of the future, one in which no people or class governs over any other or exerts power by making arbitrary laws for all to abide. One in which humans are not slaves to the irrational idolatry that is the basis for all of the organized religions today...

But with all due respect to my esteemed comrade, there exists an *ocean* between our views on how such goals can and *should* be accomplished. It was not so long ago that we both crossed a different ocean, the mighty Atlantic, in similar fashion – in third class steerage on the lower decks of vessels barely seaworthy, through rough and stormy seas that made the outcome not entirely certain. We both breathed the stench-filled air, felt sick to our stomachs, and saw with our own eyes what it took to successfully make that crossing. We both saw the heartbreak of the ones who contracted disease or were denied entry and turned back.

Certainly, if while investing my family's life savings to pay for my passage in hopes of getting an opportunity for a better life, one without the constant Anti-Semitic attacks and cursed pogroms, we were approached by a charlatan who bid us to save our money and proclaimed that we needn't take the difficult journey across the sea fraught with danger at every moment but rather could by-pass that messy and time-wasting step in favor of instant relocation and gratification, it would have been a tempting proposition indeed! But we can all agree... that such magical transformations... are just plain foolishness."

Happy watched in amazement as Fanny began to hit her stride and take on a very different persona. Rather than halting, her voice was full of confidence, her points accentuated dramatically with a pointed finger.

"So, I maintain that there are no short cuts along the path to Utopia. Indeed, it is likely a tortuous, frustrating and exhausting journey – a struggle to be sure – across wide and dangerous oceans, over long and windy roads, through hills and valleys, through all seasons of extreme weather, through generations of trials with partial victories and setbacks alike. But each step down that path... is as important as the one before. To think that we shall rid ourselves of government any time soon, is simply a nonsensical notion – no more likely...than turning a chicken into a sow! So, if our government or some form of government continues, it follows, that it should represent, the will of the people, of all its citizens."

At this point, Fanny paused for a moment to catch her breath and collect her thoughts. As she did so, she scanned the auditorium and saw many faces beaming and nodding in approval.

"Surely my learned opponent in tonight's debate would concede that emancipation of the slaves, was a step forward for humanity, would she not? "

Here she turned her head to acknowledge Goldman for added effect.

"And further, that passage of the 15th amendment to our Constitution, granting the right to vote to all *male* citizens, without regard to race... while tragically flawed because it totally disregards the plight of women, is nevertheless, welcomed by former slaves and the children of former slaves. How presumptuous it would be, for those of us who have never known the cruelty of the bonds of slavery... to pass judgment that would deny the honor, respect, and dignity to partake in the political process, that was so long denied, no matter how flawed it may be?

And can we deny that there is value, in bringing incremental reforms to the oppressed? Even if the Utopian goals that we strive for are, at this time, still beyond reach? We agree that many workers are forced to toil for long hours under oppressive conditions... would my colleague advise them not to join together and organize to form a union? To bargain for better conditions and thus improve the lives of their families, their children? Or should they continue to toil and accept nothing short of Utopian change?

So too, is the case for women. We deserve the right to be part of the process, to accelerate real reforms that will improve our lives and those of our families. Ladies and gentlemen, I contend that what is absolute folly is to maintain that progressive change is an all or nothing proposition!"

Happy had never heard much about the women's suffrage movement until he came to New York and had a difficult time following some of the detailed arguments being made. But he could sense that without the innate oratory skills of her opponent, Fanny's approach was a bit more like the Superba's style of play – she tried to make contact, get on base and make something happen. His own assessment of how she did was confirmed by the spontaneous burst of cheers and applause when Fanny completed her remarks. Granted, considering the sponsor of the debate and the makeup of the audience, Fanny was playing to a hometown crowd, but she had at least tied it up and more likely moved out to a one run lead.

Ethel and Luisa had volunteered as ushers for the debate so they were allowed to stand and listen in the rear of the orchestra section. They had known Fanny for 27 years and had never seen this side of her – while they knew she had come a long way from recent immigrant struggling to speak the language, they had never known her to be so captivating and eloquent. They each broke out into a grin and nodded their heads in approval as Fanny was reaching the end of her address and eagerly joined in the loud round of applause when she was done.

Next up was Josephine Marshall Jewell Dodge. She strode to the podium with confidence as she, like Emma Goldman, had considerable experience in public speaking. Her arguments, not surprisingly, reflected the published positions of the NAOWS in their pamphlets, which she began to recite. Namely:

- 90 percent of American women do not want suffrage or do not care about the issue,
- If women were to vote, it would result in their competing with men rather than cooperating with them,
- 80% of women who would be eligible, would only double or cancel out the vote cast by their husbands,
- Allowing women to vote will be a costly proposition, not justified by the so-called benefits,
- It would be unwise to risk the good we already have for the evil that may occur

After each point she tried to expound and elaborate but Happy found himself wondering whether these claims were true and while Dodge spoke convincingly, he noticed she provided no data to back them up. On his scorecard he noted no runs scored for the visiting team that half-inning.

Clara Lemlich was hitting cleanup for the home team and as a veteran labor leader was no stranger to being in the limelight, public speaking or providing convincing arguments for her side. She didn't beat around the bush and came up to the podium swinging for the fences. Following some brief opening remarks she immediately connected the demand for a woman's right to vote with her struggles for better wages and working conditions.

"It's all about who decides a woman's destiny. Should a woman have no say in deciding how many hours she must work outside the home, under what conditions, and for how much pay? Should she have no say in who makes the laws of the land, who decides how much tax she must pay or who decides if her sons are sent off to war? Of course not!

Most of the crowd, already primed for an exciting finish, had trouble containing their emotions and the moderator was forced to interrupt and quiet the crowd again. Once they settled down, Clara continued without missing a beat.

"The manufacturer has a vote; the bosses have votes; the foremen have votes; the inspectors have votes. The working girl has no vote. Women must have their voices heard both in the workplace and in the government! We have toiled for too long without adequate conditions or compensation. But now, because thousands and thousands of workers have organized, we speak as one to say 'Enough is enough!' We are beginning to see how powerful we can be. We bargain collectively and demand that all workers' rights are respected. If the bosses refuse to listen to reason, we take action collectively! And collectively, we win!

So, it's time... No, it's passed the time we apply these lessons when it comes to politics. It's passed the time for women to be regarded the same as men in the political arena. It's passed the time for women to enjoy the same rights as men in our democracy and be allowed a voice in our own destiny. In the destinies of our families and children.

Now how do we accomplish this? What's the recipe? It's simple. In the labor movement, we say 'In unity, there is strength.' We already represent half the population and there are plenty of men who are on our side too. We must keep women's suffrage on the front burner of our kitchens and turn up the heat!"

When Clara concluded her remarks, the hall erupted in pandemonium reminiscent of her speech at Cooper Union. Most leapt to their feet to cheer their hero, this young female firebrand labor leader as she paused for her home run trot. The supporters of women's suffrage waved banners, shaking all manner of noise makers, pumping their fists in the air and shouting over and over as if on the picket line:

"We fight for Justice and Liberty,

Join us in our Vow,

To win Equality in Democracy,

Women's Suffrage NOW!"

As he stood and took in the scene, reflecting on the arguments raised in the debate, there was no doubt in Happy's mind who came away victorious today. He'd seen it before and could sense that momentum was truly shifting and that the underdogs were rallying ahead. Women were far from declaring victory and they had an uphill battle to reach their goal, but just having the debate was a sign that they'd made it to the majors and it was just a matter of time before parity was achieved.

Deep Crimson

Number 758 read the numerals tacked above the front door. Happy quickly glanced at the paper he was holding to confirm the address that Flash had written down for him was in fact, 758 Greene Ave., between Sumner and Lewis Avenues, Bedford Stuyvesant.

When he mentioned to Fanny where he was going and to ask for directions, she told him that Sumner Ave. was named after Charles Sumner, the senator from Massachusetts, who in the time leading up to the Civil War was a staunch abolitionist. Sumner maintained a principled stand and resisted compromise with the Southern states over slavery. His words and actions resulted in a brutal assault perpetrated by Congressman Preston Brooks on the Senate floor on May 22, 1856. Brooks attacked Sumner with a gold tipped cane and didn't stop until his cane had shattered. The blows to his head knocked Sumner unconscious and almost killed him. After the attack, gleeful Southern politicians wore pieces of the broken cane as a show of their racist solidarity.

"Wow, that's a whole history lesson packed into a simple street name, Happy responded. "Back in Coquille, the streets just have names like Fishtrap Rd. and Mill Avc.!"

Still out of breath from running at a pace faster than a normal jog but not quite a sprint, he bounded up the front stoop and then tentatively tapped the brass door knocker. He didn't hear anyone stirring, so after about 30 seconds he knocked again, making sure to elicit an unambiguous announcement of his presence.

This time he heard someone call out the familiar refrain, "I got it," as if they were shagging a fly ball in right-center field and the center fielder moved over to claim it, bringing a grin to Happy's face. A woman's face appeared as the curtain in the skinny window beside the door was drawn and the wooden door soon swung open widely.

"Hello, you must be Henry. You don't mind if I call you that, do you?"

"Good evening, Mrs. Jones...No, Ma'am, been Henry my whole life 'til I showed up here." Happy paused to catch his breath.

"Sorry I'm a bit late – there was an accident – a pushcart salesman was trying to make it across the intersection in front of us but couldn't dodge the trolley in time..."

"Oh my, that sounds terrible. I hope no one was hurt!"

"No, fortunately the gentleman escaped serious injury but the trolley stopped its run, so I had to jog all the way here from the Slope, Ma'am."

"Gee, Henry... there was no need to run all that way...but welcome to our home...please do come in. And we can dispense with the formalities. My name's Florence but everyone calls me Flo."

"Very pleased to make your acquaintance, Ma'am..., uh, I mean Flo. No problem, a little extra running just helps keep me fit since I don't get to play all that often. I brought you some flowers from the flower lady in my neighborhood. She said they're fresh-picked this morning." Happy held out the bunch, which were well wrapped so they survived the fast-paced jog without much damage.

"Why how thoughtful, Henry. You didn't need to do that, but I do love fresh-cut flowers." Turning to the kitchen directly behind her down the hall she called out, "Josie, honey could you fetch a vase to put these beautiful flowers in?"

"Sure, mom. Be right with you."

An appealing but unfamiliar aroma greeted Happy as he entered the vestibule of the brick row house. Flo was originally from St. Louis, and she prepared a typical southern style Sunday dinner. The sweet and smoky smells which enveloped the whole first floor of the house were enticing. She led him through the vestibule to a cozy living room and dining room where she motioned for him to sit and relax.

The walls in the hallway and living room were covered floor to ceiling in artwork framed in wood that resembled crown molding of various shapes, plain and ornate, painted or stained that allowed each to stand out from all the others. The artwork ran the gamut from still lifes of fruit baskets, crusty bread and half-full wine glasses, landscapes of an angry sea pounding the sandy beach, and portraits of people unfamiliar to Happy. But most striking were the scenes of inner-city life. Streets with young kids playing jump rope or tag on the sidewalk, elderly folks walking slowly trying to stay out of their way, and moms sitting on stoops with babies in arms waiting for their husbands to return from work. Scenes of workers unloading ships at the docks, collecting garbage, or in overcrowded sweatshops toiling in dingy light. Several sculptures of busts and ballet dancers accented the end tables, the front windowsill and a bookcase in the corner. Happy had never been to an art museum but the Jones' house resembled what he thought one might look like. Many people decorated their homes with artwork – Fanny certainly had a fair number of paintings hanging in her house, but Happy had never encountered such an abundance of art all in one place.

Noticing Happy's awe-struck look Flo said, "As you might have noticed, I'm an artist and these are mostly my own oil paintings and sculptures. I have a hard time parting with them so that's why we've hung so many in the house. Flash made all of the picture frames himself."

"Wow, these are amazing" said Happy as he tried to take it all in.

"Thanks, Henry. I studied art in school and have been painting ever since. The sculptures and the simple still life and landscapes are mostly from my classes – I prefer to work in oils and have been focusing more recently on using my art to reflect people's everyday lives. It's all about making connections with common folks and their reality including their struggles as well as their joys."

Josie appeared with a glass vase filled with water. "Henry, this is our elder daughter, Josephine."

"Ma, would you please stop with the "Josephine." No one ever calls me that except you and Dad. My name is Josie!" And then turning to Happy, "Don't get her started – she'll talk your ear off about her artwork."

"That's all right...I've never met a real artist before. I can't imagine how you can manage to create all this great stuff."

"Well, thank you very much. Nice to see some young folks who still have some manners! I sent Flash to the bakery around the block to pick up some dessert – he should be back any minute."

"Howdy, Josie" said Happy as he belatedly jumped to his feet.

"Howdy, yourself" she chuckled.

"I'll let you youngsters talk for a few minutes until dad gets back while I finish up the preparations in the kitchen" said Flo as she disappeared around the corner of the dining room.

Josie was wearing a fashionable and contemporary simple black hobble skirt and white lace shirtwaist top. The skirt restricted her walk ever so slightly and caused her to lower her tall and shapely figure carefully into the upholstered living room chair which did not go unnoticed.

"So, I've been to quite a few Superba games this season but haven't seen you on the field," she stated matter-of-factly.

"Well, I'm not a starter – at least not yet. I'm kind of a utility player, play right field mostly when I do get in. I pinch hit and pinch run from time to time."

"How's it feel to be a ball player but not actually get to play ball very much? I imagine that would be pretty frustrating."

"Well, it does take some gettin' used to, especially coming from the amateur leagues where I was one of the better players and played every game. But geez, the Superbas are a professional major league baseball team and they're actually payin' me real money to do this so a good part of me is just happy to be here..."

"Hence, your nickname."

"Yeah, guess that's true – the competition to make the club was really intense and when my name was listed on the final roster my teammate noticed the huge grin on my face and decided Happy was an appropriate nickname for me."

"But how are you feeling about it now that the honeymoon is over and the reality of being a bench player has sunk in?"

"Hell, if I was Nap Lajoie, Ty Cobb, Tris Speaker...Honus Wagner, Sherry Magee, or Christy Mathewson, it'd be different. The guys on the field are the very best players out there. Just being in uniform and getting a chance to play – even if only on a limited basis against teams like the Cubs or the Giants is something special."

"OK, those players are certainly great - I've seen Magee and Mathewson when they've played the Superbas here at Washington Park but you're leaving out a whole other league of talented ball players."

Happy was a bit taken aback. "I'm talking about the men that play in the Negro Leagues," Josie continued, "... like Pete Hill for the Chicago Leland Giants, John Henry "Pop" Lloyd for the Philadelphia Giants and Habana in the Cuban General League, Home Run Johnson for the Cuban X Giants, Cyclone Joe Williams for the San Antonio Black Broncos just to name a few... They're as good as the best players in the Major Leagues as far as I'm concerned. Damn shame those athletes are not recognized outside our community and are certainly not making a living wage in professional baseball..."

Happy was impressed with her knowledge and passion for the game.

"We used to go to lots of games when I was little. That was when dad was a ball player in the Negro Leagues. Bet you've never been to a Negro League game, am I right?"

"Yes but your dad said he'd..."

"Well if you do, I'm sure you'll agree. It's just another example of the inequities that are ingrained in American culture. Baseball is becoming America's pastime, but in doing so it highlights two unequal Americas, white and Black. We abolished slavery almost a half century ago but are still living out the legacy of hatred upon which it was founded. Living here in Brooklyn sometimes it's easy to forget how far we've got to go until you read in the paper of another lynching somewhere or show up at the stadium and can't find a single Black face on the field except when someone gets injured and my dad rushes out to attend to them."

That didn't seem like an invitation for debate and like a newborn, Happy was still first opening his eyes to the realities of the world around him. Not only was Josie knowledgeable about baseball, but she was articulate and outspoken. He didn't have a lot of experience with women but even after five minutes Happy could tell Josie was unlike any he'd met before. A moment or two of uncomfortable silence followed until Happy changed the subject and asked Josie what she did.

"Junior at Teacher's College at Columbia University."

"Wow, that's great." Happy added that to the list of things different about the women of the Jones household compared to women he was familiar with. No woman he'd ever met attended college.

"So what grade do you want to teach?"

"Actually, I'll probably wind up going into administration rather than the classroom. I think I can make more of an impact that way, and besides the pay is much better. So what do you do in the off-season, you know to make a real living?"

"Well, after high school I worked for a time in a shipyard building boats, spent a couple of years in the Navy. Then I worked part-time as a steamboat pilot like my dad, while playing ball in the amateur leagues, hoping to get a break to come east and play professionally. Guess I lucked out."

"Sure, it's great that you got that opportunity...and hopefully you'll get to play for a while. But what's your backup plan? Most ball players don't wind up playing all that long. You could get injured and even if you stay healthy there's certainly no guarantee you'll be able to remain competitive enough to stay in the Majors."

"Gee whiz, when you say it like that it sounds pretty bleak. Truth is, I've been taking it one day at a time – that's a worn-out expression around baseball but for most of us it's kinda true"

"Tell me more."

"In some ways, not knowing what the future will bring makes you motivated to play harder."

"Like how?"

"Oh, I don't know...Let's say a sinking line drive is coming my way in right field and I'm chasing it down with as much speed as I can muster. I've got my glove extended as far as possible but am not quite there and it's clear the ball will fall in for a base hit... unless I take a flying leap through the air to nab it before it hits the ground. It's more complicated too, because if I try and make an extraordinary catch and miss, there's a good chance the ball goes by me for extra bases. So, there's a lot of risk and you've got that split second to weigh all the options and decide what to do. If playing baseball is just a hobby, and whether I make that catch has no effect one way or another on my career, there's not much incentive to make that headfirst dive onto the hard ground, possibly getting banged up or worse. So, you kinda get used to not knowing what's ahead and not being sure whether you can make the play... you just go for it, roll the dice and hope for the best."

"So your plan for the future is to leap headfirst and hope something lands in your glove?"

Whoa! This Josie is one tough character thought Happy and she's not afraid to dive right in and lay it all on the line.

"Alls I'm sayin' is, to be a successful professional baseball player you have to focus on one thing and one thing only: giving it your all each and every moment without worrying what's happening next. Hit, run, score. Field, catch, throw. One at bat, one inning, one game, one season at a time. In baseball, only the owner and manager can afford to plan for the future. For the guys on the field, thinkin' about the future's just a distraction...Look, I hope to be back here next year and for the next ten to fifteen years after that...but if that doesn't work out, I'll figure it out from there. I'm still young and this is a once in a lifetime opportunity, so I guess I'll..."

The front door opens and Flash walks in holding a white cardboard box sealed with a piece of red and white twine. "Hi folks, got a fresh-baked open top peach pie at Theresa's Bakery for dessert."

"Sounds delicious, Dad! We're in the living room. Happy's arrived."

Shortly afterwards they were gathered around the dining room table as Flo served the elaborate Sunday dinner. For the Jones family, the meal of barbecued ribs, collard greens, succotash, and homemade corn bread was simply comfort food. For Happy it was yet another culinary adventure that served to broaden his social awareness.

Happy's sumptuous journey from the simple, homogenous, rural Pacific Northwest to the modern, cosmopolitan melting pot of urban east coast life could be traced like the many stops along a gastronomical railway: Midwestern Corn-fed Beef... Pickled Herring... Hot Dogs... Lobster Shore Dinner. Next stop Chinese Dumplings.

Flash turned the conversation to sports. "So, Happy – You have any money riding on next week's Johnson-Jeffries heavyweight fight? They're already calling it the fight of the century."

"No, but Humpty was sayin'quite a few of the guys on the team were placing wagers – mostly on Jeffries. I heard that he dropped 100 lbs. while training after they convinced him to trade in his farming gloves for boxing gloves, postpone retirement and come out swinging back in the ring. Still, six years is an awful long time to be away from any sport."

"Well, pardon my frankness but considering Humpty's shit-kicker Georgian background which is kind of typical of many of our players, I'm not surprised they are betting on The Great White Hope. Most of them don't bother to hide their racist feelings even when I'm around. It's like I'm invisible to them..."

"Geez...can't imagine how that must make you feel."

"I've been able to insulate myself, mostly and just let it slide. Developed a thick skin when I was a player and we occasionally faced a white ball club, so I've heard it all. If you read about how Johnson deals with all the racist provocations every time he gets in the ring – he kind of laughs and puts it all beneath him. If you look at the photos of him in the ring, he's got this knowing, confident smile as if to say "All your racist crap don't mean shit here in the ring. It's just me and you now and there ain't no place to hide!""

"Yeah," Happy agreed, "I saw the film of the Jack Johnson –Tommy Burns fight from Australia when he first won the heavyweight title in '08. Johnson was steady and confident, dominating through the whole fight until he finally knocked Burns out in the 14th."

"By the way," continued Flash, "I don't care if he retired from the ring undefeated - Jeffries doesn't have a chance in hell against Johnson. "

"You think?"

"Absolutely guaranteed. Johnson will let it go 15 – 20 rounds and toy with him just so they can get enough film footage in the can so people will go see it in the movie theaters. He's not just a good fighter- he's a shrewd businessman too."

"Yeah, from the looks of it he does all right," Happy concurred. "Seen pictures of him in the paper riding in his fancy, fast-moving automobile. He'll be 65 Gs the richer if he wins, too. That's not chicken feed."

"Sure enough" reflected Flash, "Probably more than the entire season's payroll for the Superbas for just one day's work! Flo, could you pass the cornbread, please... You know, I think there'd be a lot of hatred of *any* Black fighter who dared to take the crown from a white champion. But the racial hatred Johnson faces goes much, much deeper, beyond run of the mill bigotry..."

"Why's that?" Happy wondered out loud.

"Part of it is just jealousy- no offense Happy, but the average white guy can't stand seeing a Black man wearing fur coats and driving fast cars."

"No offense taken."

"But the one thing that fuels the fires of racism more than anything else...that focuses the hatred of him in white America... is the fact that Jack Johnson dares to date white women – one of the most deep-seated racial fears the white man has. It's against the law for Blacks and whites to marry in 28 of the 46 states in this country for Christ's sake! And just last week, Louisiana made it illegal for Blacks and whites to even live under the same roof. Hell, you read in the papers every month about another Black man lynched just for the slightest hint that he was even *looking* at a white woman. And Johnson's not the least bit discreet – he defiantly just puts it out there and says deal with it! Ironically, this issue has created as much controversy in the Negro community as with white folks..."

Flash paused for a moment to refill his water glass and take a sip. He used the timeout like a mound visit to give the relief pitcher a few extra tosses as he formulated how best to convey his thoughts. "...Personally, I couldn't care less who he sleeps with, and as a free man in America he should have the right to date or even marry whoever the hell he wants. And unlike Booker T. Washington, I'm not much concerned when he waves that particular red flag in their faces even though it fans the racist flames... I am concerned though, with the message it sends to young Black women..."

"Dad, for crying out loud..."

"No, let me finish. I'm serious. It's hard to imagine that when one of the most famous and eligible Black men whoever walked the earth is interested exclusively in white women, it wouldn't affect the self-esteem of women of color. From that perspective, I think he does a disservice to our community. But like many of the Black leaders who have spoken out, I'm conflicted on this issue. The last thing I want is to legitimize the lynch mob mentality that is nurtured by this controversy."

"Speaking as a representative of one of the 'young Negro women' you are so concerned about, Dad, let me remind you that this is the 20th century and the world is changing. We don't want to be prisoners of history. Just as we cast off the shackles of slavery over 50 years ago, it's time to break down the shackles of narrow-minded thinking. You're right that as a free man, Jack Johnson should have the right to date and marry whomever he pleases. And as a free, young Black woman, so do I! If Jack Johnson can date white women, I can date white men."

Happy was fascinated to hear Flash's views on the controversy surrounding Jack Johnson but once the conversation turned more personal, he became self-conscious and must have started to blush.

"OK, young lady, that's enough," interjected Flo like a referee in the ring separating the fighters from a clinch. We'll continue this discussion later."

"Yes, your mother is right...but as the last word on this subject I'd also like to remind you Josephine, that playing loose and easy comes at a very steep price. If the Negro community cannot maintain the highest level of moral standards we play right into the hands of the racist lynch mobs. It is imperative that we conduct our lives with unimpeachable respectability so that we don't give them the slightest excuse for incrimination."

"But Dad..."

"But nothing, I said that's the last word and I mean it."

Josie turned her head away from her parents and looking directly at Happy dramatically rolled her eyes, which was her last word on the subject. Caught in the middle, his face turned a deeper shade of crimson.

The Tolling of the Balls

B illy Labriola and Walter (Buddy) Budzinski were enjoying their fountain drinks at Sam's Candy Store and Luncheonette at the corner of Neptune Ave. and Brighton 5th St. in their neighborhood of Brighton Beach before catching the Coney Island Ave. trolley north to Park Slope.   The pair had been neighbors and good friends since 3rd grade. Billy never ceased to enjoy introducing him to new acquaintances as his buddy, Buddy – quickly followed by, "And I ain't no stutterer!"

He polished off the last of his Cherry Lime Rickey and poked Buddy to hurry up and do the same with his Chocolate Egg Cream. It was just past 11 a.m. but Billy was eager to arrive at the stadium as soon as they opened the gates so they could get the best seats in the grandstand and watch batting practice. Maybe even say hello to his new "friend," Superba's Tony Smith and his teammates who generously provided the free passes.

Billy was wearing his newly acquired blue woolen baseball cap emblazoned with a large curvy script letter "B" embroidered in white thread in front.   He fortuitously happened upon it at the foot of Coney Island's Drop the Dips coaster on his way to work the day after his encounter with the members of his favorite team. Wondering whether it was related to their visit or merely a coincidence, he happily adopted the stray cap. It was about two sizes too big so the brim sat low on his forehead and made his ears stick out but Billy didn't mind.

Since he had a pair of free tickets, Billy invited Buddy to share his good fortune and join him at the game. Considering Billy's reputation as a storyteller and practical joker, Buddy wasn't certain if this whole thing wasn't just another elaborate ruse Billy was putting on. But after they ordered their fountain drinks at Sam's, Billy produced the evidence in the form of two, very real passes to the Brooklyn Baseball Club's Washington Park Stadium.

Both boys had already been to several big-league ballgames but never without adult supervision, so this was an exciting milestone. Considering it was a mild September day, the Superbas were hosting the World Champion Chicago Cubs, and perhaps most significantly, they were skipping out on school, spirits were flying high.

The trolley traveled northwest along Coney Island Ave. from Brighton Beach through Sheepshead Bay, Gravesend, Midwood, and Kensington, passing a variety of retail stores and stopping frequently to let passengers on and off. The boys were oblivious, engrossed in comparing their baseball trading cards, so much so they failed to notice they had passed Prospect Park at Park Slope's southern border and missed their stop at 4th Ave. Billy looked up just in time to pull the rope sounding the bell that alerted the driver to stop and they hopped off on 3rd Ave, just east of the Gowanus Canal.

They continued heading north on foot alternately racing, skipping, and marching quickly up the industrial street lined with stables and blacksmiths, lumber yards and building material suppliers, coal storage bins, a brass foundry, and small factories that produced umbrellas, motor-generators, soap, and other various and sundry merchandise.

Proximity to the canal with easy access to the New York harbor ensured that Gowanus retained its commercial inclination. The odors generated by the industrial manufacturing, the smoke and soot from the blacksmith shops and foundry, plus the pungent and ubiquitous smell of manure, all mixed with the even less pleasant aroma coming off the canal itself caused the boys to hold their noses and quicken the pace. Considering its location, depending on the wind speed and direction, foul smells within the ballpark itself were sometimes as common as foul balls. And with the way the team had been playing of late, the newspaper writers joked that the team couldn't possibly stink up the place much worse.

Just past the easternmost spur of the canal, off to their right basking in the noonday sunshine, they spotted the stadium's wooden outfield bleachers and the grandstands that surrounded the infield and extended part way along each baseline. They immediately began to sprint in earnest, hanging a right turn down 3rd St. past the entrance to the cheap 25 cent outfield grass lawn "seats." They soon saw the large white letters announcing The Brooklyn Ball Club atop the main entrance to the 75 cent grandstand seats on 4th Ave.

As luck would have it, they were just opening the gates when they arrived, so they presented their "player tickets" proudly and entered through the turnstiles. Once inside the stadium, they headed toward the first base side and found the tunnel that led to the section closest to the Brooklyn dugout. As they had both been to the ballpark and its previous incarnation before the fire, they knew their way around.

But they were far from jaded and the experience of seeing the sparkling lush green grass and carefully groomed deep brown dirt infield suddenly appear when they emerged into the daylight, an integral part of the magic of baseball, was once again spectacular. They raced to claim seats along the railing on the right field side just beyond first base. They weren't quite as exclusive as the seats behind the infield that sold for a buck and a half but their location was within shouting distance of their heroes as they took the field and returned to the dugout. The downside was that it did not allow for viewing the players in the Brooklyn dugout.

The backdrop in right-center field was the large six-story apartment building on 3rd Ave., the late morning sun glistening brightly off its bank of windows overlooking the field. Oftentimes residents sat out on the building's fire escape to get a free peek at the action. The outfield walls were covered in a potpourri of painted advertisements from Coronet Dry Gin, Old Bushmills Irish Whiskey, Perfection Scotch Whiskey, Green River (the) Whiskey, Imperial Beer, Peter Doelger Bottled Beer, White Rock Beverages, Fatima Cigarettes, Phillip Morris Cigarettes, Adams Pepsin Tutti Frutti Chewing Gum, Turkish Trophies, B.V.D. Underwear, and Ajax Tires.

As they got closer to the field, the unique sounds of batting practice baseballs ringing off the bat pierced the air as dramatically as the tolling of the church bell announcing the hour. They could see some of the Superbas huddled beside the metal mesh backstop awaiting their turn at the batting cage. The pitcher on the mound tossing to them was a Black man. The image of a Negro player on a Major League field was jarring at first until Billy realized that it must be the Superba's equipment manager, Flash Jones who was a former player in the Negro Leagues.

Those sounds were punctuated by the arrhythmic popping of baseballs on leather as other members of the team paired off to loosen up and casually toss balls back and forth. They started out about 20 feet apart and every few throws would each take a couple of steps back, gradually increasing the distance between them. This was a routine that Billy and Buddy had repeated countless times except that even when they were 100 feet apart the Superba players still seemed to be throwing effortlessly.

Still others were doing stretching exercises or running sprints to warm up. Although they were engaged in their pregame drills, the players maintained an informal atmosphere as they chatted and joked with each other. Occasionally, a ball would be overthrown and require the fielder to jump or stretch to make the catch, but even these balletic moves were choreographed with an air of nonchalance.

Many of the Superbas were close enough to be identified. Buddy shouted greetings and encouragement to each player he recognized. "Hey Buckwheat! Lookin' good, Eggie!" In return, an obligatory toss of the head and brief hint of a smile were reluctantly delivered, which the boys savored none the less.

Then Billy spotted Tony Smith as he was jogging back to the dugout from having taken a few laps. "ToeNee, *ToeNee*, over here!"

Smith looked up and appeared puzzled as if to say, do I know you? Once he caught his attention, Billy began to wave his hands wildly above his head and realizing he had about one second to bridge the recognition gap, he blurted out, "Roller coaster guy from Co-neeee *Island*!"

Bingo, we have a winner! Get the young man in the first row a kewpie doll. Better yet, another personal interaction with the starting shortstop of the Brooklyn Superbas Baseball Club. When Tony Smith recalled their night out in Coney Island several weeks earlier and the fact that he had given the Drop the Dips operator a pair of player tickets, he detoured from his route to the dugout to head over and say hello. When he arrived, he reached out to jostle Billy's cap with his baseball mitt in a friendly, familiar gesture suitable for his younger brother.

"Hey kid, glad you made it, good to see you again. Hope we can return the favor and give *you* a good ride today...We're facing Three-Finger Brown so we may be in for some different sorta drops and dips from him... plus those Cubs have a mighty fine lineup, so wish us luck." Billy said they would and introduced his buddy, Buddy (and I ain't stutterin') to his famous "friend," trying his best to take his star power in stride. "Glad to make your acquaintance, son," said Tony. Buddy was absolutely ecstatic and couldn't believe their good fortune but all he could muster in return was, "Thank you, sir."

"Well, gotta get back with the team and get ready for the game," said Tony as he tipped his cap, turned and headed off for the dugout to their left.

"Thanks Toe-Nee! Let's go Brooklyn!" shouted Billy. He turned to Buddy and the two stood in disbelief, grinning with their mouths hanging wide open but too excited to scream.

A Shoestring Catch

Josie was in the Superba's clubhouse after the 3 -1 victory over the Pittsburgh Pirates on Thursday, June 2. Since she had an unlimited general admission entry pass, she occasionally attended games and would then assist her dad complete his post-game routine required to maintain the team's equipment. There was a lot to do, and he appreciated her help. The players' bats were wiped down, inspected for cracks, and placed back in the rack; balls were inspected and cleaned; gloves were re-stitched, oiled, or had their laces tightened, as needed; shoes were wiped down, laces checked, and bent cleats straightened; uniforms were collected for cleaning. In his medical capacity, player injuries needed to be attended; occasionally Flash administered a rub down or massage to ease a player's barking muscles.

To respect the players' privacy as they showered and dressed into their street clothes, Josie remained in the equipment room until she was sure everyone was decent. Even then she kept to herself and did not engage the players in conversation – it's not that she was shy or reserved but Flash did not feel it was appropriate for his daughter to be openly fraternizing with the white ball players, which made her mission on that particular day particularly challenging.

But Josie had a plan. She was deliberate, not impulsive and had thought it through. The idea was hatched the day Happy had come to their home for Sunday dinner. She couldn't get him out of her head and was determined to follow through on her declaration. She finished working on the shoes and delivered each pair to the players' cubby and set them neatly on the bench in front. When Happy retrieved his shoes to place back in his cubby he noticed a piece of paper folded up inside the left shoe. He removed it and read the following:

"Dear Henry,

I enjoyed talking with you last week…I'd be very Happy (ha ha) to meet you for a drink if you are interested! We could meet at Marshall's Hotel, 127 W. 53rd St. in Hell's Kitchen (Manhattan). They have musical entertainment – a group called the Clef Club is playing there now; some of my friends heard them and said they were excellent. Most importantly, I've heard it is quite private and maintains a reputation for being very discrete - since it's not here in Brooklyn, there really isn't much risk in our being recognized together.

In any case, as I said when you were over the house, I am determined to live my life as a free woman and don't feel that anyone has a right to say who I can or can't have relationships with. However, I don't plan on telling my parents as I fear they would not approve. You might consider this hypocritical, but I know my folks well and feel the best way to handle this is to break it to them gradually. Please trust me on that.

I do hope you are interested and will meet me at the grill room in Marshall's Hotel on Saturday night at 8 PM. I'd rather not risk letting anyone else know about this for now (especially my Dad) so please don't try to contact me. I will be back helping him after tomorrow's game too, so if you are interested in joining me, simply tie your shoelaces together after the game when you leave them out for cleaning. If your shoelaces are untied I'll know you are not interested (or are too scared!)

Respectfully yours,

Josie

Just as he finished reading it, he heard right fielder Jack Dalton call over, "Hey, what you got there Hap, a note from a secret admirer?"

He tried hard not to blush and quickly pocketed the slip of paper replying, "Well, sort of – just something that a fan handed me as we were leaving the field wishing me luck."

Jack just laughed and said, "Must be the President of the Happy Smith Crank Club."

"Well, if so, he's also the Vice President, Treasurer, Secretary and sole member..." He then ducked into the restroom, closed the door and took the note out and read it over again and again. Although the handwriting was neat, the words were clearly written and their meaning unambiguous, Happy couldn't believe his eyes.

When he departed Coquille aboard his dad's tugboat on the first leg of his journey just months earlier, Henry knew he'd be in for the adventure of his life. Yet he didn't have a clue just how far-reaching this adventure would turn out or where it would lead. He couldn't have imagined how many new doors he'd pass through, most of which he had never even set eyes upon, let alone dreamt of crossing over the threshold. Just as he would not allow himself to contemplate his fears as he climbed aboard the Drops and Dips coaster, he decided on the spot that he'd take Josie up on her offer and made a mental note to remember to tie his shoes tomorrow.

Trapped

Henry's parents, Albert Jr. and Elizabeth Smith met and married outside Scranton, PA, the area where they were born and raised. His paternal grandparents (Albert Sr. and Margaret Smith) had settled there after emigrating from England in the early 1840s. Immigration records were not well maintained at the time and the family history has gotten a bit hazy, so the exact date isn't known. But as near as they can tell, it was sometime in 1843. Henry's maternal grandparents, William and Charlotte Evans moved to the nearby town of Wilkes-Barre, PA having come from Wales in 1858 and Elizabeth was born two years later.

Henry's grandfather had been an anthracite coal miner at the Philadelphia and Reading Coal & Iron Works Co. Potts Colliery in Locustdale, PA for almost 30 years and as a young man Albert Jr. followed in his dad's work boots. Elizabeth went to work as a spinner, winder, and reeler in the Sauquoit silk mill after dropping out of school at 15 years old. They met at a Halloween costume party and community dance, quickly fell in love, and were married on New Year's Eve. About a year later, their first son Carlton was born.

Life was not easy – the least senior workers got the graveyard shift, so Albert Jr. toiled in the dark and dank, dangerous subterranean web of tunnels from dusk 'til dawn. His dad and older brother Norton worked the day shift, so they didn't see much of each other. After Albert Jr. completed his shift, he'd return to the house they shared with his parents, wash up, eat breakfast, play with his son for a few hours and collapse in exhaustion. There wasn't time or energy for much of a social life, not that there was all that much to do in the small company town outside of Scranton. His main social activity was the Wednesday morning poker game where the miners practiced another sort of gambling.

But that all changed on January 15, 1878, just one week after Carlton's second birthday. Shortly after Elizabeth served the evening meal (her supper and Albert's breakfast), they heard a low rumble and felt the house shake as if an earthquake had just hit. Elizabeth turned ashen and started to speak, "You don't suppose..." But before she could finish her thought they heard two shrill, steam-powered site whistles pierce the early evening air, calling out the news that there was serious trouble below. "Oh my God" she murmured as Albert, speechless, tossed his silverware onto his plate and almost tipped over shoving his chair back to head out the door. They soon learned that a methane gas explosion had rocked the mine at the end of the day shift.

Albert joined the rush of miners sprinting toward the Potts Mine Emergency Assembly Area and quickly found his colleagues in the rescue squad he was assigned to. Elizabeth bundled Carlton up as quickly as she could and scurried over to the mess hall/meeting room where miners' families gathered to console each other and coordinate relief efforts.

The main mine shaft access was closed immediately to reduce the airflow into the mine and the fresh air circulation fans were de-energized in hopes of quelling the blaze raging below. That required access in and out through one of several small auxiliary safety shafts. Within ten minutes all of the miners who were able to evacuate had already made it to the surface, allowing Albert and his fellow twelve-member emergency crew access into the mine.

There was no time to spare, no time to check whether his dad and brother were among those who escaped. He passed the main triage area on his way, but it was a blur of chaotic activity. The sound of workers shouting orders as they attempted to attend to the wounded survivors was overlaid by shrieks of pain everywhere. All he knew was that there were still a handful of miners trapped and that a wall of flames fueled by kerosene tanks ignited by the blast blocked their way to freedom.

As he lowered himself down the narrow emergency shaft by the hand- operated pulley, he thought how ironic, how tragic it was to shut the mine mouth entrance. It might help reduce oxygen available to fan the flames but also reduces air needed to breathe deep below the surface. With the ventilation system shut down and the flames consuming precious oxygen, there was little chance the trapped miners could hold out for long. Their fate was sealed when the heavy steel doors slammed shut. The very act was like tossing a shovel full of dirt on their graves. And with so little air to breathe the rescue team had limited time to operate below before they too, were among those who would be grieved.

Albert was among the first to descend with buckets of sand. The crew leader told them to leave the soda-acid fire extinguishers behind – they were useless when battling a fuel-fed fire. Albert's initial fears were confirmed when they arrived at the tunnel level where the explosion had occurred, and he saw the raging inferno. He knew instinctively no additional trapped miners would be freed when he observed the ferocity of the blaze. But they did what they could and ran to douse the fire with their sand buckets, getting as close as they dared.

They had no way of knowing the fire was still spreading and while charging toward it, another wall of flames thrust out in their direction in a blast of super intense heat. Albert felt like his skin was melting and that he'd been stabbed through the nose with a red-hot poker. They ran for their lives and somehow although badly burned, managed to get all of the emergency crew members out alive.

It wasn't until he was admitted to the hospital and lying in the recovery room did he learn that his brother was uninjured but his dad was one of the five victims who did not make it out alive. Albert Jr. was among the scores of miners who sustained serious injuries. He received second and some third degree burns to his face and hands and his recuperation was long and painful. The news of dad's death was a shock. The only consolation was the coroner's report released several days later which indicated he was probably killed instantly by the blast or the tons of coal that rained upon them as the roof timbers collapsed.

Elizabeth was also devastated by grief but even more paralyzed by fear. In addition to the death of her father-in-law, she couldn't bear the thought of her husband's return to the mine. The statistics were grim. In the thirty years since federal regulators began paying attention to coal mining accidents, there had been ten serious incidents with five or more fatalities. A total of 184 workers had died and scores more were injured and/or disabled for life. Who knows how many more accidents occurred where the death toll was fewer than five as those were not considered significant enough to even record!

The lack of response on the part of the company in the days and weeks following the disaster was the last straw. Other than a perfunctory show of sympathy for the victims' families and a pitifully small compensation payment, their sole focus was to get production back to business-as-usual just as fast as possible. The other miners' families provided some support, but Elizabeth couldn't help but feel that they were all trapped and resigned to their fate.

The federal mine inspectors came and filed their report. They even had the audacity to place the blame for the incident on the shoulders of the deceased miners, stating it was their carelessness and not the lack of mine safety protocols that was the root cause. Nothing changed. Working men went down into the mines each day and sometimes they just never came back. No one –not the company, the government, nor the majority of the miners themselves – questioned or challenged the status quo.

But Elizabeth had had enough. She knew that without a sea change in mining safety protocol and proactive government oversight, there would be many more accidents down the road. She was convinced that this incident was a warning sign it was time to turn in their cards for a new hand. Elizabeth was ready to issue an ultimatum but in the end that wasn't necessary. It didn't take much effort to convince Albert.

It would be difficult leaving friends and family behind, but it was hard for them to imagine life any bleaker than their current reality. They were ready to gamble on a better future. Even before Albert had fully recuperated, they sold or gave away everything they owned that couldn't be packed in four suitcases in preparation for a journey to what they dreamed would be the promised land, the Pacific Northwest.

In Pursuit of the Promised Land

T he Union Pacific Railroad had completed the first transcontinental rail connection or so-called overland route to the West Coast in 1869.[7] A decade later, tickets were still expensive but were becoming much more accessible to ordinary folks as the railroads and Federal government collaborated to promote western settlement. The huge potential to unite the entire continental U.S. was finally being realized. For the first time in history, people not only enjoyed the freedom of the pursuit of happiness but actually had the means to move about freely to facilitate such pursuits.

So, in July 1878, Albert, Elizabeth, and Carlton Smith headed west in search of safe, decent work, affordable land, and a fresh start. Albert didn't know where they'd finally wind up or how he would earn a living but was willing to defer to Elizabeth's wishes. They took their meager savings and cashed in the paltry $125 settlement check the mining

---

[7] On May 10, 1869 the Central Pacific and the Union Pacific Railroads were connected in a ceremony at Promontory Summit, UT

company distributed to injured workers to purchase railway tickets. Although they'd need to board several different, independent lines to get to their final destination, they were able to purchase a "through" ticket and realize some savings.

After arriving at the railroad station in Scranton in plenty of time to purchase their tickets and check their baggage, Elizabeth found a bench to breast feed Carlton. Albert took a stroll outside to take in the large New York, Lackawanna, and Western Railroad passenger train they would board being prepped for the first leg of their journey ahead. He watched as rail workers conducted their routine maintenance and loaded coal from the storage silo into the tender car's hopper to feed the large steam engine. He smiled thinking the very coal he mined, and his dad sacrificed his life for would provide the fuel needed to deliver his family to a new life as far from the eastern coal mines as they could go.

Starting with the rear caboose that served as the crew's sleeping quarters, dining room, and recreation area, Albert examined with fascination each of the train's cars. The caboose and passenger cars were of wooden tongue and groove construction painted rust red and drab yellow, respectively. Each proudly bore the initials NYL&W in large black letters. A layer of soot coated the exterior, reducing visibility from the windows but Albert was thankful they'd be able to observe the changing landscape along their journey even if it was a partially compromised view.

He was most impressed by the shiny black steam engine. He stopped to read the nameplate which identified it as an ALCO, American Locomotive Co. built in Schenectady, NY. Through the cab's side window, he got a glimpse of the engineer checking his gauges and controls while the fireman shoveled coal from the tender car directly behind the locomotive into the boiler. When the engineer looked up,

Albert offered up a friendly wave which was returned with a nod and quick smile. A steady hiss from the pressure relief valve at the steam dome was building, waiting for the scheduled departure time when the engineer would engage the throttle, diverting steam to drive the reciprocating piston and get them under way.

The first leg on the NYL&W Railroad from Scranton north to Binghamton and then northwest through New York's southern tier to Buffalo took about ten hours. Despite the suspension system that was meant to smooth things out, the hardwood bench seats provided no cushion or comfort against the stiff rough ride and constant bumping due to joints in the rails. Albert and Elizabeth found that after several hours of the annoying click-clack and other various and sundry background noises they became desensitized and were able to tune it out. Carlton seemed comforted by the combination of motion, vibrations and white noise and slept peacefully for much of the trip.

The following day they purchased tickets and boarded a Union Pacific "emigrant express" train heading southwest from Buffalo to Omaha and finally due west to San Francisco. The Union Pacific cross-country express was a longer train with first-, second-, and third-class accommodations. The third-class cars were closest to the engine and thus noisiest and dirtiest; inside they were rustic with hard wooden bench seating only and no sleeping provisions included. Next, the second-class section where the Smiths were traveling included several passenger coach cars with a bit more leg room and bare bones sleeper cars with double decker sleeping berths stacked vertically – just wooden planks with thin mattresses stuffed with straw but at least they could stretch out and lie down for part of the journey. There were no provisions for them to get food on the train so they had to rely on food they brought with them and provisions they could purchase during short stops along the way.

While the amenities available in second class made travel significantly more comfortable than third class, they paled in comparison with the fully decked out luxurious Pullman coaches/lounge cars, club cars, sleeper cars, and dining car available for wealthy travelers. The coach cars which were equipped with overstuffed couches, cocktail tables, chandeliers, carpets and draperies yielded a smoother and quieter riding experience. Club cars provided card tables, a fully stocked bar, and a place to enjoy a smoke. The sleeper cars were divided into separate private rooms that featured comfortable mattresses, bedding, and a private commode. The dining car served fresh-cooked meals.

This line took them to Cleveland, Chicago, and down to St. Louis. Another switch to the Central and Southern Pacific Railroad was required there for the long journey across the plains, over the Southern Rockies, Sierra Madres, Wasatch, and Sierra Nevada ranges before they reached California. The views of wide-open country for as far as the eye could see and breathtaking mountain vistas were spectacular, but Albert was far more moved by the technical marvels that he saw and experienced. The railroads with their large steam powered locomotives were fascinating but even those seemed like toys compared with the huge steam powered ships they encountered when they reached California.

First was the Solano, the world's largest ferry boat onto which the locomotive and their entire train was loaded to cross the Carquinez Strait in California to take them into the San Francisco Bay area. She was just two years old and measured 424 feet long and 116 feet wide, with four parallel sets of tracks that ran the length of the ship. In Benecia, the locomotive pulled onto to the ferry and advanced to the front of the ship. After the sixth car, the Janney coupling was released and a shipyard locomotive pushed the remaining cars on board, shifting them to the next track. This was repeated a third time until the entire train was loaded onto the ferry. When they reached Port Costa at the other side of the Straight, the process was reversed. The whole loading operation took under one hour.

Another few hours landed them in the port of Oakland where they ferried across the bay into San Francisco. From there they boarded an ocean steamer heading for Portland.

They ultimately settled in the sleepy, river-front town of Coquille where Albert was able to get a job as an apprentice ferryboat captain. He had always loved being on the water and the new steam-powered ships appealed to his interest in machines and mechanical devices. He learned quickly, and before long was navigating solo throughout the local river network and Pacific harbors.

Later, after Henry was born, he borrowed enough money to finance the purchase of a small steam-powered ferry that occasionally doubled as a tugboat and went into business for himself.   There were more towns growing up along the Coquille River every year and Albert's and other ferry service companies allowed people direct and easy access between them.   He worked hard but was successful enough that Elizabeth could afford to stay home and take care of the boys.

Keeper of His Brother's Bat

Growing up, Henry was small for his age and not particularly adept at sports but that didn't stop him from getting caught up in the baseball fever sweeping the country. He and Carlton read whatever baseball related material they could get their hands on including the daily Oregonian Gazette newspaper which carried accounts and box scores from the Major Leagues as well as the more local semi-professional Pacific Coast League. Occasionally they would pool whatever spare change they could round up to purchase a copy of The Sporting Life, a national publication that proudly pronounced in its masthead, "Devoted to Baseball, Trap Shooting and General Sports." Of course, the information they read was days or even weeks old, but they gulped it down like cold lemonade on a sweltering hot summer's day.

They were captivated by stories of the Brooklyn Bridegrooms (forerunners of the current Superbas) who won back-to-back pennants in the American Association in 1889 and the National League the following year. Led by the outstanding hitting and defensive play of shortstop George Pinkney and outfielders Oyster Jones and Darby O'Brian, plus the superb pitching of 31 game winner, Tom Lovett, the Bridegrooms battled the Louisville Colonels to a 3-3-1 tie in the 1890 World Series.

The newspaper and magazine accounts were read and re-read and their imaginations easily filled in the action between the lines. Black and white photos and drawings helped recreate the action but the images in their minds were displayed in full color. Panoramas of large stadiums in the sophisticated cosmopolitan cities of the east and mid-west, filled to capacity with fans eating popcorn and peanuts. Players decked out in smart, woolen A.G. Spalding & Bros. uniforms with their team's name emblazoned on their button-down shirts, topped off with Peck & Snyder small billed, soft merino wool caps. They imagined a chorus of interwoven sounds including the ubiquitous baseball chatter meant to distract the opposing players, sporadic shouts of encouragement and derision from the boisterous cranks, and the usual sounds of the baseball being struck and caught. Critical game situations were re-enacted over and over again while playing ball in the weed-strewn vacant lot that served as the Coquille Farmer's Market several mornings each week but was otherwise available for double duty as their ball field the rest of the time.

Henry, Carlton, and their teammates would argue vigorously over who got to pretend to be Pinkney, Lovett or other notable Bridegroom stars during these games while their opponents proudly chose the likes of William Van Winkle (Chicken) Wolf who batted .363 or pitcher Scott Stratton (34-14) for the Louisville Colonels.

"...It's the bottom of the ninth inning here in the great City of Brooklyn NY for the final game of the World Series with the score tied at two apiece. The Bridegrooms and Colonels have each won three games so far and if there's a winner of this game they take home the grand trophy as the World Champions of Baseball. Oyster Jones is on second with two men out and pesky George Pinkney is stepping up to the plate to face the mighty Scott Stratton on the mound for the Colonels. Pinkney fouled off the first two pitches and then patiently resisted swinging at balls out of the strike zone to get the count full at 3 and 2. And here's the pitch..."

Henry's eighth birthday was around the corner and all he could think of was his wish for a real mitt, baseball, and bat of his own. Carlton had his own baseball equipment and let Henry borrow it when he wasn't using it. But most of the time the boys played together and catching the ball barehanded as had been the norm in baseball until very recently was a distinct disadvantage. Plus, several of their friends already had their own baseball gear and would often choose sides and play for hours. Henry loathed being left out.

Little did his parents know where Henry's love affair with the game would lead him. But they happily fulfilled his wish for a ball and glove. He still had to share his brother's bat, however. Only one player can bat at a time, Albert reasoned, and he couldn't see indulging his children with things that weren't really necessary. As it happened, Henry would soon inherit the bat but not in a manner he could have foreseen or would ever have wished for.

Carlton and his friends were swimming and cavorting at the local watering hole, the secluded, shady and sandy myrltewood grove just off a bend in the Coquille River at nearby Myrtle Point. Generally, the boys were inseparable but on this particular occasion, Albert had asked Henry to stay at home and help him with chores around the house.

The kids had been taking turns jumping off the adjoining twelve-foot cliff into the cold pond and at one point Carlton decided to show off. He dove headfirst into what he thought was the deep portion and struck his head on a large rock camouflaged just beneath the water's shiny surface. His friends tried in vain to stop the bleeding while one ran off to fetch the town doctor who came at once and tried to save Carlton but the head trauma and loss of blood were too severe. He never regained consciousness.

It took the Smith family the better part of a year after Carlton's funeral to come to grips with their loss and begin to move on. Each handled his passing in a different manner. Elizabeth became deeply depressed and withdrawn. She had always felt connected to the church and eventually found comfort in the belief that all things happen for a reason. She immersed herself even more deeply in church activities, religious and otherwise, and it became the backbone of her recovery. Albert withdrew and sought his salvation at sea – working long hours operating his ferry service and maintaining the boat. He had little energy for Henry, even though this was when his younger, surviving son needed his attention all the more.

Losing his older brother so suddenly and tragically left a mark on Henry. He was alone and confused. His mom frequently took him with her to church but thinking often about that fateful day, Henry couldn't help but wonder what sort of God would take his only brother and best friend in the world and he received no solace there. He even lost interest in baseball, the one thing that he cared most about.

In a tone-deaf move, Albert decided that it would help Henry cope with the loss of his older brother to pack up all of Carlton's personal effects (including his baseball gear) in a wooden crate and moved them to the basement. This had the opposite effect however, and the attempt to erase his memory of Carlton made Henry feel even more alienated and lonely. His mom decided the decision was more selfishly motivated and convinced Albert to reconsider.

One night as Albert came to say goodnight, in the dim light Henry noticed he was carrying something behind his back. He sat slowly on the edge of his bed and gently placed Carlton's baseball bat beside him.

"Son, mom and I talked and decided you might want to have your brother's baseball bat - I'm sure Carlton would have wanted you to have it. What do you think?"

Henry's jaw dropped but no words came. He tried to choke back his emotions but for the first time since the funeral, they got the better of him and a torrent of tears burst forth. He took the bat into bed with him and continued to do so each night thereafter. He couldn't explain it but an immediate sense of calm enveloped and stayed with him as long as he held that piece of lumber. He soon took to carrying it with him as his daily companion too.

At first his friends cruelly joked, "There goes Bat Boy!" but he paid them no mind and after a while everyone got used to seeing Henry hauling around Carlton's bat wherever he went. Besides, having it constantly at the ready tended to ensure that he was invited to play ball a lot more often. He swung that bat for several years until eventually outgrowing it and moving on to a larger model. He still keeps Carlton's bat in his equipment bag for good luck (and to preserve his memory) and carves the initials CS into every new bat he uses.

Wee Willie Keeler

On the morning of September 5th, Happy dressed quickly and couldn't wait to get to the ballpark early.

"*Bubeleh*, where you running so fast? No time for breakfast? What, you prefer the ballpark *chazzerai* to my cooking? *Oy vey iz mir*," said Fannie rolling her eyes as she noticed Happy gliding through the dining room and heading for the front door.

"Sorry Fannie, no time today. Gotta be there early. Pretty special day for me and for all of baseball really," replied Happy as he reluctantly and respectfully slowed his pace.

"Nonsense, a young man needs his energy in case the manager might put him into the game. Always time for a *bissel eppis*, a little something. You want I should wrap a *nosh*, you could take with you? Maybe a bagel *mit schmear*? I got fresh-baked this morning, they's still warm. And *vus machs da,* what's so special going on?"

"Uhh, sure, OK, a bagel would be swell Fannie, I can eat while I'm walkin' over to the Park. Today the Giants are in town for a double-header and it's the last time we see'em this year."

"*Nu*, what's so special about that?"

"Didn't ya hear? The Giants' Wee Willie Keeler announced he's finally throwin' in the towel and givin' up his playin' career. This'll be his last appearance as a major league player in Brooklyn."

"Hmm, Mr. Keeler was certainly a big *macha* on the Superbas[8] - helped win us a couple championships some years ago and I read in the papers that he was born and raised right here in Brooklyn – went to PS 26 in Bedford; they say he's a nice man, a real *mensch*, lives at home, takes care of his mother... So, I see how it's a *farklempt* time for the Brooklynites. But why such a special occasion for you?"

"He was one of my idols growin' up," responded Happy. "I was a huge baseball fan and read every newspaper account and magazine about the game I could get my hands on and

---

[8] At a slight 5 feet 4.5 inches and 140lbs., the diminutive Keeler was not your typical sports icon but with just under 3,000 career hits, two consecutive batting crowns and a lifetime batting average of .321, he was among the most elite and accomplished players to ever play the game. Over the course of his career, he played for the Orioles and all three NY major league teams (Superbas and Giants in the National League, and the Highlanders in the newly formed American League) but his time playing for the Brooklyn Baseball Club were his best days and the fans fell in love with their hometown hero. His productive hitting, prodigious fielding and speed on the base paths helped bring the Superbas the pennant in 1899 and 1900.

watched lots of local amateur games in Oregon. But since I was kind of a scrawny kid when I was younger and not much good at sports, it was pretty frustrating for me. Then, when I discovered that this little pip squeak of a guy could be so talented and successful on the field, it kind of opened my eyes and inspired me. 'Course it didn't hurt that shortly afterwards I went through a growth spurt an' shot up like a beanstalk but mostly it had to do with developing confidence and puttin' in the time."

Happy paused for a moment to reflect. "Makin' it to the majors was a pretty crazy dream but gettin' to play in games with Wee Willie Keeler himself is way beyond my wildest dreams. So, to think I'll be in the stadium for his last game in his hometown, as a member of his former major league team to boot..." Happy broke out in an uncontrollable grin. "...That's just pretty darn amazin'."

"Well, now I suppose that is something to *kvell* about. *"Zei gezunt."*

The Committee of Fourteen

The two well-dressed gentlemen walked into the corporate offices of the Brooklyn Base Ball Club with a determined look and approached Dorothy's desk straight away. She was Charley Ebbets' executive secretary and usually did an excellent job screening his visitors so that he was not bothered with trivial or unnecessary matters. These callers, however, had made an appointment and represented The Committee of Fourteen, the highly powerful self-appointed "advisory" group on social vice. Established in 1905 originally as an attempt to fight the spread of prostitution, they were a well-known and respected group in the community. If they wished to have an audience with Mr. Ebbets, she was confident there was good reason for such a meeting and thus scheduled it at the earliest opportunity.

She knocked lightly on Mr. Ebbets' door and then opened it to announce the arrival of his visitors. With his consent, she ushered them into his office.

"Come in, come in, gentlemen" said Charley as he rose from his desk and came over to welcome his guests with a firm handshake. "Good afternoon. Charley Ebbets, President of the Brooklyn Baseball Club."

"We are most appreciative of your time, sir. I'm Reverend Dr. John P. Peters, and my colleague is Mr. Frederick H. Whitin. We are here however, representing the Committee of Fourteen, as Chairman and General Secretary, respectively."

"Yes, of course..." responded Ebbets. "Please make yourselves comfortable. I am quite familiar with the wonderful work your committee has done to help rid the city of the blight that brothels have brought upon us. Can Dorothy bring you some coffee?"

"Yes, thank you, sir. And thank you for your kind words of support for the ideals of our Committee. As you probably know, the ill-conceived liquor law reform back in '96 that allowed hotels to serve on Sunday was the origin of the so-called Raines hotels, which are just glorified bars with a few rooms attached. They could not have been better suited to fertilize the growth of this evil cottage industry if they tried...but we're starting to make some progress. Through our direct efforts the number of these so-called 'hotels' was cut in half from 1904 – 1908 and we are continuing our work every day."

"Legislators in the pockets of the liquor industry..." thought Charley aloud. "Those politicians are spineless I tell you!"

"That's true. But it's even worse when you consider that the city and the police in particular, just look the other way. We don't have any proof yet, but many of us think that bribery is at the heart of this from top to bottom... the cops on the beat, precinct captains, police commissioner and perhaps the mayor himself. That's why it was incumbent upon community members like ourselves to come together and do the job the city refuses to do."

"You should be applauded for your courage and tenacity in battling this evil!" said Charley. "How, may I ask, are you able to apply the necessary pressure to close down these sinful establishments?"

"It's fairly simple, really. We employ a network of undercover agents – we've found through experience that immigrant working-class types are less likely to be suspected and can pass as potential customers more effectively than more, shall we say upstanding representatives of the community, such as members of the committee. These agents circulate at the suspected bars and Raines hotels and gather information about the clientele and the establishment and then observe the behavior and interactions between the female and male customers. In cases where illicit, indecent, or immoral behavior is reported we then pass that information to beer and liquor distributors or landlords to see whether they care to be associated with this sort of lifestyle. Often, the economic pressures that can be brought to bear are very persuasive."

"Ingenious. If you are looking for donations, I am happy to contribute to your cause."

"We're so glad you see it that way, Mr. Ebbets... we most definitely appreciate any monetary support that you can afford to contribute... but it's your strong spiritual and moral support of the greater cause that is most important... which leads me to the delicate mission that brings us here today."

Charley looked up a bit startled and for the first time since their arrival he felt a touch uneasy. "Of course, what can I do for you gentlemen?"

"Perhaps I'll let Mr. Whitin fill you in on the details. He supervised this particular case and is more familiar with it..."

"Case? What case?" inquired Ebbets with increasing anxiety.

"Fred?"

"Yes, of course Reverend…" said Whitin… "but because of the sensitivity of the material we'd like to discuss with you, Mr. Ebbets, we are hoping you would be willing to sign a non-disclosure statement. No reflection on you, of course, just standard procedure in these sorts of cases. I'm sure you understand."

Whitin removed the document from his briefcase and provided Charley with his fountain pen, pointing to the lines he needed to sign. Ebbets thought for a moment about deferring until he could consult with his attorney but that seemed like a defensive move, and he certainly didn't want to appear to have anything to hide from the Committee. So he quickly gave the page a once-over and took Whitin's pen in hand, signing the statement acknowledging that under no circumstances would he disclose the information revealed to him.

Whitin retrieved his monocle and perched it over his right eye to examine the signature. A moment later, he continued, "Very good. OK, so one of our experienced investigators by the name of Harry Kahan, a Jewish immigrant from Russia has been focusing on several so-called Black and tan clubs in Manhattan. Some of these establishments, often but not exclusively owned and operated by Negro proprietors, have been implicated to be directly involved in the facilitation of prostitution and of course, we are pursuing these aggressively…"

"…But the Committee has recently become alarmed with the increased popularity of these types of establishments that tolerate, or worse, encourage the sexual intermingling of the races. The proprietors of the Black and tan clubs turn a blind eye to the negative impacts that inevitably result from comingling with those of lesser moral certitude. Don't misunderstand me, we are very much in favor of freedom for

Negros but like Booker T. Washington, we believe that neither race benefits from assimilation." Charley nodded his head in agreement.

"Frederick Moore," continued Whitin, "editor of The New York Age, which as you know is the largest Negro paper in the country, is a member of our advisory board and has published editorials supporting these principles. We just can't ignore the fact that some elements of society have different standards for ethical and moral conduct and if left unchecked, these values will pollute our sense of decency. Are you with me so far?"

"Yes, of course. I share all of the concerns you have so eloquently described thus far," replied Ebbets.

"Very good. So, getting back to the particulars of this case... in a recent stakeout at the Marshall Hotel in Hell's Kitchen, Kahan reported about how the joint is laid out. There's a long bar with stools as you enter the place and these tend to be occupied by Negro patrons. But if you walk all the way to the back there are a number of more secluded rooms where patrons of both races were congregating together. On the floor right above the bar were rooms available for rent on an hourly basis. Kahan observed this over multiple visits to the Marshall and it is all very well documented."

Whitin took a moment to sip his coffee before proceeding. "I should add, by the way, that Harry Kahan is a resident of Brooklyn and is a very devoted Superbas crank."

This brought a momentary smile to Ebetts' face. "And as such, he is quite familiar with your players. One night last week he was alarmed to identify one of the Caucasian male patrons as none other than a player on your ball club..." Adjusting his monocle and looking down at his notes to recall the name... "A Mr. Henry Smith."

Charley noted to himself that Whitin was clearly not much of a fan but acknowledged that Smith was in fact one of his employees.

"Mr. Smith was drinking and conversing with an attractive young Negro woman whose identity is unknown but whom we assume was a hooker." Whitin paused to gauge the reaction from Ebbets, which was one of serious concern.

"Who else knows about this? Did your investigator confront or publicly expose Mr. Smith at the bar?" asked Ebbets.

"Certainly not. Kahan's report indicates the ball player was operating anonymously. We train our people to be most discrete and preserve their undercover status so they can continue to be of use to us. In addition, coming to you with this information is typical of how we work."

Whiten paused to let his revelation sink in and give Ebbets a moment to collect his thoughts. But it didn't take long for Ebbets to respond, "Well, thank you very much gentlemen for your discretion and for bringing this to my attention. This kind of information would make excellent fodder for the gossip pages in the papers and would undoubtedly be the talk of the town, which I can assure you would not be good for business. You can rest assured that I will deal with this appropriately, quickly and decisively."

A Jersey Bull

On the way to the plate from the on-deck circle, Happy could hear Tex Irwin's voice over the noise of the crowd, shouting, "Hey Henry, fetch us some more worms, will ya?" which sent him straight back in time 20 years and landed him 3,000 miles to the west of home plate on the banks of Hammond's Creek. The appeal was actually for a run-producing base hit to "fetch us some more runs," of course, but in his mind's ear he heard the familiar request of his brother's friends while on a lazy summer afternoon's fishing expedition.

Happy's happiest moments as a child were the ones he spent with his brother, especially those times in which Carlton included him when playing with his friends. They all had nicknames to refer to each other: his brother was Constable because he tended to enforce the rule of law among the group when disputes arose. Then there was Lawrence who was called Shorty for obvious reasons, Taylor who was mostly quiet unless you got him angry when he was known to let the punches fly so his nickname was Sully (after heavyweight champion John L. Sullivan), and Alexander was simply Lex. Horace was part Lakota Indian and was thus referred to as Sitting Bull (or just Bull for short). John was called Big Fish based on his proclivity for exaggeration when it came to reporting on his success with the fishing pole. Walter, the most ardent baseball crank among the group (and a fairly talented player himself) went by King Kelly, after the star outfielder of the Chicago White Stockings.

Mostly they tolerated Henry tagging along, although there were plenty of times he was ordered around for their convenience or amusement, as the case may be. While fishing down at the creek with his brother and friends he'd often be asked to replenish the bait supply and since he knew some good places to dig for Night Crawlers, Henry would eagerly scamper off in search of fertile ground. More often than not, he would soon return with a can oozing with the slimy critters, which afforded him some level of respect among his brother's peers and the nickname, Digger. When not digging for worms he was baiting his own hook and dropping his line just as the others did from the rocky outcrop just past the sharp bend in the creek where the water tended to pool. He occasionally got lucky and landed a decent sized trout which inevitably earned him kudos along with an ample potion of jealous ribbing, both of which Henry would savor.

In addition to fishing, there were lots more opportunities to spend time with Carlton and his cronies. When not at the fishing hole they were apt to be assembling an impromptu sandlot baseball game. They mostly played at the farmer's market field in town but when it was unavailable they settled for a mostly level portion of the lower pasture of Grady's Dairy Farm, down the road a piece from their house.

While he wasn't considered good enough to play with his elders at the time, Henry was kept busy as their official ball boy, and it was his job to retrieve balls hit in foul territory. He would bring a mitt along and play catch with the boys before the games started. Occasionally, on especially hot days he'd be sent back to the house to request some more of their mom's thirst-quenching lemonade. He didn't mind – it gave him a reason to hang around and if not part of the action, he at least had a front row seat.

It was here that he first developed a fascination with baseball. He studied the games intently and soaked up the strategies as second nature. But none of the boys, least of all Henry, ever dreamed it would be his fate to pursue baseball as a career.

Of course, every once in a while, Henry suffered the usual rites of passage that all younger siblings do. This meant being the subject of the random taunt or good-natured ridicule bestowed upon him by his elders.   While Carlton was a loyal brother, he was no saint and unless Henry was in any real danger, he might bend to peer pressure and remain silent while his brother twisted in the breeze. Sometimes, adding insult to injury, he'd even join in. In such cases, there was nothing to be done but try to smile his way through and move on.

On one hot August afternoon, the boys answered a challenge from their rivals in the neighboring town of Riverton, playing a closely matched game at their "home field" of Grady's farm. When they arrived in late morning to practice before the game, some of Grady's herd were still enjoying an all-you-can-eat Sunday crabgrass brunch while others, having had their fill, were sunning themselves and swatting flies with their tails. As the cows were occupying a large portion of what was to be left field, Henry was sent to chase them off while the others set out some square wooden boards that served as bases and a small 2x4 for the pitching "rubber" and began to toss the ball around to loosen up.

So, Henry grabbed a couple of bats which he hoisted above his head to mimic the horns of a ferocious bull. Shaking his head with rage and screaming at the top of his lungs with all the malevolence he could muster, he galloped in their direction, attempting to stir an outsized ruckus. The boys rolled hysterically in the grass as they watched the spectacle unfold.

The cows, on the other hand, appeared bemused but definitely not amused. As the charge continued in their direction, they began to become concerned. Jersey cows are considered relatively docile but tend to be a bit nervous when stressed. Several began to shake their heads and moo in response, but their calls quickly morphed to short snorts of disgust as if to warn the "bull" to steer clear and not mess with these ladies enjoying a few quiet moments to themselves. Tails went from random fly swatting to defensive rhythmic swishing mode.

But this hint of resistance just inspired Henry to turn up his bullishness a notch until he was fully channeling a three-quarter ton, pure bred Jersey bull, (considered by many to be the least docile of any breed). He bellowed a long, deep-throated growl ("aaaahrrrooooh!") that resonated into a series of higher pitched screeches ("aarheeech!", "aahrooh!!" and "aireeehya!!!")

The cows began to stir – those already standing started to scurry off the field and head for calmer pastures and those lounging quickly rolled onto their knees in preparation for a hasty retreat. Meanwhile the boys were practically peeing in their pants and laughing so hard snot was involuntarily spewing from their noses. The "Jersey bull" returned in triumph to a rousing round of applause and pats on the back.

The mood was jovial following the game as they barely edged out their Riverton rivals 6 - 5 in 10 innings. After Shorty popped out to lead off the bottom of the tenth and Sully struck out, Big Fish doubled and scored when King Kelly connected for a line drive, walk-off base hit. As they gleefully walked back home, recounting and reliving the highlights of the day's victory, their reverie was suddenly punctured by the pungent smell of fresh manure. The odor cloud seemed to be tracking their movements, its acrid smell undeniable. Constable stopped dead in his tracks and demanded,

"OK, who stepped in it?"

After vigorous accusations and denials, King Kelly made everybody stop and examined the soles of their shoes in search of the culprit. And one by one, Constable, Shorty, Sully, Lex, Big Fish and Bull, were exonerated. King then put his arm on Shorty's shoulder for balance while he voluntarily lifted his left shoe, then his right for inspection by the group.

When all of Carlton's buddies and the self-appointed inquisitor were declared innocent there was just Henry left to be checked. He had been aware of the shit smell most of the day but since they were playing in a cow pasture, didn't give it much more thought. He warily raised his right foot. Clean. But his moment of relief was short-lived.

As he lifted his left shoe off the ground all were greeted by the unmistakable sight of a generous portion of a squished-up cow turd partially crusted and well smeared into the sole and stitching of his shoe. A unanimous chorus of "eeeewh!" and "disgusting!" left Henry with no doubt that he would be ostracized for the remainder of the day, if not longer.

They skipped the trial and accepted his red-faced, embarrassed shirk as a plea of guilty as charged. He willingly accepted his sentence of having to walk 15 paces downwind for the remainder of the walk home.

Too Many Giants

Happy was eagerly awaiting the three days off between their home series with the Cincinnati Reds (in which they were soundly defeated, three games to one) and the St. Louis Cardinals who were coming to town next. That last series with the Reds was sobering and returned the team's collective spirit to terra firma following the Suberbas seven game home winning streak against the Pittsburgh Pirates and the Boston Doves which temporarily and unrealistically inflated expectations.

Most of the players were looking forward to a rare few days in a row they did not have to report to the ballpark, some to rest their weary muscles, others so they could nurse their hangovers from back-to-back-to-back late night excursions through Brooklyn's finest drinking establishments. Since Happy was not a starter he wasn't particularly physically drained, and while he was no teetotaler, one night out on the town per week was more than enough for him. Ironically, what Happy was looking forward to most was going to a ballgame.

Flash planned to take advantage of the break and bring Josie to a Negro League game on Sunday and she suggested they invite Happy since he'd never been to one.   The game was between the Brooklyn Royal Giants and last year's western division champions the Chicago Leland Giants, originally organized and managed by the legendary Frank Leland. However, he recently sold the team and started a new one, which precipitated a protracted legal battle and ironically Leland lost the rights to using his own name. So he named his new team the Chicago Giants and the Leland Giants retained the name but were in fact, Leland-less.

The game was held at Brooklyn's home field, Meyerrose Park, which was actually just over the county line in the farmlands of Ridgewood, Queens. They set out from the Johnson residence in Bedford Stuyvesant around 11 am in order to be at the ballpark in plenty of time for the 1 pm start time and caught the Brooklyn Rapid Transit Company's DeKalb Ave. trolley heading east. They rode in an open-air car with no sides, soaking up the warm breeze as they eased down the wide boulevard. Happy had made a point of seeing as much of his new hometown as he could in the limited time available to him and took in the many and varied commercial storefronts along the way.

Josie sat between her dad and Happy on the streetcar and was bubbling over with anticipation. She talked Happy's ear off the entire time while her dad sat quietly except for an occasional baseball-related clarification. For the most part, New Yorkers minded their own business and there were no incidents but Happy was aware of an occasional less than friendly stare he got presumably because he was traveling and fraternizing in public with a good-looking young Negro woman. Flash and Josie were well dressed and maintained a confident air, seemingly oblivious to any negative feedback. Happy noted it seemed if you were Black you'd need to turn a blind eye to racial prejudice whenever possible just to survive.

"So, you know we're gonna see Dad's old buddy and teammate, Grant "Home Run" Johnson? He's still playing ball for the Leland Giants...Dad, I'm guessing he must be ancient like you, probably pushing 40 years old, no? "

"Now wait a minute there, young lady. I may not be playing ball anymore, but I'm no dinosaur. As for HR, I reckon he's a couple of years my junior so that would put him around 37 or so. He's not hitting for power like he did when he was younger...but he's still helping his team win ballgames."

In fact, Grant Johnson had only hit one home run thus far this season... but just as the team retained Leland's name, HR did not relinquish his well-earned nickname. Although his bat speed and strength were not what they once were, he remained a smart and dependable situational hitter, currently batting a better than respectable 0.326.

"But the big star on their team though..." continued Josie "is their short stop, Pete Hill. He's hitting over 0.500!"

Happy's jaw dropped. "Are you kidding me? That's unreal – never heard of anyone with those kind of numbers in any league!"

"Well, it's true. I saw it printed in the box score for their last game plus I read an article about him in the Amsterdam News sports pages. They've got some other great batsmen too, plus a fine pitching staff, so it's no wonder they are tearing up the League."

"You sure do know a lot about baseball for a girl."

Josie shot him a lethal glance. Happy quickly recovered. "Sorry, didn't mean any offense, It was actually meant as a compliment. It's just that I'm not used to talking baseball with women. As a matter of fact, other than you and my landlady Fanny Goldfarb (and my mom of course), I've never met any women who are the least bit interested – let alone knowledgeable about the game. I guess considering your upbringing, it's no surprise though."

"Well, yeah...kind of inevitable I suppose. Definitely inherited my dad's love of the game. I'm not much of an athlete – take after my mother that way – but I do enjoy playing occasionally too."

"Girls play ball too?"

Flash burst out laughing. "Now you've gone and done it. This should be fun to watch."

"Dad, please. Don't go there... but seriously, Happy, you really are behind the times. Of course we play! Mostly for fun, but there are some semi-professional women's teams being organized now too. Just this year they started a team here called the New York Bloomer Girls."

"OK, ok, I'm learning...bear with me. What can you tell me about today's game? How does the Brooklyn Club stack up?"

"Should be exciting. Both teams are leading their leagues in the standings...Brooklyn's ahead in the Eastern Independent League but they're probably not quite as good as the Chicago Leland Giants who are way out front of their Western Independent Club rivals: the Kansas City Royal Giants, Chicago Giants, Indianapolis ABCs and the Kansas City Giants."

"Lots of Giants roaming around out there!"

"Yeah," said Flash, laughing out loud. "Guess the owners ain't too creative in the naming department. Does get a bit confusing, I'll grant you that. But the West also has the Minneapolis Keystones, St. Paul Gophers, Stars of Cuba, Oklahoma Monarchs, and my favorite, the West Baden Sprudels."

"Did you say Sprudels? What's a Sprudel?"

"Some kind of legendary gnome that supposedly protected the town's mineral springs and eventually became the name for their drinking water and hot springs which draw people from near and far. They built a hotel there for rich white folks... the Negro league team was started for their entertainment and the Sprudel was their mascot. That's how a bunch of the Negro teams got their start, by the way. Fact, the very first team of Black players back in 1885 was the Cuban Giants who were waiters, bus boys and porters at the Argyle Hotel in Babylon Long Island. The white owner of the hotel fielded and sponsored the team as a form of entertainment for his guests. Nothing to do with Cuba either except for the color of their skin I suppose – I guess the owners figured their clientele would be more accepting of seeing dark skinned players on the field if they thought they were foreigners. The players talked gibberish to each other on the field thinking it sounded like Spanish."

"That must have been quite a sight!"

"Indeed," continued Flash. "Eventually Black businessmen like Frank Leland and John Conner saw baseball as a lucrative opportunity and began to invest in the game. Leland was a former player and very familiar with the game but Conner is strictly a money guy – he runs the Royal Garden Café – essentially a nightclub, over on Myrtle Ave., a few blocks north of here."

"Yeah," said Josie. "I hear it's a Black and tan club."

"And what would you know about that?" asked Flash, suddenly concerned.

"Well, nothin' really" replied Josie, as matter of factly as she could muster. She struggled not to glance at Happy who fidgeted uncomfortably and turned to gaze out the side of the streetcar. "Just what I heard on the street is all."

"Let's keep it that way, Miss."

Sensing she needed to quickly change the subject, Josie said "Speaking of restaurants, I'm starving. Can't wait to grab a hot dog when we get to the ballpark!"

Just Another Mercenary

❖

May 11, 1910

Dearest **H**enry,

    I hope your adjustment to big city life continues to go smoothly and that the excitement of playing **b**aseball at the professional Major League level is as exciting and rewarding as you'd always dreamed it would be. Of course, we cherish your letters and each time we find a letter from you ~~jas~~ has arrived at the post office in Coquill**e** it makes our day!

    Things are still pretty routine here – it seems more and more people are moving to the Pacific Northwest and as a result, Dad's ferry **b**usiness is doing quite well. I continue to keep myself rather busy working with the Ladies Auxiliary at church, reading, and with my new hobby: quilting. My quilting group meets once a week on Thursday mornings and we work together on various projects – For example, Mrs. Weld**o**n (up river a piece), just gave birth to twins and poor Mr. Weldon recently lost his job. So, the Ladies Auxiliary arranged to get them some hand-me-down cribs and our quilting group made them a set of matching quilts. Of course, we ladies talk and talk and talk as we work so the time goes rather quickly and it's been fun. My background working in the mills years ago definitely comes in handy, but I really don't miss factory work one bit!

Speaking of which…there is some news from your Uncle Norton. As you recall, he retired from mining after putting in 30 years at the Philadelphia and Reading Coal & Iron Works Co. mine where Dad and Grandpa Albert Sr. also used to work. I don't know how much of the story has been covered by the New York papers, but there's been some trouble at the coal mines in western Pennsylvania's Westmoreland County, near Pittsburgh. The workers are trying to unionize and they organized a massive strike of more than 10,000 miners calling for an 8 hr. work day and some basic improvements in safety.

As soon as the companies found out, they fired hundreds of workers and brought in their goons from the Coal and Iron Police, which is their private security force plus troopers from the Pennsylvania State Patrol, attacking and arresting workers, their wives, and their supporters willy nilly. In most cases, miners live in company-owned towns near the mines as we did before you were born, and many families were evicted to try and scare the others into submission.

The mining companies didn't want to lose one minute of operations, so they immediately put out the call far and wide for strike-breaking (scab) workers. They made a special recruitment effort in other mining towns, trying to lure experienced workers to fill the striking workers jobs, offering free transportation and tempting cash incentives.

Your Uncle Norton, who was never very socially minded, couldn't resist their offer and joined with hundreds of other scabs to make a quick buck. What's worse is he feels superior to the strikers, most of whom are recent immigrants of Italian and Irish descent. In a thoroughly un-Christian, intolerant, and bigoted manner, he complains about the "Dagos, Wops, Donkeys, and Coal Cracker union troublemakers." It makes me so mad!

While Dad would never condone bigotry, he says he doesn't see anything wrong with his brothers' actions. But frankly, I'm rather troubled. I know firsthand (and Dad should know even better than I) the difficulties and dangers of working down in the mines. The men risk their lives every day they go to work, struggle through 10-hour workdays, six days a week, for about $2 a day…and they're paid by the ton so they don't get paid at all for the work that is required in preparation for mining and cleaning up afterwards. Did you know that the workers even have to buy their own safety helmets and lights?

Coal powers our boats and trains, provides the energy to run our great iron works and steel mills, heats our houses and even powers the electric plants that are popping up all over the place. As a result, the owners of the mines are sitting on mountains of profits for many years to come. And yet they deny the workers on whose backs those profits are derived a decent wage, safe working conditions or time to enjoy life with their families and communities. I don't regret for one second our decision to leave that life behind but I feel deeply in my heart for all those who have not been able to escape and are stuck dealing with those crooked mining companies every single day.

It makes me angry to see other workers take management's side and sick to my stomach that our own flesh and blood has become just another mercenary. It's no use arguing with Dad about this – he just can't bring himself to judge his brother's actions objectively.   So, I share my thoughts with you and just pray that the strike is settled quickly and we can ~~pot~~ put this family embarrassment behind us.

Write soon.
With much love,
    Mom

    P.S. Please excuse my sloppy typing. My fingers are rusty and so is this beat-up old typing machine!

Another Sort of Beanball

The Superbas were gathered in the clubhouse locker room for a pre-game meeting scheduled by the manager. These were not all that unusual, especially when the team was playing as poorly as they'd been. They generally covered activities on the field to inspire greater effort or reviewed fundamental aspects of the game to improve the team's performance. It was more than half-way through the season and despite their poor play thus far, both cranks and management alike (as well as most of the players) still believed the team could turn things around and have a respectable if not fully competitive season.

But every once in a while, a meeting was called to review expectations for team conduct on and off the field. For example, there were several meetings last year devoted to reminding the players of the need for appropriate behavior. These were inspired by repeated infractions of the rules of conduct by Harry the House McIntyre. Even when he had a beef with how his players were performing "Big Bad" Bob Dahlen preferred to mke his case calmly, without threats or raising his voice. So, the players were loose and joking noisily amongst themselves as he stepped up.

When Happy noticed none other than team owner Charles Ebbets emerge from Dahlen's office and stand just off to his left, it was clear that today's get-together was not the usual pep talk.

"OK, folks, pipe down now...this will be short and sweet. Mr. Ebbets has something to talk with you all about, so listen up."

"Thanks Bill, of course our focus is always on the game itself, but the Brooklyn Baseball Club takes pride in being upstanding citizens of this great borough of New York and we have worked hard to establish and maintain a good neighbor policy. As ballplayers, you are both cultural ambassadors in the community and role models to our youth. That is why we sponsor team visits to hospitals and orphanages and spend time reaching out to encourage sandlot ball..."

The noise in the clubhouse had evaporated. His teammates were uncharacteristically serious now – some out of sincerity and others merely reflecting an understanding that Charley meant business and had proven he would not tolerate a smartass attitude.

"...As most of you know, we have a code of ethics that we expect you to respect and abide."

Through the quiet, the creaking of wooden benches and scraping of metal cleats on the concrete locker room floor could be easily heard as a few of the more boisterous Superbas squirmed, hoping one or more of their recent transgressions had not been exposed. Happy sat calmly taking it all in.

"It has come to our attention that one of the players in this clubhouse, a member and employee of the Brooklyn Baseball

Club was recognized in one of the many houses of ill repute that pollute our great city."

Having gotten to know many of his teammates, this news did not come as a shock to Happy. But then, out of nowhere, the beanball pitch was upon him.

"Worse yet, it was at a so-called Black and tan club called The Marshall Hotel, in which races intermingle and the player was seen with a Negro prostitute."

Henry felt dizzy. Could it be that he and Josie were spotted, someone recognized him as a member of the Superbas and assumed she was a prostitute? He wasn't often recognized in public when not accompanied by some his better-known teammates and it hadn't occurred to him that he may no longer be anonymous. Henry looked over at Flash but he didn't seem to connect the dots.

"I will not embarrass the player by identifying him here. He knows who he is and now knows that we know and that we are watching. But I wanted to announce this to the whole team so we can nip this kind of behavior in the bud. Associating with prostitutes or interracial liaisons will not be tolerated on this club!"

Happy's face flushed and his whole body tensed as he considered the possibilities. He glanced around at his teammates to see if anyone else was looking as guilty as he was feeling. In contrast, the usual suspects all seemed relieved after Ebbets announced the infraction occurred at the Marshall Hotel. Their own specific indiscretions had apparently slipped through the cracks.

"One last thing gentlemen...So far, we've managed to keep this story out of the tabloids. God help anyone who is responsible for leaking the incident. With the level of play you guys have managed lately, it's hard enough to get paying cranks into the seats. And I needn't remind you, that's where the money comes from that pays your salaries. Now let's get behind Manager Dahlen and go out and win some ballgames!"

No Joy in Mudville

Dearest Henry,

Sorry… under the circumstances I just can't bring myself to use your nickname – there really is no joy in Mudville today…

After Charley Ebbets met with the team this morning, my dad put 2 and 2 together. He didn't come right out and accuse me but got angry and said he wasn't going to allow me to date white men while living under his roof. Said I'd have to choose between their support to finish college or continuing to see you. As much as it pains me to say it, that's just not a sacrifice I'm willing to make.

I am so ashamed of how my dad reacted but even more ashamed that I don't have the courage to stand up to him and fight for what I know is right. Maybe someday folks like us won't have to deal such small-minded bigotry. But that day seems like it's a long, long way down the road.

We'll never know if the feelings we shared could have grown into something more, but I like to dream they could have. We'll always have fond memories of our short time together. That's something no one can take away from us.

So, this is a sad goodbye. I wish you the best – both on and off the field and hope you'll be "Happy" all of your days. Even though we can't be together, I'll always be in the stands watching you from afar and lamenting what might have been.

Your friend,
Josie

The Unhittable Pitch

◇

June 23, 1910

Dear Mom,

I apologize that it's been longer than usual since my last letter to you. We are getting ready for a road trip to Boston to play the Doves and since I've finished packing, I have a few minutes to write. Fanny let me use her typewriter, so you won't have to read my lousy handwriting.

First of all, hope you had a HAPPY BIRTHDAY! Wish I could have been there with you - hope you and dad did something fun to celebrate.

I've been enjoying your frequent messages - the detailed news from home and my busy schedule have kept me from getting too homesick. Sorry to hear about Uncle Norton. It's disappointing that he can't see the big picture. Being around Fanny and her friends in the Women's Trade Union League has made me much more aware of the problems workers face in this country.

I haven't had many opportunities on the baseball field – most games, I'm not in the starting lineup and just watch from the dugout. Occasionally, I get a chance late in the game as a pinch hitter (but not when the score is close or in important game situations). A few times I was put in the game in the eighth or ninth inning as a defensive replacement (I'm as good an outfielder as Jack Dalton who usually starts in right field.) And I have a better arm so I can throw the ball to the infielders more quickly and more accurately. But the players on the team are a great bunch of guys and have looked out for me.

Sorry I haven't gone to church very much, except on Easter of course… and I already told you about that really big Old First Reformed Church down the street from us.

You asked whether I've met any nice young women, and I have, except circumstances have kind of gotten in the way. It's a bit complicated but I'll try and explain, knowing you always have an open mind. Flash Jones, our equipment manager, physical trainer, and team nurse is a former player in the Negro Leagues. He knows a heck of a lot about the game and is really friendly. His wife Flo is an artist and they have a daughter named Josie. Anyway, they invited me for Sunday dinner about a month ago which was really very nice - Flo cooked a traditional St. Louis meal of barbeque - not sure what everything was but it sure was tasty. If nothing else, I've been exposed to lots of different kinds of foods since coming to Brooklyn!

Josie is good looking and very smart - you'd really like her mom. She is even enrolled in college and wants to be an education administrator when she's done. To make a long story short, we got a chance to talk during the afternoon and I wasn't sure, but I thought maybe she took a bit of an interest in me. A few days later she was at the clubhouse helping her dad out with equipment and although she didn't approach me, she did manage to sneak me a note asking if I'd like to get together for a drink. Lots of things are different here in Brooklyn and across the bridge in Manhattan, but interracial dating, while it does occur, is certainly not done openly.

Needless to say, I was pretty shocked, but I did agree to meet her at a music club in Manhattan for the evening. The place was considered a "Black and tan" establishment because they catered to both Negros and whites. I was really nervous on my way there and the whole time until I managed to find Josie. The ragtime music was amazing, and we talked all night long. I'm sure you'll

understand that I couldn't take her home –
despite being very open about most things,
Flash made it clear to Josie that was a line
she shouldn't cross. I think we both felt
the evening was pretty special though.

A few days later, Flash took me and
Josie to a Negro Leagues game at a ballpark
in eastern Brooklyn. Those fellas were
excellent athletes and could play ball just
as good as any white players.

A few days later, I was trying to think
of a way Josie and I could meet again but
got another huge shock before I could make
any arrangements. Charles Ebbets, the owner
of our club held a players' meeting and
announced one of the players (he wouldn't
say who) was seen in a Black and tan house
of prostitution! This is obviously against
the rules but I'm afraid someone might have
seen us and recognized me from the ball club
and just assumed that Josie was a
prostitute. Nothing could be further from
the truth, but I found myself in a situation
for which there was no winning solution. I
can't confess what really happened and don't
know whether it would even make a difference
from the team's perspective. Ebbets said it
was a warning and they'd be watching us
carefully. And Flash, who figured it was us
told Josie she had to choose between dating
me or continuing to get their support to
finish college. It's just not fair!

So, I'm chalking this up to just
another learning experience in the big world
beyond Oregon. As I mentioned in previous
letters, I've learned so much in the short
time I've been away.

Missing you and Dad...

Sincerely,
Henry

Strike Two

F anny stood and tapped her water glass to signal to her guests it was time to start the meeting.

"Welcome to this month's seminar for the Park Slope Chapter of the Women's Trade Union League. We are fortunate to have with us tonight, a young woman, who while still in the prime of her youth, is already a veteran union organizer. Four years ago, at the age of just 16 years old, Pauline Newman, helped organize, what turned out to be, the largest rent strike in NYC history."

Happy remembered Fanny mentioning Newman as one of the possible replacement speakers at the women's suffrage debate and the fact that because she and others were out of town Fanny was asked to fill in as a last-minute replacement. He was surprised both at how young Pauline Newman was and her unconventional appearance. Closely cropped hair, white button-down shirt with broad solid black necktie, and sharply creased wool tweed trousers.

"I'm sure you'll remember," Fanny continued, "that the country's economy, was in a big depression at that time - thousands of recent immigrants and others, struggling to make ends meet, were faced with enormous increases in their housing costs, at the hands of a few, greedy landlords. For her leadership role, the New York Times, called Pauline Newman the Joan of Arc, of the lower East Side. They said, and I quote,

> *The young woman who is recognized as the real leader of the movement is Pauline Newman, who is employed in a shirtwaist factory on Grand Street. Although most of her daylight hours are spent in the shop, she has, for a week or more, devoted six hours out of twenty-four, to visiting the tenements and arousing the interests of the dwellers there. She has organized a band of four hundred women, all of whom earn their own living, whose duty it is to promulgate the doctrine of lower rents.*

"The rent strike was a big success, but she did not stop there... The following year, the Socialist Party of America, asked her to join their ticket and run for Secretary of State in New York. This was really just a symbolic act of course - as women, we are not even allowed to vote! But Pauline took this opportunity, to campaign for another important struggle, women's suffrage."

"Today, Pauline is a rising new leader for us at the WTUL, and is also working for the International Ladies Garment Workers Union. So, she is dedicated to making a better life for workers in the future... but tonight, she will take a few moments, to look back and tell us about her experiences as a young union organizer, and a leader of the rent strike. Please welcome, a dedicated activist and my dear friend, Pauline Newman."

"*Oy gevalt,* such an introduction!" Using both hands to hide her grinning face for a moment, she basked in the warm welcome and then quickly motioned to acknowledge their applause and continued, "You're making me blush! Thank you so much Fanny. And let me say, that it is strong and smart women like *you*, who continue to inspire me and who make it all possible..." Then, gesturing to the group assembled in Fanny's living room, "And thanks to all of you, for coming tonight."

"When Fanny first asked me to speak with you about my life and my experiences, I immediately said no! I don't like to focus attention on myself. Besides, it is not about Pauline Newman or any one of us for that matter. As working-class citizens of this great country, and especially as women, we must act together, struggle together, to fight for a better life. But as most of you know, Fanny can be very persistent and very persuasive, indeed. In the end, she convinced me, that if my experiences can inspire others, I should make every effort to do so."

"So, here I am... I should probably start by telling you a little about my background. I was born in Kovno, Lithuania, and was raised in a poor but religiously observant Jewish household. My father died when I was about ten years old and like so many others, my mother decided we'd have many more opportunities here in America. So, she bravely packed up my two sisters and me, and we came here to join my older brother who had emigrated a few years earlier."

"I wasn't able to attend school – we all had to work to help make ends meet. My first job was at a hairbrush factory but shortly afterwards a relative who was working at the Triangle Shirtwaist Co., was able to get me a job there. When I told the foreman at the hairbrush factory I was leaving, he told me that I was very lucky to have gotten a job with that concern because they are the largest manufacturers of shirtwaists in New York and there is work all year round so I would no longer have to look for another job."

"On the one hand, I felt fortunate to have such job security... but on the other hand, I quickly realized that after 70 or 80 hours a week for a mere $1.50, we did not earn enough to keep body and soul together. I will never forget the sign which was posted on Saturday afternoons on the wall near the elevator that said: 'If you don't come in on Sunday you need not come in on Monday!' So, what choice do we have?"

"In many ways these sweatshops make you feel like a slave. If you are just five minutes late to work because of a trolley or subway delay, they deduct from your meager wages as a penalty. You rarely hear the foreman or the boss sneaking around in their rubber heels, but they are constantly watching to make sure you don't stop working even for one moment. You are watched even when you go to the lavatory and if you stay a minute or two longer than the forelady thinks you should have, they threaten to fire you. They routinely search your purse or any packages you have before leaving work, to make sure you didn't take bit of lace or thread. The conditions that still exist in the factory of the Triangle Shirtwaist Co. and most of the other factories in this country are the height of exploitation perpetrated on defenseless men, women, and children - a sort of punishment for being poor and vulnerable."

"But somehow, we put up with intolerable and even unsafe conditions and continue to work for these companies. What good would it do to change jobs since similar conditions exist in all the garment factories? Plus, you kind of get used to a place, get to know the people you work with, develop friendships, all of which help you get through the day. These things make us complacent, and we tend to stay put. Of course, despite the deplorable conditions, the threat of losing our jobs, is a huge barrier to organizing and fighting for decency and a better life."

Happy thought back to the locker room grumblings he'd overheard during Spring Training and started making some connections. While ball players were mostly paid more than average wage earners, they were still beholden to the owners, were bought and sold, were not free to seek work with other competing employers and were prohibited by law to organize unions to represent their interests.

It's a real challenge, but we are starting to make progress," Newman continued. "This past year, things reached the boiling point and as you recall 20,000 women garment workers realized we can make a difference if we stick together. Even though we didn't get all of our demands met, the garment workers' strike was a wakeup call and a turning point, marking the beginning of our struggle."

"And the struggle goes far beyond the workplace. Four years ago, when I was 16 and still working at the Triangle factory, the economy hit the skids. To make up for some of their shrinking profits, landlords started jacking up the rents, 10,20, 30% in just a few months' time! Since our salaries, for those of us still fortunate to have a job, were frozen, the noose around our necks was getting tighter and it was a nightmare just trying to survive. We were getting fed up and needed some time to think."

"So that summer, a group of about 60 of my fellow women workers and I decided to take a break – since business was very slow our employers were more than happy not to pay us for a while. And a generous patron from WTUL, who owns some property in the country on the Palisades overlooking the Hudson River, allowed us to pitch some tents and camp for a few weeks. We organized lots of social activities to unwind and keep busy - swimming in a nearby lake, volleyball tournaments and baseball games, crafts such as jewelry making and (believe it or not for those who missed being at work) even sewing, cards and other group games, folk dancing and sing-alongs – it was a much needed break from the sweatshop... but the main focus of the camp was social activism."

"We wanted to find a unifying issue we could rally around so our political action would lead to measurable and meaningful impact on peoples' lives. There was no shortage of good ideas – from trade union organizing, to women's suffrage. Margaret Sanger spent several days at the camp and lobbied for adopting the issue of birth control and women's health. Others lobbied for more mundane issues like protesting the high cost of fresh meat especially from kosher butchers. All just causes, but in the end, the issue of affordable housing won the day."

"Our tenements are overcrowded and run down and the outrageous and unjustified increases in rent the building owners have been imposing just wind up lining their pockets rather than making much-needed repairs or improvements. We decided hitting the landlords in their wallets would be the most effective approach and called for a general rent strike demanding a halt to runaway rents with little or no improvement in living conditions."

Newman was mostly preaching to the choir of course, and there were scattered remarks acknowledging agreement with her assessment of the problem and the selected course of action so she paused for a moment to take a sip of tea. Happy on the other hand, was hearing of these issues for the first time and found himself paying close attention. He wondered what it must be like to live in a crowded tenement and struggle to be able to pay your rent. Even though he was far from wealthy on his salary as a professional ball player, he realized he had much to be thankful for.

"Our strategy was to first recruit a dedicated cadre of women who would spread the word and act as local coordinators in various buildings and neighborhoods. When we returned home at the end of the summer, the word spread like wildfire and we quickly gathered strength – before long we had around 400 women canvassing their neighborhoods to encourage people to join the rent strike. They knocked on doors, handed out flyers on street corners, and attended organizing meetings. The response was much greater than we ever dreamed!"

"Ultimately over 10,000 families joined in and it turned out to be the largest rent strike in New York history. As a result of the strike, rents were lowered for about 2,000 families... but even more importantly - these actions, sent a message to the wealthy landlords, that they cannot continue to raise housing costs just for their own greed... and if they do, there will be consequences."

A round of applause broke out, but Newman just shook her head and motioned with her hands to let everyone know she was not looking for accolades.

"I got a lot of personal credit for my role but am truly just one voice among many."

Newman continued to speak of her more recent activities including her campaign for state office on the Socialist Party ticket, working as an organizer for the ILGWU and her efforts on behalf of the WTUL.

There was a short question and answer session and when the meeting adjourned Newman stuck around to speak with small groups of people. Happy continued to sit by himself listening in to the sidebar conversations. Finally, as most of the guests had filtered out, Pauline noticed Happy on the side of the room and wandered over.

"So you must be Happy Smith, utility player for the Superbas?"

"Yes, ma'am, that's me. How'd you know that?"

"Fanny's told me quite a bit about you and since I've played some amateur ball myself and just love the game, I must admit I took more than a passing interest. Ever hear of the New York Bloomers?"

Thanks to Josie he was better informed on the subject. "Is that the new ladies' team they started this year that's barnstorming across the country?"

"Yes, don't like to brag but I'm proud to say I was invited to try-out for them in the Spring. They were looking for a catcher and that's where I usually play... but I've been so busy with my political activities I had to decline. Still play in pick-up games whenever I can though."

"Well, if you play ball half as good as you talk politics, you'd be a cinch to make the team. Learned a ton listening to you tonight, by the way."

"You're too kind. But I often wonder what it'd be like to get to play in front of a packed stadium of cranks. Must be a dream come true for you."

As usual, especially when talking with women, Happy felt a bit uncomfortable when the topic of the conversation turned to him. "I suppose you can say that, but I'm no star player and don't get to play much. But I've loved the game for as long as I can remember so getting to play in the Bigs is pretty special. You get to Washington Park much to see our games?"

"Well, I have to confess... I was born and raised on the Lower East Side and still live there– so I've been a Giants fan since I was a little kid. Hope you don't' hold that against me!"

"Nah, you're entitled," Happy replied with a smile. "I keep forgetting New York is such a big baseball town that there are three major league teams with plenty of fans to go round. And they're all loyal as hell."

"That's true. I follow the scores in the papers and try and get up to the Polo Grounds for a few games a year. Saw Christy Mathewson pitch against the Pirates a few weeks ago. Mighty impressive."

"You're telling me? Never had the pleasure of stepping into the batter's box with him on the mound but watching him up close from the dugout is intimidating enough."

While he was usually awkward talking with women, Happy began to feel strangely at ease with Pauline. Her passion for baseball helped of course, but he was also impressed by her intelligence, fiery spirit, and dedication to fighting for what she believed in.

Their conversation continued another few minutes until Pauline excused herself – she was running late for another speaking engagement. After she left, Happy asked Fanny about her and whether she had a boyfriend.

"Let's see, how is it I should say this? In the language of baseball, I wouldn't put on that play if I were you" said Fanny. "Pauline is quite a ballplayer in more ways than one, but she plays for the other team. *Farshteyn?* Know what I mean?"

"Yeah, I think so." Guess that's strike-two, he thought to himself.

Baltimore Chop, Medium Rare

Back at the plate where he was also two strikes down, Happy felt his opportunity drifting away. He'd certainly been in countless pressure situations on the field, but this particular at bat had taken on a surreal quality unlike any he'd experienced before.

Happy couldn't believe the absurdity of how badly he was overmatched. He was facing one of the game's best twirlers, who in turn, had some of the best defensive players in professional baseball backing him up. What the hell was he even doing here? Besting Mordecai Brown would be a feat on the order of the greatest of Houdini's great escapes. Hell, getting a decent swing at one of his pitches, making contact and getting good wood on the ball would be an accomplishment in itself.

It was a typical September day, not particularly hot, but beads of sweat had begun to streak down the sides of his face. The frantic cheering of the crowd spread to a fever pitch but to Happy's ears faded into a mere din supplemented obliquely by the blended indistinct shouts of encouragement from his teammates standing on the top step of the dugout.

The perspiration on his hands made it difficult to get a good grip on the handle of the bat so Happy stepped out of the box, balanced the bat between his knees and bent down to grab a handful of dirt. He rubbed it between his hands and rubbed some on the bat handle to dry off any sweat that had accumulated there. Next, he wiped his palms on his pant legs to finish drying them and get off any excess dirt. Then he grabbed the middle of the bat where he had a reserve supply of dark brown pine tar and applied an ample amount of the gooey substance to his palms. Finally, he slid his hands toward the handle with both wrists open, left on top, right on bottom. Tightening his fingers around the narrow bat handle he squeezed it gently while rotating his wrists in opposite directions three times to redistribute the sticky pine tar on the bat handle. When he was satisfied there was sufficient goo to hold the bat securely while swinging, he automatically readjusted his grip so that his left thumb was pointing straight up to the end of the barrel. He positioned his right wrist against the nub on the bat handle, his left just above and touching the right.

Happy knew he needed to regain control of his emotions. He stretched his bat out across the plate to tap the dirt, reset his stance and closed his eyes for a moment, taking the deepest breath he could muster. Exhaling deliberately and fully, he tried to flush the tension from his head. As he got set for the next pitch, a disembodied high-pitched scratchy voice pierced through the fog and startled him.

"Psst, Hey kid!"

It was not at all like the catcher's sarcastic tone or the umpire's stern rebukes, but he quickly swung his head around just to make sure. Both were silent for the moment. Then it was back.

"Yeah, that's right...I'm tawkin' to you son."

What the hell? Was his tension-induced imagination getting the best of him? The mystery voice was distinctly louder and clearer than any of the background noise coming from the stands or the dugout. The voice sounded strangely familiar as if he'd heard it before, but it was definitely not anyone he knew personally. It appeared to be coming from just above his right shoulder, which Happy knew was impossible, so he shook his head and tried to ignore it.

"Didn't mean ta spook ya kid. Willie Keeler here... jes' thought you might wanna couple pointas'."

Holy shit! Happy turned toward the stands and whipped his head back and forth but of course there was no sign of Keeler. In fact, the Giants were hosting the St. Louis Cardinals at home in the Polo Grounds so as far as he knew, Keeler was at least 15 miles away in northern Manhattan's Coogan's Bluff. But he sounded a helluva lot closer than that. In fact, if Happy were in the funny papers of the Brooklyn Eagle Sunday edition, Keeler's voice would be depicted by a free-floating word balloon emanating below a NY Giants baseball cap suspended in mid- air just inches off to the left of Happy's head.

"Calm down, no need t'get axcit'd. Just some friendly advice from an ol' vetran whose been heya befaw. Youse a bit like me, Smith – ya ain't neva gonna hitfa power. So ya gotta hit 'em where they *ain't* if ya wanna get on base an' help yer team out. Ya know what I'm sayin?"

Happy still had no clue what was happening but listened intently and nodded imperceptibly in agreement.

"OK, great. So, it's all 'bout controllin' yer bat. Why don'tcha try chokin' up some? Move yer hands up da handle a cupala inches. Be surprised how much eazeeyah it's gonna be t'make contac' and punch da ball where ya wanna. Hey, whattaya say kid?' Let's seeya givita shot."

Happy slid his left hand up a couple of inches and then his right hand, extending the bat in the direction of Three-Finger Brown and quickly drawing it back behind his head to test out the increase in bat speed he could generate. "See what I'm tawkin' about?" asked Keeler.

"Ya can really whip that thing around much fasta when yer chokin' up a bit. OK, so now ya wanna figya out where ya gonna place da ball. They ain't gonna be playin' ya to pull an' they ain't gonna hol' da runners close on da bases 'cause a base hit'd probly score two runs anyway, so there's no big holes to shoot for. But they're playin' you mid-depth in the infield so they have a shot at a force at any base. So, ya could tryta surprise 'em witta bunt for a squeeze at da plate but I reckon Dahlen's signs are calling for you to swing away. Ain't that right?"

Happy double checked the third base coach who swiped his jersey, pulled on his left sleeve, tapped the bill of his cap, and pulled on his right ear... all of which simply meant swing for a base hit. Happy smiled at how much Keeler knew about the game and how he had the specific situational strategy dead to rights. Noisy spotted this and of course had to add his commentary, "Hey kid, you won't think it's so funny when Three-Finger strikes your ass out."

At this point Happy was locked into his "interaction" with Keeler and barely heard Noisy's latest distraction. He glanced out to observe the Cubs infielders. Sure enough, they weren't holding the runners close on the bases. Steinfeldt at third base was just two steps closer than usual and getting set in his crouch. Tinkers was carefully leveling the dirt at short with the toe of his left shoe. Evers was pounding his mitt just a few feet off second. Chance was off the first base bag staring at the third base coach trying to decipher his signals but as Wee Willie indicated, all of them were keeping their options open, playing about halfway between the infield and outfield grass in the middle of the manicured dirt surface.

"So, lemme tell ya... what I'd do in dis heyah *sit'yation* is I'd whirl 'round ta show yer buntin' jus' as soon as TreeFinga gazinta his stretch windup. Hold it as long as ya can, t'get them infielders ta charge in... but then get the bat back real quick see, and use that short stroke ta *chop* one. Swing down hard on the ball jus' like a butcher slicing through a nice big piece'a T-bone *steak* ta bounce it innuh dirt. Ya know what I'm sayin'? Hit it right and it'll land just over their heads and scoot out slowly inta da outfield grass. Get ya one, maybe two runs dependin' on how fast da outfielder charges and how good his arm is. That's jus wonnada l'il tricks I came up wit' back in Bawltmore– the one they named da Baltimore chop. Hey, byda way...Nex' time yer at PedaLooga's Steak House, check out the "Wee Willie Baltimore Chop" named in my honor. Don't be fooled by the name – nut'n small'bout da porshun – a double tick loin'a lamb, grilled medium rare ta perfection that can't be beat. And don' fuhgettabout' a peasa der apple strudel wit' schlag for dessert."

Freedom and Exhilaration

The thought of celebrating a victory over the World Champions with a gourmet meal at Peter Luger's, one of Brooklyn's finest restaurants was a welcome diversion from the mounting stress, allowing Happy a very brief moment of respite. He took full advantage by gathering another deep breath and relaxed his hands just as Brown began his stretch windup. Without further contemplation, he responded instinctively by squaring around to a bunting position, slid his left hand toward the end of the bat to steady it horizontally and positioned himself perpendicularly to the first base line to drag a bunt up the line.

At this point everything slowed down so that each millisecond felt like an eternity. The entire ballpark was wondering what was going on. Bill Davidson, the runner on third was not expecting a squeeze play and thus was not bolting toward home. Superba's Manager Dahlen was kicking himself for being coerced into sending up such an inexperienced player in a crucial game situation. He hadn't put on a bunt play and clearly, Smith misread the signs from the third-base coach.

The first baseman, Frank Chance took the bait and began to charge aggressively toward the plate so he could field the bunt and either have a force at home, tag the runner out, or throw to Evers who'd be covering first to get the final out. Then as Chance was four or five steps toward home plate and Brown was completing his windup, Happy quickly moved his left foot back and swung his body into a conventional stance. He moved his left hand down so it was touching the right, but in the choked up position.

The ball was released from Three-Finger's grip and came sailing toward him. Fortunately for Happy the pitch was an off-speed changeup, which gave him an additional fraction of a second to readjust his position and timing in preparation for his swing. Although it seemed things were unfolding at the speed of an Edison Phonograph that needed to be re-cranked, it all happened quickly and as soon as he detected Happy's decoy, Chance threw on the brakes and tried to abort his charge toward the plate. In doing so, his cleats tangled with the infield sod causing him to lurch forward and downward. He didn't hit the ground, but his vertical reach was temporarily impaired. The pitch was shoulder high and very likely out of the strike zone but was well suited for the type of swing Keeler had suggested. Happy timed his attack to clobber the ball on a downward trajectory into the hard packed infield dirt in front of home plate. He felt like he was back in Oregon splitting logs for the winter.

The sound of the ball off the wooden bat was a firm thwack quickly followed by the dull thud of it ricocheting on a single bounce off the dirt. As he connected, Happy was reassured it was solidly hit off the sweet spot of the barrel just around the diamond shaped Zinn Beck Bat Co. Model 400 trademark – both by the auditory feedback and by the lack of the characteristic vibration one feels when the ball is hit off the thin handled section of the bat.

The next sound he became conscious of was the overwhelming response of the cranks as they watched along with Happy, the ball bounce high in the air and take flight well over Frank Chance's outstretched glove at the end of an awkward stumbling leap and trickle past him up the first base line. Washington Park erupted into a wild uproar which lifted him like a huge gust of wind and suddenly he took flight, soaring effortlessly down the line to first base.

Happy pulled off the deception in a manner that would make Houdini proud. Like the great magician in flight, the funny thing was as soon as he connected with Three-Finger's pitch, all the tension and strain left him. Like the conversion of the aviation fuel's chemical energy into the thermal energy of combustion and finally into the mechanical energy that powered the propeller on Houdini's 80 horsepower British ENV engine allowing him to defy earth's gravitational forces for 2.5 minutes, Happy sensed the pent-up nervous energy stored in his muscles release from his body and transfer through his bat in the form of kinetic energy to drive the baseball. He felt all his muscles relax and he floated down the base path feeling a sense of ease. Freedom and exhilaration, that's what it was.

Ordinarily, a well-placed and successfully executed Baltimore Chop like the one Happy had just managed was an automatic base hit. So, despite the fact that the opposition was the league-leading former World Champion Chicago Cubs, no one in Washington Park, least of all Happy, anticipated what happened next.

Chicago's scrappy second baseman Johnny Evers appeared out of nowhere as he saw Chance on the move and wisely was positioning himself to take a throw to make the put-out at first. Thus, he was fortuitously positioned and continued to charge at full speed as the ball sailed over the first baseman and rolled up the line. As he got closer, Evers took a flying horizontal leap with his glove at the end of his fully extended left arm. He hit the ground hard, dislodging a reddish cloud of clay dirt that temporarily obscured the play. The ball disappeared from view and his forward momentum carried Evers and his mitt careening right for the first base bag in one single motion. They arrived and touched the base seemingly the instant before Happy's foot landed atop the bag. But where was the ball?

The first base umpire leaning in as close as he dared with his legs apart and arms on his knees for balance, was adjacent to the bag just over the chalk line, in perfect position to make the call. On close plays at first in which the umpire must judge whether the player or ball thrown by an infielder arrived first, they can rely on the high-pitched thwack of the ball hitting the glove vs. the dull thud when the player's foot strikes the bag to assist them. In this case however, the umpire had to rely solely on a visual assessment of the play.

For a long moment, however, the decision was in limbo. The umpire did not immediately indicate one way or another whether Happy was safe or out. As soon as he passed the bag he glanced over his shoulder waiting for the call but the umpire seemed frozen, poised over the bag. After colliding with first Evers got to his knees and held his glove up revealing that he had and maintained secure possession of the ball. At that point the umpire dramatically pulled his clenched fist with his thumb pointing upward across his body, and yelled, "Yer out!"

The sold-out crowd let out a collective sigh of frustration and disbelief over the unlikely and spectacular defensive play. The insurance runs to put the game out of reach were not to be and the pressure to keep the Cub's bats in check and seal a Brooklyn victory for starting pitcher Doc Scanlon would now be in the hands of Kaiser Wilhelm, one of the team's two relief pitchers who had been loosening up on the sidelines.

Happy, who had sprinted to first with every ounce of energy he possessed, shifted into neutral and coasted after passing the bag. His momentum carried him an additional 30 feet into the nebulous purgatory where infield and outfield met as he slowed to a deliberate walk, then turned and headed back toward the dugout. With hands on his hips, elbows bent, and head tilting slightly forward, he paused to catch his breath. He glanced up and noticed Dahlen motioning that he would stay in the game for defense. Tony shouted that he'd deliver his glove on his way out to the field so Happy could have an extra moment to recuperate.

While he stood waiting for the delivery of his well-worn mitt so he could take his place in right field, Happy reflected on what transpired. It was not the ending he dreamed of since his days as a sand-lot wannabe. He was given an opportunity to be the hero of the day but came up short. Some of the hardcore Brooklyn fans saw his failed at bat as proof of his limited abilities but were even angrier at Manager Dahlen for choosing the inexperienced Happy Smith in such a critical game situation. Despite their lead, a small chorus of boos could be heard throughout the stadium.

It wasn't clear to Happy whether he'd get a chance at redemption later in the game or if that was his last at bat for the season or even his career. But somehow, he didn't feel crushed. He'd given it his all and felt ok.

Happy Smith's first season's improbable roller coaster ride from amateur in the rural Pacific Northwest to professional Major League ball player in the urban capital of the baseball universe of New York was coasting to an end. He'd dodged adversity, weathered numerous hairpin turns and kept his nerve as the bottom dropped out. It was a thrill he'd never forget.

But it was his off-field experiences that lifted him up to provide a vista onto the world beyond baseball that Happy knew had changed his life in a much more profound and lasting way.

Epilogue

◆

Here ends the story which took place during a single at bat in a meaningless ballgame between the Chicago Cubs and Brooklyn Superbas on September 21, 1910. From this vantage point we're able to look back in time at the back stories of our on- and off-the-field "players" but have no crystal ball to see into the future. Did the Superbas (who of course soon became known as the Dodgers) hold onto their lead and win? What became of Happy and the rest of the people in his world? One can only imagine...

This book is based on real-life characters (e.g., Happy Smith and the other baseball players, team owner Charles Ebbets, labor and political leaders Claire Lemlich, Pauline Newman, Emma Goldman, and Alfred Steers, leaders of the Committee of Fourteen Dr. John Peters and Frederick Whitin, boxing champion Jack Johnson, and cultural icon Harry Houdini.) It weaves the fictional story within a framework of real-life events (e.g., the avalanche and devastating train derailment in Washington, the arrival of Halley's Comet, the Uprising of the 20,000, Coney Island and the annual Brooklyn Mardi Gras parade). The story itself, and most of the other characters, however, are total fiction.

The idea for the book was born when I read an article in the New York Times about an exhibit at the Metropolitan Museum of Art that consisted of old and extremely rare baseball trading cards. It mentioned a player on the Brooklyn Superbas by the name of Henry Joseph Smith (nicknamed Happy), who enjoyed just one season playing in the major leagues in 1910.

Somehow this sparked my curiosity. Who was this man? How did he manage to find his way from rural Coquille, OR to the hustle and bustle of big city life? In what ways did this influence his view of the world? How was he impacted by getting a chance to rise from sandlot and amateur leagues to play professional Major League ball? What was his life like? Who did he meet and how did they influence him?

Writing historical fiction requires attention to detail and once I began to research life at the turn of the 20th Century, I became fascinated by current events and the social and political issues of the day. Automobiles, trains, and trolleys were quickly replacing the horse and buggy. Electric lights and phonographs were becoming ubiquitous. Halley's Comet was well known but still a bit of a mystery. With the challenges facing immigrants, struggles of the labor movement, the early days of feminism, the women's suffrage movement, oppression and lynchings of African Americans, and self-appointed social vigilantes, it was a dynamic and volatile period in American history. And baseball was quickly becoming America's favorite pastime.

Thus, the stage is set for the emergence of the book's fictional characters including Happy's landlady and friend, Fanny Goldfarb, Happy's extended family, team equipment manager Flash Jones and his family, and Superba fans Billy Labriola, Walter Budzinski, and Kevin Kearney. These disparate characters intersect the world Happy enters (either directly or indirectly), as he steps up to the plate against Three-Finger Brown and all have an impact on molding who the fictional Happy Smith will become.

Glossary: Yiddish – English Translations

Bissel eppis – a little something (to eat)

Bubeleh – term of endearment, sweetheart

Challah – traditional braided bread typically eaten on ceremonial occasions

Chazzerai – nosh or junk food

Chutzpah – impudence or gall; speaking your mind without regard to consequences

Dos Meydl Fun der Gheto – The Girl from the Ghetto

Farblunget–hopelessly lost; out of whack

Farbrente Yidishe meydelech –fiery Jewish girls

Farklempt – choked up

Farshteyn – understand

Flanken – flank or side of beef

Forverts – Forward (formerly The Jewish Daily Forward; popular Yiddish newspaper published in New York City)

Gay shlofen - Go to sleep

Genug – enough

Haggadah – (Hebrew) "telling"; Jewish text that sets forth the order and story of the Passover Seder

Hamantashen – triangular pastries filled with fruit or seeds and served at the Jewish holiday Purim

Hak mir nisht keyn chaynik! Stop bothering me! (literally don't knock a teakettle at me!)

Ikh bin eyner fun yene vas suffers fun di abiusiz diskreybd do – ... I have no further patience for talks as I am one of those who suffers from the abuses described here

Kanehura – jinx

Kashes - questions

Kneidlach – matzah balls (usually served in chicken soup)

Kugel – baked casserole often made from egg noodles or potato

Kvell – express intense joy or pride

Latkes – potato pancakes

Landsman, landsmen – fellow Jew(s)

Lieb – to love

Macher – big shot

Mandelbrot – a classic Jewish brittle cookie; similar to biscotti

Mensch – person of integrity and honor; kind and thoughtful

Mishegas – craziness, silliness, insanity

Mit – with

Mohn - poppyseed

Nosh – snack

Nu – Well? So?

Oy –to express exasperation or dismay

Oy gevalt – Oh, violence (to express shock or amazement)

Oy vey iz mir – Oh, woe is me!

Oysgematert – utterly exhausted

Schlep – carrying or dragging something

Schmear – spread on bread, e.g., with cream cheese

Schmudda – melted farmer or "pot" cheese; name possibly derived from "*schmatta*" or old "

Seder – (Hebrew) "order"; traditional Jewish service which recounts the events prior to and during the journey to freedom, celebrating the start of the Passover holiday

Shadchanis – matchmaker

Shule – school "

Tchotchkes – small decorative objects

Tsuris – trouble

Un ikh makh az mir geyn oyf a general shlogn – And I move that we go on a general strike!"

Varnishkes – bow-tie noodles

Vus machs da – what's with that

Yahrzeit – anniversary of a death

Zei gezunt – go in good health (a goodbye greeting); alternatively, *Gei gezunterheyt*

Zetz – a poke

About the Author

Paul Kalb recently retired from Brookhaven National Laboratory where he spent 40+ years conducting and managing research in environmental science. Paul and his wife Terry are devoted Mets fans and live on eastern Long Island and in Manhattan with their cats, Kasha and Knish. They have two adult children and one grandchild.

Paul has always enjoyed writing and has published a blog called Opinion8ed2 for over 15 years. It contains an eclectic assortment of mostly non-fiction articles on the arts, entertainment, politics, the environment, and miscellaneous rants. The latest issue and a link to more than 200 previous blogs written by the author are available at Opinion8ed2.wordpress.com. His memoir entitled, *The Mystery Boy and Other Stories* was published in 2023 and is available through Amazon and Barnes & Noble online. Comments and feedback about *Happy Smith Goes to Brooklyn* are always welcome and can be submitted in the comments section of the blog.